# AEROSPACE:

# The King's Payload

## by

~

## Renné Siewers

DEDICATED TO THE FOLLOWING:

I dedicate "The Aerospace: The King's Payload" to my loving husband, Jon Siewers, and all the dedicated Aerospace Personnel who make Space Exploration a reality.

Acknowledgments:

Dennis Morrison, Ph.D. co-developed and co-implemented the Microencapsulation Electrostatic Delivery System (MEDS) treatment against cancer for his life work. The MEDS experiment was renamed the Micro Encapsulation Crystallization System (MECS) and patented. The MECS experiment went full round when the MECS process was used to save Dennis Morrison, Ph.D., from Non-Hodgen cancer at MD Anderson. This is truly a miracle. God made this happen.

To my friend Yvette Perry, who helped me edit the book, my editor, Kathy Russ.

# Table of Contents

## Introduction

I gasped for air, unable to defend myself. Hands grasped around my neck, squeezing savagely. Pain emanated throughout my body. I tried to speak, to shout, "Help me. Don't kill me."

Fighting for my life, I clenched both hands into fists and began beating against the unknown dark force. I thrashed back and forth. I felt my eyes bulge from the threatened attack. I tried to scream, but I could not. I felt the executioner's hot breath against my naked body. His rough hands tightened even more ferociously as my life was ending.

My inborn fight for survival renewed my strength. I fought desperately to protect myself. I grabbed the perpetrator's hands, pushing them away as hard as possible. It was useless; I didn't have the strength to fight anymore.

Suddenly, the assault stopped as quickly as it had begun. My eyes stung as I blinked, searching for the assailant.

I saw a shadowy figure lurking in the early morning light, an ominous form, white from the head down, but the face was a dark, black mask.

A taunting voice mixed with a sinister laugh spoke, "You will suffer a gruesome death. I will bring death to you and to the one you love. It will happen when you least expect it. You will die."

"Who's there?" I cried out.

The shadowy figure disappeared. Was the attack real? Was I going crazy?

Powerless, I could not move, caught half in a dream state of sub-consciousness and terror. My body, dripping in sweat, shook uncontrollably.

## Chapter 1 – Questions

I opened my eyes, repeatedly blinking, trying to focus on reality. Slowly, I began awakening from the recurring dream. I felt tangled in a web of horror.

"Who's there?" I cried out. I heard an internal voice, "Susan, Susan, wake up; it is a nightmare." My body, dripping in sweat, shook uncontrollably. *Was the attack real? Was I going crazy? Unfortunately, real, or not real, the pain was real.* The throbbing soreness still penetrated my neck.

The nightmare began shortly after the Space Station tragedy. Dr. Dalton Masters, a biomedical research scientist's Micro Encapsulation Crystallization System (MECS) payload experiment, had gone awry. All hell had broken loose on the Space Station. I have lived with the memory every day since the occurrence.

Sweat trickled down my body. I tried to calm myself. But, somehow, my nightmare kept the mysterious Space Station catastrophe alive, repeating the tragedy repeatedly. It left many unanswered questions. Every day, the death of my astronaut hero and Congressman Dan Fletcher broke my heart.

Yes, the culprits were Leona and the deceased Dr. Daryl McKnight, an astronaut physician. The double experiment introduced anthrax into Dalton's MECS and his life-saving cancer experiments.

I tossed in anguish back and forth in the master quarters. Who was the mastermind behind the death of Congressman Fletcher? It had to be an unknown culprit, someone other than Leona or Dr. McKnight. In the end, the crew killed Dr. McKnight when they realized what was happening, but it was too late for Congressman Fletcher. He died not from the cancer treatment but from the diabolical plan implemented by

Leona and Dr. McKnight.

Who was the entity responsible for turning Dalton's cancer experiment into a chemical warfare weapon? Whoever it was, they had to have immense power and authority, and I suspect no one will ever know the real guilty party.

Ironically, the hypothesis proved successful when Leona and Dr. McKnight used Dalton's experiment for chemical warfare. The anthrax is delivered using oxygen as a catalyst. It proved that the experiment could destroy many people's lives by dispersing the chemical into the Earth's atmosphere. It had the capability to kill the people but not the country's real estate and valuable resources. It would leave the territory open to new pioneers to claim the deceased belongings at no cost except for precious human life.

I didn't believe Leona and Dr. McKnight could have acted alone. So, who contrived the catastrophic incident?

I remembered Dalton, my aeronautical protector and sweetheart. He was on deck helming the beautiful sailboat, *La Dulce Vida,* the sweet life.

I had fallen in love with Dr. Dalton Masters, the biomedical Ph.D. from NASA who had changed my life and the cancer research world. Maybe Dalton could make the hideous nightmares go away.

Groggily, I slowly prepared myself to get out of the sailboat's berth. I was still shaking as I put on my well-worn silk tee shirt. I stumbled up the companionway. I looked up and saw the back of a tanned, broad-shouldered man on the deck of the beautiful *La Dulce Vida.* Dalton and I were returning to our home in Kemah, Texas, after spending three weeks in the Bahamas, the Abacos Islands, truly a paradise. [1]

Watching Dalton turn the wheel, I composed myself, "Good morning, Sweetie. Thank you for letting me sleep."

Dalton replied, "Susan, you didn't sleep well last night, so I let you get some extra rest."

I said, "Thanks, but none of the sleep was restful."

My thoughts turned to the time I read that infamous note.

---

[1] The poem "Clear Blue Water" is located in the Poetry Section.

I believe it said, *"Dr. Dalton Masters, keep the MECS formula safe. It may be the beginning of life and death, not as we know it. The future is in your hands. Your life may be in danger. Be careful. Yours truly, Dr. Jon Keller."*

I haven't had a good night's sleep since my eyes read the note. My curiosity about this note led me into a suspense-filled journey with Dr. Dalton Masters, Ph.D. Unfortunately, I found out later that Dr. Jon Keller and his wife died in a house fire. Now we are returning to civilization from the Abacos, Bahamas, where the culture is laid-back, mañana, and Bahamas time, so don't get in a hurry.

I thought of the beauty of the multi-deep aquamarine blue Bahamas seas. It is so different from the open, dark space one sees when looking down onto Earth and its beauty, but going back to civilization after the retreat was hard for me to handle. I had gotten used to the easy life: snorkelling in the tranquil sea amidst the beauty of the coral reef and the multitude of colorful fishes.

Now I remember the death of the first astronaut murdered by the deceased astronaut Dr. McKnight and Leona, his accomplice. I paused and said, "I wonder how Leona is managing in the Titusville, Florida, jail."

Dalton said, "I heard she was isolated in a small cell with no one to talk to except herself, which she does all the time. She keeps chatting about her darling Dr. McKnight and her plan to avenge his death."

He continued, "Her Doctor called and warned me about her confusing behavior. He said she told him she loved me and wanted to be with me forever, but she hated Dr. McKnight in the same breath. The only thing consistent in her story is you, Susan. Yes, she wants to kill you; she wants you stone-cold dead."

This report sent chills down my spine. Leona's threats frightened me.

I whimpered, "She can't harm me. Can she?" My thoughts on her in prison didn't give me comfort.

I still felt her thin, strong, rough hands around my neck. The memories are still alive in my head, dancing into my repeated nightmares, rewinding to the time she almost choked me to my death.

My hands instinctively jumped to cover my neck; the black and blue marks remained. It is a constant memory, and the recollection does not fade. It had been months since the episode, but the bruises kept the pain alive and real. It is a constant reminder and a sign. Yes, I should keep my guard up.

Dalton knelt and kissed me on the forehead. "I will always protect you. She can't harm you," he said lovingly.

I responded. "I know Leona is locked up. I should always remember my first instinct about situations."

Dalton said, "You never know who you can trust in this world. Instinctively, you do. But do we always listen to our instincts?"

I said, "No, sometimes your friends end up being your enemies, and mysteriously, your enemies end up being your friends. Life is funny. Even families can be the ones who hurt you the most. But, regardless, the pain generated from people you trust, people you care for, the ones who are the closest."

He said, "How do you know when to trust and whom do you trust? What do you look for, and how do you know how to read the signs?"

I said, "Did you see the signs in Leona? Poor Leona, all alone, I do feel sorry for her. She is so confused and so alone. Did Dr. McKnight use her, or did she use him?"

Dalton said, "His charm and charismatic personality made someone as plain as Leona easy prey. Additionally, her history made her an easy selection, with all the information about her grandfather's experiment."

I continued

, "It makes me wonder whether the twosomes were alone in performing the historical space murder."

Dalton said, "Don't forget about the double experiment: chemical warfare and cancer research. What were they thinking?"

"How could they possibly get away with such a high-profile murder? Poor Congressman Fletcher, it seems strange that the two planned the espionage, murder, and the switch in your MECS solution."

Dalton replied, "Who else was behind the murder? I can't

see Dr. Daryl McKnight or Leona being masterminds. Do you think more people are involved?"

I said, "I'm not quite sure; I don't believe it is over, Dalton. There are just too many unanswered questions."

Melancholy consumed me as I walked to the bow of the boat. *My thoughts went back to my biggest question concerning Dalton. Could I trust Dalton enough to marry him? He has asked for my hand in marriage, but this is a conflict for me.*

*My heart says yes, yes, yes, but my head says no, no, no. Will he be faithful? Will he cherish me? Will he get bored? Will he cheat? Will I arrive at our boat to find him with someone else younger, prettier, or perkier?*

I mentally slapped myself, thinking that I must stop these constant questions. I must remember that Dalton is an honorable man who asked me to spend the rest of my life with him until death do us part. Again, I touched the bruises on my neck, which Leona left while trying to strangle me. Yes, death until we do part.

## Chapter 2 – Return

I gazed at Dalton, and his eyes met mine, and then the bright, hot orange sun over the horizon blinded my eyes. His smells, lovemaking, and quirks were part of me.

The recurring nightmare made my well-worn satin tee shirt drenched in salty sweat. I felt uncomfortable and slowly removed the damp tee shirt. It smelled of the jasmine that permeated the air. I hung it on the safety line next to the bow pulpit to dry.

The warmth of the new morning sun felt terrific on my bronzed body. The dampness evaporated as I lay on the deck.

My thoughts turned to Dalton's marriage proposal. *Ironically, it triggered my distrust of men. But, of course, Dalton is a man. Why I had included him in this dilatory category, I asked myself. It must be my history with men who lied about undying friendship.*

*On the other hand, was it cheating? Maybe I am damaged goods. Should I trust Dalton? I wondered whether he had an affair with the madwoman, Leona, his crazed Hardware Quality Assurance Engineer. He certainly had many opportunities during his long business trips with her.*

*Thankfully, Leona sat in jail, awaiting trial for the death of Congressman Fletcher and the attack on me.*

Dalton walked toward me, "Susan, what are you doing up here all alone? I miss you, beautiful lady. I can't get enough of your smiles and sparkling eyes."

I turned with my arms open, anticipating his touch. "Dalton, my captain, who is at the helm?"

"Mr. Auto Pilot, he sails very nicely. We are on a direct course to land and will be coming into port in approximately two hours. I'll take over when we get near the jetties. But, right now, it is clear sailing." He kissed me on my nose, forehead, cheeks, and neck, making his way down to the softness of my breasts.

I gave a breathless moan, "Now Dalton, we may have to

heave to and spend a couple of hours offshore before we enter a port. You are getting me excited."

Dalton immediately returned to the helm and turned our fine sailing vessel directly into the wind, adjusting the mainsail and backwinding the jib.

We left topside and went below, stopping at the companionway. Dalton kissed me slowly as I sat on the stairs. I anxiously anticipated his every move. He continued kissing my lips, gently touching the center of my back. His hands moved down my body, stopping to satisfy me in every way. My body responded to his every move, but my mind kept thinking about the return to civilization. Finally, I gave out a sigh.

It's inevitable that we return to reality: his vital research, the Nobel Prize of Medicine ceremony, and Leona's trial. They are all on our plates. Dalton's wounds healed, but his internal scars remain deep. His pain is my pain, which permeates deep into our hearts. For me, the bruises around my neck are a constant reminder of the disasters on the Space Shuttle, the International Space Station (ISS), and the Kennedy Space Center (KSC).

Congressman Fletcher, the awesome man who made space history, is adored by the whole country, and cherished even in death. I questioned why he had to die.

Why would anyone want to kill America's hero? It didn't make sense that Leona and Dr. Daryl McKnight tried to recreate her grandfather's World War II bio-chemical warfare experiments. Death had once again occurred from the Nazi's evil plan of world domination, this time killing Congressman Fletcher, the hero.

Ironically, Dalton almost saved him from cancer by reversing his illness with the MECS. The experiment exhibited signs of destroying cancer and even changing the aging cycle. It seemed surreal that this happened to my hero. Grief overwhelmed me as tears ran down my large, sad eyes. I stared out the aft cabin porthole. The emerald sea flowed majestically as the tears streamed down my face. The sadness slowly drifted into the turquoise blue waves as Dalton stroked the softness of my body.

I threw my head back in ecstasy and sorrow as he grabbed my long, curly hair between his fingers. Grief sometimes releases your pleasure. He kissed me, from my lips to the wetness between my thighs. His touch felt breathtaking; I am accustomed to his touch. What would I ever do without him?

The boat lunged forward as the sails clanked against the mast. A deafening noise blasted our tranquillity. Naked, we flew up the companionway. The boat rocked and vibrated as if a cannonball hit it.

The sun blinded our eyes as a menacing fast boat turned toward our sailboat. The fast boat swerved at the last minute, causing the waves to hit violently against the hull. The La Dulce Vida ferociously rocked back and forth as the unknown, ominous boat returned. My heart stopped. I panicked, screaming, "No, not again. Are we under attack?"

We saw a 50-foot black Scarab splashing water across our boat. It was happening so fast. It looked like a tall, ominous man was pointing a gun at us. His appearance was that of a madman, laughing hysterically.

I couldn't handle any bloody chaos. Ducking down in the companionway, I reached for the flare gun. It was the only weapon aboard. The best I could do was to shoot at the engines.

I grabbed the VHF and began calling the Coast Guard on channel 16. "Coast Guard, Coast Guard, this is the sailing vessel, La Dulce Vida, located off the Galveston Jetty. We are under attack from an unknown speedboat."

The Coast Guard said, "Please go to channel 11."

I said, "Going to channel 11."

The boat made another pass at us. This time, Dalton recognized the man driving the Scarab.

I started to shoot, pointing the gun at the engines, when Dalton shouted, "It's okay, Susan. It's Ken."

Perplexed, I said, "What?"

I saw a familiar face, Ken, but I never noticed his dark olive complexion as I looked up. It was Dalton's hardware supplier in a sleek black Scarab. He was laughing his head off like a hyena. I screamed back at him, "One of these days, I will get you back."

I quickly returned to the radio, "Coast Guard, Coast Guard; this is the S/V La Dolce Vida. Please ignore the emergency call; everything is in order. It is a friend playing a joke. The S/V La Dolce Vida is signing off."

The Coast Guard stated sternly, "La Dulce Vida, it is a high penalty for calling the Coast Guard a joke. Please never call the Coast Guard unless you have a real emergency.

or there will be fine."

I said, "Coast Guard, yes, sir. It will not happen again."

I heard, "Coast Guard going back to channel 16."

I said, "La Dulce Vida, going to channel 16."

We looked at each other in disbelief and scurried below to throw on our clothes. Dalton laughed as I fumbled to get dressed; he said, "This guy is going to make me mad. Wait until I see him. I will get him back." With that statement, I knew our mystical journey in paradise was over. * [2]

Ken screamed, "Pull into the Galveston Bay Fuel Dock. I have scheduled a press conference at the Galveston Bay Yacht Club and a feast fit for a king. It is time for you guys to rest after the long crossing from the Bahamas. Dalton, your fans await you."

Dalton and I looked at each other in disbelief, but I heard him say, "Sounds great. We wouldn't miss it for the world." With that statement, Ken revved the 427 Corvette engines and took off toward Galveston Yacht Basin.

The renewed silence was welcoming. I felt so comfortable with Dalton by my side as we returned to our sailing routine.

---

[2] The poem "Paradise" is located in the Poetry Section.

Dalton was at the wheel, lazily steering with his feet, while I sat on the bow with the wind blowing through my hair. At times like that, we are one with the wind. The wind lets us be free, free to go anywhere in the world. I knew what would happen once we went ashore. It was inevitable that we would return from our dream-filled cruise. Oh, yes, going back to civilization is now a harsh reality. Shortly, we would arrive at the Galveston Bay Yacht Basin.

I saw a dolphin pod swimming in front of the bow as the boat sailed through the water. The almost-human creatures were such graceful mammals playing in the water with their young. Instinctively, I wanted to join the beautiful creatures to escape returning. But unfortunately, it was inevitable for us to return to concrete civilization. Still, it would be a dream come true to swim with the dolphins.

We passed the safety Fairway Anchorage, where all the ships were waiting for the Homeland Security check for terrorists lurking on board. Any attack on the Ship Channel would be devastating, stopping all supplies into the Houston shipping docks. Sad, but after 9/11, life had changed on land and the sea.

I could see the jetties ahead. "Dalton, this reminds me of the Harvest Moon race from Galveston, Texas, to Port Aransas. Once, I crewed on a 35 J boat, which had no motor. It had quit at the mouth of the jetties. That didn't stop us. The captain forged ahead, and we went all the way to Port Aransas without a motor, which is what you are supposed to do in this race. Still, a motor, to me, is a huge safety factor. In the middle of the race, a huge shrimp boat bigger than a house came toward us, and there was no way we could get out of his way without a motor. I told the captain to point a bright light on the sails."

Dalton said, "What happened?"

I explained, "It worked. Finally, the commercial shrimp

boat saw the light shining on the sails and turned just in time. The shrimp boat was a gigantic house."

*I looked out to sea, daydreaming about yesterday, today, and tomorrow.* * ³ *I didn't want to go back to the States.*

Dalton asked, "Penny, for your thoughts?"

I smiled and said, "Just thinking about all my racing days and the near misses. But the sea is where I think the best."

The waves were swishing against the boat as we approached Bolivar Roads. "Susan, please watch out for the barges coming out of the chute so we can cross."

"I know, Dalton. It is treacherous at night, but today, the sun is out, giving us great visibility," I said.

The perspiration gathered, making the sweat bubbled on my forehead. Fortunately, the breeze kept us from being too uncomfortable.

*My thoughts turned to the devastation of Bolivar Island, the nightmare when Hurricane Ike destroyed the whole barrier island. I thought of friends who didn't leave or could not leave the island. Hurricane Ike left only debris and remnants of beautiful beach homes; slowly, rebuilding will start.*

Dalton commanded, "Let's take down the sails before entering the busy nautical highway."

"Dalton, you know the ocean is not the problem, but its boundaries. So now we are going into the channel edges," I said.

"Let's miss the edges. Turn on the motor and head up into the wind, Sweetie," Dalton commanded.

The wind blew directly on my face as Dalton brought down the mainsail. The lazy jacks caught the sail.

He came to the cockpit, and we brought in the jib. I held the lazy sheet for him as he brought in the sail, using the furling line. We worked together like a finely tuned, well-oiled machine. We make a great team.

I said, "Dalton, look at the Bolivar Lighthouse. It's welcoming us back home."

"Yes, it is — what a welcome sight. I'm glad to see you

---

³ The poem "Yesterday, Today and Tomorrow" is located in the Poetry Section.

home again. The Robert C. Lanier Ferry Boat is welcoming us home."

We passed it on the port side. Everyone on the boat was smiling and waving at us. We waved back, watching two little girls playing on the boat's starboard side.

"Look, Dalton, the dolphins are welcoming us back to shore." Three dolphins rose out of the water: a father, a mom, and a baby. It was a magnificent sight. It made me feel exhilarated.

I reached over to Dalton, "Sir, I don't want to return. Let's turn the boat around and go back to the Bahamas. Please."

Dalton gently lifted my lips to his. "Darling, I wish we could stay out here forever, but I know I must return to my research. We'll travel more one day, and I promise we'll go to the Caribbean and British Virgin Islands."

I looked at him like a little puppy dog and pushed out my bottom lip, pouting, "I want to know when my dear, and I will begin packing now."

"We will return to our paradise after the MECS payload flies on the next Space Shuttle mission to the Space Station," he said.

"Promise," I said, remembering the touch of the beautiful crystal blue water caressed between my fingers, reminding me that through the water, I was touching the whole world. Now Dalton was my entire world.

"Promise," he said.

The turn inside the protection wall of the Galveston Yacht Basin was tight. I turned the wheel clockwise to position the fuel dock to the port side. I threw the boat's transmission in reverse and, little by little, approached the pier as dusk approached. *I thought to myself, go slowly, so it won't destroy the boat if you hit the dock. You never want the boat to go faster than you want to hit something.*

Docking the boat was as natural as breathing. The wind picked up as I maneuvered the boat up to the dock. I turned the wheel to starboard, bringing the boat around. Dalton jumped off the boat to get the lines as the boat went into reverse. It caused the forward motion to stop. When it stopped, I put it into neutral.

I ran to the bow and threw him the starboard line when I noticed a dock boy waiting for the stern line. I made my way back as quickly as I could. I hadn't even noticed the constant camera flashes in all the commotion of docking the boat. Bright, blinding flashes exploded in my eyes. Panic set in. I wanted to run like a turncoat and head out to sea again. The whole scene was frightening.

## Chapter 4 –Paparazzi

I said, "Who told the paparazzi we would be here? What do they want this time? Why can't they leave us alone? We have been out to sea. I still have the memory of the beautiful full moonbeams playing with our hearts. I remember sleeping on deck using the cushions as pillows and the dolphins playing and dancing ballet in the moonlight. Two would fly into the air as if they were kissing each other and then fall backward. I loved the wonderful days spent on the beach with cold tropical drinks that went down too easily. This time has been special; our loving, our holding, our desires, as if no one else existed except us. Please don't make me go back. Not now."

He turned and acknowledged me with a smile. My heart stopped when reality hit as I whispered to myself, "Hopefully, Dalton will invite me to Stockholm, the most beautiful city. It has dark cobalt blue water, boats sailing between islands and reefs, surrounded by culture, history, and magnificent grandeur."

Another bright flash brought me back to reality. Dalton talked to the reporters. "Everyone, give us a chance to get presentable, and we will meet you in the Galveston Bay Yacht Club. It's been a long trip, and we must freshen up."

We showered on board and dressed very quickly. I took out a white sundress with intricate embroidery around the neck and bust. I sat in front of the mirror and applied my makeup for the first time in weeks — sigh, back to civilization and the formalities.

I realized the news media had left, except for one last ominous man who stood in the fuel house looking at us with piercing eyes. I said, ignoring the man staring at us, "Dalton, where did the news reporters go?"

"Susan, don't get your hopes up. The reporters are probably waiting at the Galveston Yacht Club, would be my guess." He said, ignoring the man standing nearby.

We walked briskly to the Galveston Yacht Club. I

continued to look back to see if the strange man was following us. He was not. As soon as we reached the club, the camera lights began flashing.

Ken ran up to us and said, "Your table awaits you. I have an exceptional menu for your return. I've convinced the media they have only half an hour of questions. That's the best I could do."

"It's okay, Ken. I know you did your best. Susan and I became spoiled by being isolated on the islands. It's time to get into the real world. Our Caribbean sabbatical away from the unfortunate incident was necessary for our sanity. Unfortunately, the time passed too fast." He grumbled as we sat in front of the sea of newscasters.

A man in a sailing hat asked the first question, "Dr. Masters, how do you feel about winning the Nobel Prize in Medicine?"

Dalton spoke deliberately, "I must admit I feel honored, but still, there is more research to be completed to find answers about the MECS Experiment. Each day brings me sad memories of the most cherished man I've ever known, Congressman Fletcher, who died in my care. I will share the Nobel Prize 10 million (SEK) between research and Fletcher's family. Perhaps their suffering will lessen with the reduction of the family's financial problems."

Unfortunately, astronauts cannot get insurance for their hazardous duty, and their family suffers. I administered the MECS Experiment to a great man, but his cruel death shouldn't have happened. Yet, he didn't die in vain. His death has helped us answer any questions concerning life and death. Do you have any more questions?"

A beautiful blonde reporter asked, "When do you plan to leave for Stockholm?"

Dalton hesitated, "Hi, Valerie. I'm leaving as soon as I can. The Nobel Prize award ceremony is on December 10, and I want to be back at KSC to prepare for the next flight scheduled on June 29."

I watched Dalton, and my heart sank. He didn't say to us, nor could he take his eyes off the attractive reporter, Valerie. I turned away and wanted to die.

I put my arm around his waist, and he turned away. The

rejection vibrated through my body as I spied the man from the fuel dock, watching.

He said, "Ladies and Gentlemen, not only did I win a Nobel Prize in Medicine, but I also won a lifetime prize. It's Susan, my fiancée. May the world know I have found happiness and happiness in the future. It is truly a gift to both of us. We will be going to Stockholm soon to prepare for the celebration. I will never forget how I got this award, the high price of success. May Congressman Dan Fletcher's family know I will never forget him and his life was not in vain."

All the troublesome thoughts floated away. Silently, I thought. *Dalton loves me. Yes, he loves me. Cute little Valerie can just take that and there.* I grinned from ear to ear. Yet, my *insecurities kept returning as I thought of all the cheaters throughout my life and the mentally abusive men who had taken advantage of my open heart. Yes, this time, I have chosen wisely.*

Dalton turned to me before God and everyone. He announced, "Now, Susan and I have a lot to plan: our wedding and the trip to Stockholm. So please excuse us; we are exhausted."

I almost fell, tripping over my own feet. I looked up just in time to see Valerie's jaw drop. I felt empty inside. What was this all about? Dalton didn't look her way but took my hand.

I whispered into his ear, "Dearest, when do you think this will take place?"

"Well, you know we are traveling to Stockholm for the Nobel Prize, and I possibly thought we could get married before the launch." He grinned, smiling from ear to ear.

"Dalton, you know I said before we would have to know each other for four seasons, my dear," I jokingly said.

Dalton's face changed, seeming angry and distant, and he didn't respond. I felt shut out. I finally said after the silence engulfed us, "Dalton, look at me. What is going on? You know I want to marry you, but you haven't even given me a ring."

"Well, I can take care of that-" he reached into his pocket, pulling out a small stainless-steel clamp from the boat and putting it on my right ring finger. "This is just temporary; the real one is coming just for you, my Sweetie. It's in the mail, so to speak. I don't have it now, but you have my heart, soul, and future. I'm just a man in love, Susan."

I was speechless. The sun looked brighter, the sky looked bluer, and I felt the best I had ever felt in my life. I wanted to scream at everyone, especially the girl, Valerie.

"Dalton, I, too. I can wait for the real wedding ring, but not forever," I began laughing, and so did Dalton.

He turned to the reporters and said, "Please leave us. We want some private time."

I saw the Elissa, the 1877 Iron Barque, sail past us. It was a magnificent ship, a British merchant vessel, and a real traditional "tall ship." It was a sign. It took dedication and money to preserve her impressive status. So, too, our relationship will be preserved and stay as strong as Elissa with her riveted iron hull.

"Susan, look at the Elissa; she is under full sail." Dalton continued. "You know, a Swede once owned her in 1912. It made two visits in the 1800s to Galveston. Ironically, now Galveston, Texas, is her permanent home over one hundred years later."

"Dalton, look at the three towering masts with ten square sails. It is incredible." I smiled from ear to ear.

We stared at Elissa for some time as we watched her outline pass in front of the beautiful, bright, orange-red sunset. Finally, the bothersome reporters had left. Dalton turned to me and took my hand. "What a beautiful ending to a beautiful vacation. I have never had such an amazing time. You are everything; I want to stay with you forever. The days can't pass fast enough until you are Mrs. Dalton Masters."

I started to respond, but the words weren't to come. Then, in the corner of my eye, I saw the ominous man again. He was staring at us. I grabbed Dalton's hand and said softly, "Let's get back to the boat. I want to go home to Kemah."

The following day, we were headed northwest through the ship channel, leaving the intruders behind.

We proceeded through the five-ship channels, then Bolivar Pass into Galveston Bay, bouncing through the water. I felt the salt-water spray felt salty on my lips. I licked them, tasting the salt and thinking of how I wanted to taste Dalton's lips. Then, my mind started thinking about the days we had just spent on faraway beaches, with tides moving against our bodies. I knew those days were going to be far and few between from now on.

I said, "Look to the starboard side. It's the USS Seawolf submarine."

Dalton laughed, "You must be mistaken, my friend; the USS Seawolf is a lost submarine, probably destroyed. However, you see the USS Cavalla, a memorial to the USS Seawolf in the Seawolf Park, Galveston. It's very confusing, and many people often mistake it."

"Isn't Cavalla a Gato class sub? I read somewhere that she was designed and built in the summer of 1943. On her maiden voyage, she sank Sharaku, a Japanese aircraft carrier." I asked.

"You are right. It's amazing how many people don't know about the submarine. Nor do they take the time to visit our famous park. Isn't that so," said Dalton.

"Remember, guy, I'm the blond." We both laughed. I just adored Dalton. He was not only a lover but also a real friend and so easy-going.

We passed by the Texas Dike, and I cringed, remembering a Poker Run race when a new boat owner raced to the next stop for a card. He came to a dead stop, didn't win the race, nor did he get his poker card. He ran into a sunken ship, and I watched them life-flight the team away. The captain didn't have tribal knowledge about the sunken ship. It is a harsh lesson to learn a deadly lesson.

I enjoy watching ships, whether they're a container or tankers or just yachts parading down the seafaring nautical highway. We headed to Portofino Marina. I had purchased a dockominium slip there, so I would always have a place to dock my boat. I felt safe in the marina. Everyone is family inside the gated community. No one could even work on your boat unless they are insured. Yes, it is a hole in the water, but not any hole. This hole had a luxury clubhouse and a swimming pool right on the waterway. I like swimming and watching the assortment of floating homes – yachts, pleasure boats, and fishing boats on the liquid highway.

Soon, we were at the Number 2 marker at the beginning of the Kemah channel, heading toward the Kemah Boardwalk. My heart raced in anticipation of returning home. As soon as we turned into the channel, alongside us was a floating procession of our friends. I couldn't believe my eyes when I saw Plankton, Half Moon, Shangri-La, Anastasia, Present Moment, Fishing Frenzy, Reality Check, Remedy, Fun Sun, Foot Loose, Iron Maiden, Miss Bez, It'll Do, Double Trouble, Andante, and the JonNe'. All the ships are beautiful and unique boats, some seafaring, and some just bay boats. All enjoyed afternoons on the bay or fishing offshore with everyone who was waving and smiling. It was good to see my friends again. It felt like we were gone an eternity. I realized they hadn't even met Dalton but had only heard about him in the News and tabloids.

When we turned into the marina, the clubhouse displayed a sign, "Welcome home, Dalton and Susan." One look at the banner told me Party Bill had designed the intricate, colorful sign.

All my friends gathered on the dock to help us tie up. Dalton pitched them the dock lines. Everyone hurried, winding the dock lines on the cleats. Surprisingly, the procedure went like a well-rehearsed play. Finally, we were safe in our harbor.

I noticed that even Ken was there to meet us. It was lunchtime. They prepared a feast on the island for all boaters, and everyone brought musical instruments. They began playing Kelly McGuire's original song, *Where Did Red Fish Go?*

I couldn't believe the turnout. I jumped with joy, kissing everyone. This time, Dalton just observed all the people in amazement. He didn't know what to think. He was now in my hood.

## Chapter 6 – Home

We partied the rest of the day without the interference of reporters. I was happy to return; it had been a long trip. Eventually, we had to batten down the hatches and head for Dalton's home on Clear Lake. As we drove down the street, I remembered his neighbor, Nancy. Her house looked closed up tighter than a drum. I said, "Dalton, look at Nancy's home. It looks like she isn't home."

Dalton said, "First thing in the morning, I'm going to give her a visit and see what's going on. I still don't understand what happened to my stuff."

I answered, "Dalton, I don't think you can blame her since it was her sister who was at home when I got there. The whole ordeal was very suspicious."

Dalton said, "I'm worried about Nancy and plan to find out some answers tomorrow. Right now, I'm beat and need sleep. Let's go to bed."

Looking into his room, I could see the glistening of the lake through a massive window. The view was mind-blowing. I noticed there was no shade or curtains. Dalton seemed to be reading my mind. "I wake up with the sunlight. I don't use an alarm clock, and I've never been late."

I began laughing, "Did you forget about The Bahamas when you left me waiting at the airport?"

"Oh yeah, guess you are right, but wasn't I worth waiting for?" he inquired.

"I guess you will do it…just a little bitty bit." I teased.

He threw me on the bed, and I bounced. I couldn't believe it. I felt like I was on a trampoline. I lifted my head, balanced myself on my knees, threw my head back, and giggled.

Dalton jumped next to me, and I fell on top of him. We kissed passionately, forgetting the world around us.

Soon, it was the next morning, and the sun's rays entered our secret haven. Dalton was stirring before he jumped out of bed and stood before me. "Would you like a cup of my specially brewed coffee?"

"Of course, I would, my darling," I purred as I propped myself onto the pillows.

I looked around the room, thinking this was my first time seeing Dalton's home. He had a life before me, and the surprise was Dalton's waterbed. That night, I enjoyed the comfort and the incredible sensation of being in a warm waterbed.

He soon returned with freshly brewed coffee. I took one sip. "Oh, Dalton, I like the cinnamon in the coffee." I was about to take another sip when a banging caused me to spill coffee all over the bed. Dalton ran to the front door.

I could barely hear voices when Dalton called for me. "Susan, come quickly; we have a visitor."

When I showed up, there stood a woman with the warmest smile in the world. I could only smile back. Dalton introduced me. "This is Nancy, my neighbor."

*I thought she didn't look anything like Carol, the woman I had previously met.* I held out my hand and smiled back, "It is so nice to meet you."

Nancy said, "I can't explain what happened when you came to my house that day. I had gone to the store, and when I returned, someone hit me over the head, locked me in the back bedroom, and gagged me. It was horrible."

Her face became distorted and angry. The anguish and pain were emanating from her blue eyes. I could tell the pain hadn't diminished even though it had been a year.

Dalton said, "I'm so sorry. I didn't know you would be in danger. I didn't know what was happening. I guess you read about Leona. Somehow, I think what happened to you is intertwined with the murder of Congressman Fletcher. Someone is trying to steal the formula."

Nancy responded, "I know you would never put me in harm's way, and I don't want you to feel bad. Since that day, I have kept one eye open when I sleep. Oh yeah, I want you to meet Magnum, my Doberman. He protects me day and night. Don't let his nice personality fool you. He would rip apart anyone who tried to harm me."

The beautiful, dark, shiny coat made me want to pet

Magnum. So, I stuck out my hand, and he growled.

Nancy spoke, "It's okay, Magnum. Let the nice lady pet you."

I said, "That's okay, are Magnums just so beautiful. I will get to know him when I spend more time at Dalton's home."

"I hope you spend as much time as possible. It would be great getting to know you. Dalton needs a woman around. Did I hear you guys are getting married?" she asked.

Dalton said, "News travels fast! Yes, we are, and very soon."

I chirped in, "So, we are. I'm looking forward to our wedding, and it will be in Sweden. Of course, an international wedding will be a first for me."

"Me too," Dalton gleamed with pride as he took my hand. Magnum growled and showed his teeth. We all laughed.

"Dalton, I don't think he likes men too much," I said.

"Well, I don't blame him. I like women, myself," he said.

Nancy said, "I'm just so excited about you two getting married."

"Thank you, Nancy. It means a lot to me. I wish you could join us in Sweden," Dalton said.

"No, I don't want to leave Kemah. I don't do so well traveling anymore," she said.

After our visit, we walked Nancy out the door. I surveyed Dalton's home. It was a rustic older home right on the water. The peace and tranquillity made me feel like I had been there forever. It was a fortress, a safe place from the photographers and nosy people. I was looking forward to spending time living on the water.

The days passed like the beginning and end of the ever-moving Clear Lake tide going back and forth to the sea. Dalton worked in the lab every day, early in the morning, until the sun went down. At night, the moonbeams hid his emotions. I felt his pain. * [4]

His devotion to the deceased Congressman Fletcher Dalton continued his life work, the MECS Experiment. His burning

---

[4] The poem "Forever In Time" is located in the Poetry Section.

passion for the success of the MECS experiment balanced the death of such a great man. It would prove Congressman Fletcher didn't die in vain.

We saw little of each other until, one day, he came home early, announcing a turn of events.

"Susan, come here quick; you will never guess what has happened," Dalton shouted.

I ran to him as he stood at the door like a little boy on Christmas morning.

I responded, "Tell me, I want to know the good news."

He said, "Susan, NASA assigned me as an astronaut on the next flight, STS-144. NASA wants me to perform the MECS Experiment again, perform a spacewalk to install additional MECS functions and protect the MECS capsule. My dream has come true: I will go into space. The long wait has ended.

"However, that leaves my job open, which means I have good News. You will run the MECS Experiment project from the ground. Your training will begin immediately."

I kissed Dalton from head to foot. "I'm so excited. All your dreams can come true, and I am proud to be part of them. I live happily every day, knowing you will be by my side. You are my professional space traveler."

Dalton kissed me, unleashing the affection he had stored up since his wife and children died.

Our eyes locked as he said, "I love you." We slowly walked to the bedroom. I wanted this time never to end.

He said, "You didn't answer me."

"About what," I questioned.

"About you're managing the MECS project while I'm in space," he said.

"Dalton, I didn't even hear you ask," I said.

"Well, since I'm not going to be available, and you know the experiment better than anyone else, I want you to be the project manager of the MECS experiment. So, he asked, "Who better than you?"

"I'm flattered, but this is such a big job. I don't know if I can do it since I have only managed small projects, but nothing like this," I responded.

"Susan, you can ensure the formula is correctly completed

just before the flight. I will be in quarantine at KSC. I need someone I can trust, and that is you. We are a team, Susan. I wouldn't say I like it when you sell yourself short. You are very good at what you do and a strong woman who knows the business. Are you up for the challenge?" Dalton said.

"Dalton, I don't know. Give me some time to think about it before I make a decision. I'm a perfectionist, and if I don't think I can do a perfect job, I don't want to take on such an incredibly high-exposure job. I know that I'm good at project management. Still, I don't know about managing a project so visible after what happened. When someone sabotaged the program, everyone will be watching me. Let me think about it," I said again.

I felt awful, but Dalton encouraged me. "Susan, life is always full of challenges, and this is just one. When life is storming, adjust your sails and point toward the stars. All you need to do is adjust your sails, and you will find the answer. I have faith in you, Susan. I know you can do it."

I said reluctantly, "I will do it; my sails may luff a little, but I will do my best."

The next day, Dalton began teaching me how to manage the project. We spent days going over the procedures. It was grueling, but I knew this was something I had to do if I was going to succeed. It was just what had to happen.

Later, I called, "Uncle! Dalton, I can't look at another document to save my life. I just want to go to bed. My eyes are killing me. Please, let's go to bed."

# Chapter 7 – Clear Lake Outing

The following day, Ken picked us up on Dalton's pier in his jazzy black go-fast boat, which reminded me of a sleek Cuban cigar on fire.

I joked, climbing aboard, searching for adventure. "This is fun. I am now one of those girls with looks and no brains. Now you don't have to talk to me."

Dalton smiled, "You have one part right; you are beautiful, Susan, and brilliant. You fit well on a sailboat or a motorboat, just like a precision engine."

I laughed. Dalton made me happy, and he made me feel so treasured. All my life, I had felt that I wasn't good enough. His continuous positive remarks blew my insecurities into the wind.

I watched the man I adore take the wheel. He looked as comfortable on a go-fast boat as he had on the sailboat.

Ken focused on Dalton, "I hear you are going up in space. Who is going to run the MECS project?"

Without hesitation, he said, "Susan is my project lead. She will manage the project."

You could see Ken's veins pop out on his forehead. I couldn't believe my eyes. I waited to see what Ken's response would be.

His reaction surprised me. "Do you think Susan is ready for an assignment as enormous as the MECS Experiment?"

Dalton said, "Of course she is; her experience in Software Quality and Hardware Quality makes her a natural. She also has a project management certification."

"Dalton, I would like to take the challenge. I know the equipment, the process, and I've been your right-hand man for years," he said.

"This is not about history. It is about who I consider would be the best in the position. Your job is to work as a partner with Susan at every step of the project. I know she is new, but I have all the confidence in both of you to perform the process according to the requirements," Dalton said adamantly.

Ken seemed to calm down; at least his veins weren't protruding.

I smiled, "Ken, I'm looking forward to working with you. It's going to be so exciting, and I need someone I can trust. There is so much to do and remember. Do you know where you store the documented procedures after the last flight?" I inquired.

"Yes, I do. Once we get to Kennedy, I will bring them to you, and we can get started. Of course, Dalton will supply the MECS solution as he did last time," Ken said.

"The solution is formulated and is ready to mix right before the flight. However, it will take all night to mix the solution just like the last time," Dalton explained.

"We will do whatever it takes," Ken said.

"Yes, whatever it takes," I said. The wind blew against my face. I held on for dear life. The boat rolled back and forth as we went by the red markers going through the Galveston Channel. I couldn't believe how fast we were going. My body bounced as we hit each wave.

A container ship passed with a leading wave splitting at its bow. I knew we were in for some rock-n-rolling. Here it came, "Ride'em, Cowboy," I screamed and laughed as my hair blew away from my face.

We headed back to the restaurant row, and the aromatic food smells made me hungry. I looked at the familiar places, all the restaurants that had recovered from the last hurricane. I was glad to see the boardwalk back to normal. Unfortunately, there was still debris in the water. It reminded me of all the hardships everyone went through because of the most massive storm surge Galveston Bay had ever seen.

I said, "Let's stop at the Aquarium Restaurant and have lunch."

"Sounds good to me," Dalton said.

"Me too," Ken agreed.

We tied the boat up beside the Aquarium Restaurant and made our way into the sea-designed building. In the middle was a huge aquarium with sharks swimming back and forth. Dalton had gone to the restroom, and I was staring at the fish, going back and forth.

Ken came up behind me and said, "Wonder what it would be like to be ripped apart by a shark"?

Cold chills went up to my back. I got spooked but turned around and said, "Let's hope none of us ever experience such a terrifying death."

Ken just stared at me until Dalton arrived.

When we sat at the table, Ken approached Dalton, "Do you remember my telling you about my backer, Research Underwriters for Specialty Hospitals, RUSH? They want to do an article about the MECS Experiment. Would you have time to meet with them?"

Dalton paused for a second and said, "I don't think I will have the opportunity, but maybe after the mission, I will."

Ken looked disappointed and said, "Well, maybe later on, but the board of directors are some of the most powerful oncologists in the world. You would be impressed with the Who's Who list from hospitals specializing in cancer research in New York, Philadelphia, Houston, Paris, Rio, and Luxemburg."

Dalton responded, "On second thought, it would be interesting to meet some of my peers."

Ken said persuasively, "Even Ed Hart, one of your fellow astronauts, is on the RUSH board of directors. I can arrange an interview with them when you are ready, my friend."

Dalton said, "Well, let's see when I have an opening in my schedule."

After we finished eating, Dalton said, "I have a surprise for you, Susan. We are on a mission to find your wedding dress. You can go to the Galleria and shop at Neiman Marcus, Saks, Nordstrom, Lord, and Taylor, or anywhere your heart desires."

Ken said, "I'll take the boat back to the Endeavor Marina and meet up with you two later. I'm afraid clothes shopping is neither my cup of tea nor the Galleria."

"Bye, Ken. Dalton, you are full of surprises. You want me to find a wedding dress. I have never met a man who would go shopping with me, yeah," I said, walking through the restaurant door.

## Chapter 8 – Shopping

A black limousine Hummer was waiting in front of the Aquarium restaurant at the Kemah Boardwalk, with a fully stocked bar. I climbed into the luxurious leather seats, waiting for my soon-to-be husband.

He entered into the backseat, and I purred, "Dalton, this is perfect. I feel like I'm in fantasy land."

Just then, as we were going over the Kemah Bridge, I looked over and saw a navy-blue car with dark-tinted windows. I gasped. Someone was following us. I didn't know who, but I certainly didn't like it. It was such a horrible feeling. I must have turned pale as a ghost.

Dalton asked, "What's wrong?" I pointed in their direction, but the car had accelerated and was out of sight.

"Dalton, it's them. I don't like it. Someone is following us again. We are not safe. I want us to head out to sea again and be safe. But, please, Dalton, let's not stay," I begged.

"Susan, it's just your imagination. I know we have had some stressful times, but you are shopping for your wedding dress today. It will be a wonderful day. Nothing can go wrong on this special day," he said very persuasively.

My stomach sank, but I smiled. "I will trust my fiancé." I held his hand, squeezing it very hard. I knew it wasn't over, but whom could we fight? The enemy had no face.

The day I should have been my happiest, I wasn't happy. Instead, I felt the navy-blue car watching us, watching me.

The car hummed, and soon, we were in front of the Galleria.

The chauffeur opened the door directly in front of Neiman Marcus. I pretended I was a movie star as I got out, feeling as if I were famous. The entire world was mine. "Dalton, I'm on a mission. I will pick out my wedding dress, which you cannot see until the wedding day. Please meet me in one hour."

"I've never seen a woman who could find an article of clothing in an hour. So, hmmm, but, you know, there's always a first time," Dalton said.

He was so right. Two hours later, after going in and out of

ten stores, I finally found a simple white satin dress with a long train. It had delicate tiny pearls surrounding the low, revealing neckline.

Next, I picked out a simple headpiece to wear. I wanted to look elegant like a white trophy white rose standing next to Dalton. Reflecting, I had come a long way from the time I saw Dalton sawing on his rudder, as he said, fixing it.

*Little did I know one day, we would become man and wife. I had only wanted a sailing partner but had gone on an incredible adventure, and now I was to be married. My excitement was boiling over like a volcano, ready to burst.*

*The honeymoon could not come soon enough, even though it would be in cold, dreary Stockholm. I would have preferred the Caribbean, lying barefoot on a deserted beach with warm breezes. Now, the wedding would be in the frigid air, which cuts through your soul. This new location was unsettling. No matter what, our love will keep us warm, I thought.*

*Across the store, I saw a mannequin wearing a beautiful white, longhaired fur coat. It would keep me warm. It was calling me.*

*I told myself; this is perfect, white on white with my blond curly hair. Red roses will offset the white beautifully."*

*I wore the soft, white fur fox coat, which fit me like a soft kid glove. The matching white fur hat framed my face. The fur coat would complete my trousseau.*

The sales clerk approached, "Darling, you look so gorgeous. It matches your hair, and you look just like Julie Christie in <u>Dr. Zhivago</u>. It's an incredible look. I see you have a wedding dress. Must you be getting married? Have you tried it on? Let me get the perfect bridal veil for you. Please tell me, when are you getting married?

She reminded me of Chatty Cathy, the woman I met at Ellington Airport when I met Dalton in the Bahamas. How could I ever forget the beginning of my adventure with Dalton?

I asked, "Where is the dressing room so I can try on my wedding dress?"

"Follow me, young lady. My name is Pat, and I'm here at your beck and call," she said with authority, taking all the garments.

I looked at her for a second, analyzing her. She was of a small frame, dyed dark hair, makeup overdone, and dressed to kill. Yes, she had done this for a very long time.

Therefore, I turned and said, "We are getting married in Sweden in a couple of weeks. How long have you been a saleslady?"

With encouragement, she burst from the seams with energy, "I have been at this store for many years. I started before I finished high school, and I have dressed many fine women like you. Once, I even dressed the President's wife, Barbara Bush, with pearls and everything. She is a charming lady and so gracious."

She placed the clothes in the dressing room, "My name is Pat. If you need anything, please let me know."

I couldn't believe the prices of the clothes; they were on sale. "Fifty percent off, praise the Lord," I screamed with excitement.

The dress looked so elegant. I walked out of the dressing room, and Pat handed me a veil with tiny pearls embroidered on the headpiece. She positioned it on my head as the trail fell gracefully to the ground. I stood back, gazing at the reflection in the mirror. I looked stunning.

Instantly, the paparazzi surrounded me. Once again, flashing lights blinded me, as I froze in my steps.

Pat took my shaking hand. She led me blindly back to the dressing room. I couldn't see anything but bright, indistinguishable images in my constricted pupils. All the way back to the dressing room, the five reporters badgered me with questions.

"When are you getting married? Are you going to Sweden with Dr. Masters? Has he found the fountain of youth? Can he cure cancer?" they all asked simultaneously.

Pat knew this was very uncomfortable for me and asked, "Who are you, and why are these reporters following you? Are you famous?"

I started laughing, "No, I'm not famous, but I'm marrying a legendary aeronautical scientist. The reporters want to know anything and everything about us. It is so difficult. I have no privacy."

The next minute, tears started running down my cheeks from the excitement of the marriage and the memory of Congressman Fletcher's death entangled in my heart. The stress kept multiplying as the hounding photographers shattered my happiness.

All of a sudden, I wanted to leave, to escape from all the excitement. The only thing I hadn't gotten were my shoes, but to avoid the reporters, I would make do with what I had at home. I sat down in the dressing room with the door closed. I was afraid to leave the dressing room. Then, I heard the reporters begin asking questions to someone.

Pat said, "Should I check?"

"Please do," I asked, hearing their voices outside the room.

Pat left, and soon Dalton entered. He saw the tears running down my face. He leaned my face up and passionately kissed the tears away.

Dalton said, "I will not let anyone hurt you. Let's get out of this place. First, have you paid for your wedding outfit?"

As soon as the words came out of his mouth, Pat came in, "Here is the bill. How would you like to pay for it?"

Dalton handed her his credit card. "Use this, and please be discreet about what Susan bought."

"Oh, I understand; your confidentiality is of utmost importance, but the news reporters took a million pictures in her gown," Pat said in her ladylike fashion.

Pat handed me the garment bags. I held them close to my body as if someone would steal them from me. I tried to compose myself before leaving the dressing room. My eyes focused on Dalton as he led me from my safe haven. Pat followed, watching the reporters have a barrage of questions while they took unlimited photographs. It was a wild exit.

# Chapter 9 –Shooting

Suddenly, we heard a loud shot. The mannequin next to us exploded into a million pieces. Dalton threw me to the ground, and my body crashed to the floor. The force was incredible. The reporters scurried to take cover.

Dalton fell on top of me, "Don't get up! Susan, we have to protect ourselves."

He gripped his cell phone and dialed 911. I could see the veins bursting in his intense face. The trauma magnified as Dalton said, "Shooter at Galleria Mall. Come quickly to Neiman Marcus Ladies' department."

"Dalton, why is this happening?" I whispered.

"I think it is a warning of some type. I'm not sure," Dalton said fervently. "Let's get out of this place. I don't know how yet!"

Dalton didn't want anything to happen to us, and neither did I.

I felt someone grab my feet. Spontaneously, I screamed. It was from Pat. I almost had forgotten about her. She whimpered.

I said, "Pat, are you okay?"

She responded, "So far, I am. Susan, what is going on? Are you a target?"

I answered, trying to cover up what I felt. Yes, we were targets, but I didn't want to tell Pat the truth since it would scare her more than she was already. I couldn't get rid of the picture of the navy-blue car, and now this is in the back of my mind.

Dalton answered, "Well, Pat, lately, there have been killings in malls all over the country. It could be a random act. I'm not sure. All I know is that we need to take cover and wait for the police to protect us. I wish I had a gun."

Pat looked at me and said, "I have a gun if I can get to my purse."

"Where is the gun? I'll get it," Dalton whispered.

"It is behind the counter across the room in a Coach black

purse," she said.

"You girls stay here. I'm going to find it," he commanded.

*My mind was racing with fear. Not again! The nightmare was happening again. Was someone trying to kill Dalton again? Were we ever going to be safe?*

Suddenly, a man appeared in a turban. He was visibly shaking when a loud reverberating shot into his white turban as blood gushed everywhere. He fell on top of us. The dead man had no gun, and I decided he wasn't the mall assassin.

Pat whimpered.

"Shhhh, Pat, the killer may hear you," I was afraid to say anything else and didn't move the man's body. His hollow eyes were staring at me. Had I not seen him gunned down in front of me, I would have thought he was the shooter. His was the perfect description of an assassin. Looks are sometimes deceiving; one must remember. I cringed as I heard several more shots.

In the corner of my eye, I saw a young, blond-headed man with crystal blue piercing eyes in a sculptured model's face. He held a .357 magnum.

I stopped breathing. Did the shooter see us? I could hear Pat gasp. She had tears running down her eyes. I prayed, "Please, Lord, don't let us die."

He glanced in our direction and moved toward us. His face had no emotion. Where was Dalton?

I could see the assassin, sweat dripping down his handsome face. His pupils looked dilated, with a wild, reckless look searching back and forth for more victims.

Please, God, don't let him see us. He turned little by little, coming toward us. I felt something warm on my leg. Pat wet herself. I thought, oh my God, this is worse than Bahamians shooting at us on the wild boat race. At least we could move and not be trapped like a wild hunted animal. Now, time passed in slow motion. My future wants and desires began to disappear with each of the shooters' steps.

I looked up, taking a shallow breath. The shooter spotted us. His voice vibrated through my head, "Stand up."

My legs shook as I stood up. Pat, just lay there. I tried to help her up. She began whimpering and crying, "Please don't hurt me."

I stood in silence. What could I do? The helplessness of the situation froze me into a statue, just like a mannequin. I held my breath, waiting for the final shot. It didn't come.

He put the gun down Pat's throat. Then, laughing, the murderer screamed, "I want to see you beg."

*I thought how strange he would want to hear her beg when he had a gun down her throat. She couldn't even talk. Finally, I understood he meant me.*

I was speechless. The shooter was staring as I eased over to one side. He removed the gun from Pat's mouth and pointed it in my direction. I looked at him directly into his deep, crystal blue eyes, waiting for the inevitable death.

I heard a single crisp shot explode loudly, vibrating through my body. I grabbed my chest, feeling for blood, and felt no blood. Instead, I realized the assassin had fallen across the lifeless man in the turban, both dead.

Dalton ran beside me, holding the smoking gun, "Are you ladies, okay?"

Pat trembled. I held onto Dalton, wondering, "Are we still in danger?"

"No, I don't know, but I believe he acted alone."

The paparazzi, hot on our pursuit, had witnessed the whole ordeal. They began pelting Dalton with questions. It was apparent he was a hero again. We had so many unanswered questions. But unfortunately, we would get no answers from a dead man.

Dalton chose to protect me. The unknown man had to die, or we would be dead. Death seemed so close to us, as if always hovering around the corner like a vulture.

I felt sure my retired father had viewed the whole episode on TV since he watched the News endlessly. He was probably wondering if I were still alive since the News broadcasted, I was a hostage.

I searched my purse for my cell phone. I quickly called. "Daddy, I'm okay. Dalton and I are both okay. It is shocking. I almost died, but Dalton saved my life. I saw two men die in front of my eyes."

Irrationally, I exclaimed, "I just bought my wedding dress,

and this happened. Is it a sign?"

Daddy patiently answered, "No, Susan, this is not a sign about you and Dalton. It may be a sign of Dalton's work and safety and yours. You have to be careful. Why don't you come home to Mom and Daddy? I will keep you safe."

I glanced down at my wedding trousseau covered in blood. Tears flowed down my face. The tears soon turned into sobs. On the phone, I heard Daddy say, "Susan, are you okay? Speak to me, honey."

Dalton took the phone away. "Sir, this has been a difficult situation. We will call you back when things settle down. Susan is okay. She is safe with me." With that, he said, "Goodnight, Sir."

The police questioned Dalton and me. We told them what we knew, which wasn't much. Next, they questioned Pat since she owned the gun.

After the interrogation, he took my hand and led me out of the mall. I left my beautiful white wedding dress, a white fox coat, and the veil dripping with crimson blood lying on the floor.

I heard Pat call out, "I will get you replacements and call you, Susan. It will be okay. We are all okay."

I mumbled, "Yes, we are all okay. We are not dead. Dalton, did this have anything to do with the MECS Experiment?" I asked, still in shock.

## Chapter 10 – Police

"I don't know, Susan. We may have been in the wrong place at the wrong time. I am tired of being a target practice. I need to investigate. I'm going to call Security at the Cape," Dalton said.

I yelled, "I want to leave the States away from this chaos. This event is déjà vu. Three months ago, in The Bahamas, it was the same bloody scenario. Maybe Sweden will be safe for us. Let's go now."

Dalton said, "Be calm and let me think. Then, I will figure out something."

As soon as we arrived home, I took a long bath, trying not to close my eyes. When I did, I could still see the helpless victim falling on top of me with his glaring eyes staring into nothing. He was dead. I wondered if the man had a family. Were they praying to Allah to speed his soul to his seventeen vestal virgins in heaven? The visions were in my brain. Make them go away: the assailant dying, the blood seeping into the white linen veil, my veil. I closed my eyes, trying to make the visualizations disappear. The hot, steamy water eased my aches and pains but didn't remove the memory of the horror.

Dalton entered the room slowly. He watched me as I lay in the sweltering heat, moisture bubbling on my forehead dripping down my cheekbones.

He gently kissed the moisture away from my forehead and cheekbones, moving down to my breasts. Then, Dalton climbed into the bathtub in his shorts.

I opened my eyes to see the Dalton, which made the day melt away. All the badness disappeared, just for a little while. I wanted to feel his tenderness as his muscular arms surrounded me. I traced his features with my hands. I tried to capture every line in his face, his shoulders, and the muscles in his arms and chest. It is what I want to remember for the rest of my life. Never did I want to forget our life is so short. It could end today or last until eternity. We enjoyed the minute, not speaking of what had happened.

The doorbell rang, interrupting the moment. Begrudgingly, Dalton got out of the tub, dressed, and opened the door. I heard the police enter.

They waited for me to dress. The interrogation began when I entered the living room. I dreaded questions of any form.

One detective and two police officers stood at the front door as if they were rigid columns built into the house. Finally, the questions began, and we both answered their probing questions.

The tall detective with the chiseled face began, "I'm Ed Davis, the homicide detective. I have some questions. I am going to ask you about the events of this afternoon. Did you recognize the man who tried to kill you?"

Dalton responded, "No, I have never seen him."

"Neither have I," I stated.

"Let me show you what I removed from his jean pocket," he said as he showed us an evidence bag containing a single sheet of paper, tattered and torn. There was a scribbled message, "Destroy Dr. Masters, kill Susan."

I gasped, and Dalton turned pale, as white as snow. I wanted to scream hysterically. While I tried to compose myself, Dalton began speaking in a slow and thought-out manner. "Can you find out who wrote the note?"

"Not sure. It might be the murderer's handwriting. Maybe he got a message from someone and wrote it on this paper. I'm afraid your lives are in danger. We will have the two police officers guard you and Susan. I understand you have plans to go abroad. I believe in Sweden."

"Yes, we will be traveling on December 5, five days before the Nobel festival day on December 10. In Sweden, we will marry on December 12, Susan's birthday."

Ed left, leaving the two police officers to guard us until we got on the plane.

I was exhausted with fear. Having a relationship with Dalton had been so dangerous. I believed the running, hiding, and looking over our shoulders had ended, but it hadn't. The monsters were still after us. They wanted Dalton dead and now me -- whoever they were.

Early the following day, the doorbell rang. I heard Ed open

the door. I ran down the stairs and found a delivery guy with three huge packages. In addition, there was a note from Pat, the saleslady. "I hope this will cheer you up from all the stress of shopping."

I smiled and opened up the packages. The first package was the veil with tiny pearls on it. I held it close to my face and gently placed it on the top of my head. It fell in folds around my face. Again, I smiled, making Ed grin.

I tore open the large box and pulled out the beautiful white fox. I put it on, wrapping it around me and feeling its smoothness, feeling the tingly fur pressed against my fingertips. I closed my eyes and immediately saw blood all over the coat. I screamed, threw it down, and began crying.

Dalton came running down the stairs, seeing the packages. He instinctively knew what had happened. He held me while the fountain of tears flowed down my cheeks and onto the beautiful veil. His fingers wiped away the wetness.

The detective went into the kitchen. Dalton said, "Let's go to Sweden tomorrow. We can go skiing, snowmobiling, and ice skating. I haven't been ice skating in such a long time. We will have so much fun."

My blotchy face somehow murmured, "I do want to go." That's all I could say. Yes, I would feel safe in Sweden, away from danger."

The next day, the police escorted us to Houston Intercontinental Bush Airport. I was relieved to get away from the States and all the chaos. I returned the beautiful white fox and veil to the store, along with the tragic memories.

## Chapter 11 – Sweden

The Scandinavian Airlines System treated us like royalty. I had never been overseas, so the excitement bubbled inside me. The first class was luxurious; the champagne flowed like water. Dalton and I were holding each other's hands, thankful to be leaving the traumatic mall events.

Dalton said, "I would like one more, please, to toast my beautiful fiancée, the woman I have dreamed of for years. The special lady I want to spend the rest of my life with, enjoying every waking moment." He started to kiss me when the cute airline attendant interrupted us.

She handed us the glasses of champagne, "Here's your bubbly. My name is Lynn Townsend; if you need anything else, ring your bell."

I looked out the window, looking at our approach into Stockholm.

"Dalton, if I didn't know any better, I would think we were flying into Minneapolis. It is unbelievably beautiful. Look at all the lakes; it is a winter wonderland."

"Yes, look at the lakes." A voice came from behind me. I turned around, and there stood Ken.

Dalton said, "What a great surprise."

The silvery-white snow covered the lakes with cabins tucked away on the icy shores. I imagined the couples inside the cabins snuggled close together by the warmth of the comforting fire. The billowy smoke drifted out of the chimneys. I tried to imagine what it would be like in the summer. I envisioned green pastures, making a design like a well-planned quilt. I saw a marina with all the sailboats onshore and a land bed for a long winter's sleep.

I looked at Dalton and said, "Too bad we can't go sailing."

"No, we can't go sailing, but after the ceremony, we can go skiing. The Swedish built a slope in the middle of town for the Olympics. You can ski, can't you?" he asked with a sheepish grin on his face.

We had never discussed the subject.

"Well, my Darling, I have tried, and I will try one more time with you. I'm not exactly a skilled skier, but I can make it down an intermediate slope; slowly, that is, very slowly," I said without making a fuss. I want to say, no, I don't want to ski, but maybe, just maybe, I can get down the hill. But, wow, I wish it were summer; the place would be full of sailboats.

I said, "I heard that in the summer, the Jubilee Sailing Regatta takes place with local sailboats and invitations to Olympians of all sports. It is held right here in Stockholm each year in June. Dalton, why couldn't they have the Nobel Prize ceremony in the summer?"

Dalton responded, "I believe it is in remembrance of Dr. Nobel's birthday, December 10. You can visit the Stockholm Swedish National Museum inside, away from the freezing weather. It is the oldest museum in Sweden and displays the painting "The Scream," which someone stole mysteriously. It is a famous theft carried out in daylight before security got tight, a sensational art heist."

We started our descent. *I thought about the events that created chaos in life. My eyes twitched, remembering the close encounters. I assumed I could now relax, being far away from Texas and The Bahamas during our landing. The bad guys are not here.*

I asked Dalton, "I still don't understand. Why is someone trying to kill us?"

Dalton looked at me with deep concern in his dark brown eyes and said, "Susan, I think they want to kill you or me to get the MECS formula. If they can get to me through you, then they will. I won't let them hurt you, and I'm not going to give them the satisfaction of hiding. I want to have a normal life. We will live life the way we choose, but you have a choice. If you weren't near me, you would be much safer, and I've thought about this numerous times. I know it would be best for you to leave, but part of me is very selfish. I want to keep you near me to make sure nothing happens to you."

I almost quit breathing, thinking Dalton would send me back to the States. No wedding and no honeymoon.

"Dalton, I couldn't leave even if I tried. It's where we are going to get married and our honeymoon." I turned and kissed him with the emotion I felt deep inside me. My whole body shook with fear. I didn't know what would happen next.

## Chapter 12 – Grand Hotel

After we got through customs, we went directly to our hotel, an old, established Grand Hotel that had been around for centuries. It reminded me of a castle. The hotel desk clerk pointed us toward an old ornate elevator, which opened and stood an elevator operator who looked ancient. His hands twisted, but he had a broad smile as we entered the elevator.

"Hi, my name is Jon DeJongh. Which floor, please?" He said in a heavy accent, but his English language was surprisingly good.

Dalton said, "The sixth floor."

I felt as if I had gone back in time as he closed the gate, securing the door.

The elevator opened onto an ornate hallway trimmed in gold and burgundy. Dalton found the door to our room, which opened to a setting of elegance beyond my imagination. I felt like a princess waiting to marry my prince. I twirled in circles, holding my skirt out like the belle of the ball.

Dalton put his arms around me, and we danced across the room as he hummed the Blue Danube waltz. It was a dream that had come true. I was in heaven. *Never would I have believed I would have a man who could make me feel special; to top it off, he was romantic.*

Dalton whispered into my ear, "I have made all the plans for our wedding. The honeymoon will be a total surprise. Let's go see the city."

The same elevator operator, DeJongh, took us down to the lobby. He asked, "Would you like to hear some history of the Grand Hotel?"

I immediately said, "Of course."

He began, "Ever since 1901, Stockholm hosted the Nobel Prize of Medicine laureates, and they have stayed in the Nobel suite, as you are. In addition, we hold the gala banquet in the venerable setting of our very own hotel's Mirror Room."

I could tell he was very proud of his heritage and his hotel. I said, "This is certainly an elegant place, and thanks for the information. It is the most beautiful hotel I've ever visited."

DeJongh said, "If I may say so, you two make a beautiful couple."

Dalton replied, "Thank you."

I blushed.

We walked outside to the main street. I peered down the boulevard, observing brightly lit quaint restaurants and exclusive shops. The smells emanating from the restaurants reminded me of my hunger pains. My stomach started growling.

Dalton laughed, "I know someone who could use something to eat."

I smiled, "Please feed me; feed me."

We walked by a charming place with low lights and a romantic ambiance. Music drifted to the streets.

"Let's go into this place."

The Matre'd showed us a corner table with fresh linens. Everything looked clean and crisp. I remembered our first meal in The Bahamas before the chaos began.

A slim, handsome young man with slicked back blond hair ventured to our table. "My name is Sven. Here menu, sir, for the beautiful lady."

He spoke in broken English; however, it sounded unpleasant. Dalton saw me inquisitively looking at him.

Dalton said in a broken foreign accent, "Can I choose dinner? I will make a surprise."

I laughed at his accent, "Of course you can."

"Sir, like dinner with an appetizer? We have champagne good for you," he said in his new foreign accent.

The exquisite gold and burgundy room had an opulent chandelier with crystals that scattered rainbows around the room. Out the window was displayed the crisp white snow blowing in the breeze. I could barely see the Grand Train Station with the mounds of snow swept over the sidewalk.

Another brawny waiter with dark black hair came up to our table, announcing in perfect English, "I will be your new waiter."

When I looked at him sternly, he explained, "He had a family emergency and left. So let me retake your order.

The hair on the back of my neck stood up. It didn't sound right. I politely said, "What happened to Sven?"

I whispered into Dalton's ear, "Let's leave."

Dalton looked surprised but accommodated my request. "Sir, we have decided that we have to leave." We both got up and made our way to the door. The man followed us to the door, trying to persuade us to stay. The more he spoke, the more his personality became sterner.

When we entered the fresh cold air, I took Dalton's hand, "He gave me the creeps. Do you think the bad guys followed us?"

"Anything is possible, but right now, my stomach is growling. So, let us not dwell on the subject; this is a night for a romantic dinner, even if we have it in the hotel room. As a matter of fact, let's go back and get room service," he suggested.

"I ditto that. Sorry if I ruined our meal, but sometimes intuition is the best call. Thank you for being so understanding," I said.

As we walked back to the hotel, I glimpsed into the park and saw two lovers. A heavy mink coat surrounded them, and it was apparent they were making love. Next, I saw another couple, but it was two women passionately kissing each other.

I pointed their way; "There is love in the freezing arctic air right in the downtown area, naughty, naughty. Who would have thought it?"

Dalton gregariously said, "I've never seen anything like this before in all my travels."

"Well, we must be in Paris of Scandinavia. Romance is in the air, and I know Cupid must live here. I know what I want for dinner."

Dalton took my hand, hurrying me back to the hotel.

At least the same elevator operator was at the hotel — no mysterious changes had been made since we had left.

The bewitching hour had passed, and it was too late for room service. The only thing we could get was a bottle of wine and cheese. Both of us were very hungry, but the cheese and crackers satisfied our rumbling stomachs. I would rather go hungry than be in danger. Soon, we were sound asleep, safe in each other's arms.

## Chapter 13 – Romance

The following day, I felt Dalton moving beside me. He began stroking my back with his smooth hands. I lived for his tender touch. He made me feel incredible; his warmth illuminated in all his movements. His kisses were sweeter than wine. This song went through my head as we made love, and afterward, I began singing.

"Well, when I was a young girl, I've never been kissed

I could feel his breath against my skin. It made me feel treasured more than life itself.

Because he had kisses sweeter than wine
He had, mmm, mmm, kisses sweeter than wine
(Sweeter than wine)

I knew that love didn't come like this very often and that he was so much a part of me now. I was soon to be his wife and would be with him forever.

Yes, he had all my love, caresses, and me with him forever.

Because he had kisses sweeter than wine
He had, mmm, mmm, kisses sweeter than wine
(Sweeter than wine)

All our work on the MECS program made it worthwhile. The accomplishments of the cancer program and all the sacred lives saved. All that mattered was the two of us. Even with all the risks, dangers, and adventures, our love made it all worthwhile.

Because he had kisses sweeter than wine
He had, mmm, mmm, kisses sweeter than wine
(Sweeter than wine)

**JIMMIE RODGERS lyrics - Kisses Sweeter Than Wine**

He was incredible. Each touch brought shivers over my body. His hands ran down my back, bringing my body toward his lips, and I trembled in excitement. My breasts rubbed against his chest, making my nipples hard just as he entered me. I let out a sound of satisfaction as his rhythm quickened, and he came to a climax. I didn't know that lovemaking could only get better and better. I wanted it to last forever.

Afterward, I lay in bed as I peeked out of the window. Ice was hanging from the windows of the hotel. It reminded me of a winter wonderland. Children were ice-skating out on an ice rink in which the town had flooded with water. We called for room service and spent the day in bed.

We ordered movies and lazily watched for a little while, slept when we wanted, and made love all day. Soon, it was time to go to the banquet at the Stockholm Concert Hall. The elegant, red, sophisticated, princess-cut dress fit me like a glove. As I put it on, I saw Dalton's eyes brighten.

"My Princess, you will be the belle of the ball. Please remember with whom you went to the ball and only come home with me," he said as he kissed me on the neck.

"Since you are my prince, I can only come home with my one and only," I said.

I had never been happier in my entire life. The world had changed since I had met my soul mate, and he was my soul mate. I couldn't imagine life without Dalton.

## Chapter 14 – Nobel Banquet

Dalton and I walked hand in hand in silence to the banquet at the Grand Hotel. *I thought how wonderful tonight was, with his incredible research accomplishments rewarded. He certainly deserved such a great honor.* As we walked into the Blue Room, many strangers smiled and greeted us. It was evident that they knew Dalton was one of the Nobel Laureates at the banquet given by the King of Sweden, Karl Ásgeirr **XIII**.

Dalton said, "Look, there is the King of Sweden, Karl Ásgeirr XIII."

I looked toward him and saw a handsome man with dark, wavy hair looking our way. Our eyes met, and his gaze sent out an overwhelming sense of lust. My body got as cold as the snow outside, with an icy breeze going through my body. I didn't know what to do. I just felt so helpless in his presence. Could Dalton sense my anguish? I wanted to run; however, I just stood still, mesmerized by his hypnotic charisma. I felt very uncomfortable. His reputation had preceded him. He was every woman's dream, and he knew it, a true womanizer.

I finally turned away, and Dalton was not beside me. He was nowhere in sight.

Before I knew it, the king strode deliberately across the room, stopping in front of me. Our eyes met, and he said, "Hi, you look as if you are lost. What can I do for you? I can show you all of Stockholm. It is a very naughty town with temptations for any desire. I would enjoy showing you the beauty and life in this frozen land."

*My thoughts were going wild, and I felt very vulnerable. The King's advances were bold. He was making a pass. Where was Dalton? I wanted him to be by my side. I didn't know how to handle this powerful man,* so I took a deep breath and said, "Your Majesty, I'm afraid I already have an escort. You may know him, Dr. Dalton Masters, recipient of the Nobel Prize of Medicine."

"I apologize. Your pictures in the news don't give you justice; you're certainly stunning. I knew it was you. I heard so much about you, Susan, and your companion, the amazing scientist Dr. Dalton Masters.  It will be an honor and my humble privilege to give him his award tomorrow."

Just then, Dalton approached us.  The King turned away and held his hand out to Dalton.  I was still gasping with surprise.

Dalton said, "It is a pleasure to see you again, Your Highness.  I have heard so much about you."

King Karl Ásgeirr XIII said, "And you, please call me Karl, in private.  I would like to discuss a sensitive subject in my private chambers after dinner.  It's rather personal.  Susan, you may attend."

*I thought I knew everything about Dalton, but I didn't think he knew a king.  How surprising.*  Ken approached us, asking Dalton the same thing I was thinking, "When did you meet the king?  You certainly are full of surprises."

Dalton grimaced, "Ken, you are too nosy.  My relationship with anyone is my private business."

His response took me back.  It reminded me of when Ken kept asking about the MECS formula ingredients.  He got defensive.

I was glad I hadn't said anything.  I didn't understand Dalton's reaction.  However, I knew he had his reasons, but I was as curious as Ken.

I felt like royalty when the royal trumpet fanfare vibrated through me.  We entered the elegant red and gold banquet hall.  I pretended to be a queen.  We found our Nobel menu and sat at the long banquet table, which seated 80 people. The dinner began with sole, Swedish shellfish, and a filet of veal, accompanied by seasonal vegetables and potato terrine. It all melted in my mouth.

Dalton and I ate until our heart's content.  Everyone was trying to ask him questions about the King.

Dalton politely said, "I'm having dinner with my soon-to-be wife.  Please respect our privacy."

With that message, everyone left us alone to enjoy the most incredible meal I have ever eaten.  It was a night I'd never forget.  Not many people ever get to participate in such an honorable event.

I said, "I have never had such excellent cuisine, and the wine is smooth. The décor is just elegant everywhere I see."

A server asked, "Would you like some coffee with Remy Martin VSOP or Cointreau?"

I said, "Yes, coffee with Cointreau."

Both Dalton and Ken wanted coffee with cognac and the Remy Martin VSOP. I didn't want dessert. I was full and didn't want to add more food to spoil my contentment.

All night, I watched the King. I couldn't help myself. He seemed to be gracious and personable with both men and women. He was undoubtedly well-groomed, and he mingled with the entire crowd. However, I got the feeling he kept glancing in my direction. *At the time, I thought I must be wrong, but regardless, it made me feel uncomfortable.*

The setting was a beautifully restored building. I felt like Cinderella at the ball, experiencing elegance and sophistication for the first time. Words could not describe how I felt. It was the most thrilling evening I had ever spent.

That night, I dreamed I was Cinderella and having the time of my life at the ball. Soon, I heard the clock bells ringing, alerting me to leave the ball. I was dancing with a gorgeous man. Who was this man? He stared down at me, and when I looked up, I realized it was the King.

I awoke, seeing Dalton lying beside me. My heart raced as I snuggled against him. He was my love, my hero, and my lover. No one could replace him, yes, no one.

# Chapter 15 – Nobel Prize Ceremony

The next evening, we dressed in layers for the freezing weather at the City Hall of Stockholm for the Nobel Prize of Medicine ceremony. I wore an elegant black gown embroidered with black pearls with a plunging neckline that showed off my pearl necklace. Under the beautiful gown, I wore silk underwear and knee-high boots. Dalton looked very handsome in his white tie and tails. I had put on my elegant white mink coat and hat. Only then was I ready to brave the frozen land.

We walked in the cold winter wonderland. Ice crusted the trees, and icicles hung from the eaves of the buildings.

When we arrived at the City Hall of Stockholm auditorium, the grandeur surrounded us. We found our seats in the front row.

*I thought Alfred Nobel, in 1895, gave his fortune to promote all the sciences. It was an honor to be associated with such a man. He had started a tradition, and now his name would go on forever. Now, the Nobel Foundation would give my Dalton the most significant honor globally. It thrilled me to be a part of the ceremony and his world. I wanted to find a way to show him how much this meant to me, but it wasn't about me; it was about him. His success and honor are what we celebrate today. He received such a significant award from His Majesty, the King of Sweden, King Karl Ásgeirr XIII.*

The King opened the ceremony, **"Your Majesties, Your Royal Highnesses, Honored Laureates, Ladies and Gentlemen,** the Laureates will receive their awards. The ceremony takes place on the anniversary of the death of Swedish industrialist Alfred Nobel, who established the prizes in his will.

This year, I would like to welcome everyone to the Prize Award Ceremony on behalf of the Nobel Foundation.

We would especially like to welcome the Laureates and their families to this ceremony to honor the Laureates and their contributions to physiology and science. I present Dr. Dalton

Masters for the discovery of the MECS methodology to encapsulate cancer human immunodeficiency tumors. He has made great strides in the science of medicine. He has come from the United States of America with colleagues to receive the award for contributing to the 'greatest mankind benefit.' It is an exceptional example of Alfred Nobel's wish for everyone deserving of winning a Nobel Prize. It is a stepping-stone highlighting the accomplishments of the highest human intellectual development. His incomparable cancer research will move us into unknown territory. The experiment is not an ordinary achievement. It is truly an extraordinary accomplishment. Let's give the honorable Dr. Dalton Masters a round of applause."

Dalton walked to the podium,

"Thank you for that outstanding introduction. It warms my heart. I am just a man who has spent most of my life performing cancer research on Earth and beyond. The MECS Experiment began as a college fellowship. Performing this fellowship as a young adult has since grown into a guiding ray of hope for humanity. MECS is a destroyer fighting the unannounced illness and cancer, which doesn't respect life's boundaries. It can strike elders, children, babies, and anyone in between. I want to let everyone know I am continuing my research on the next shuttle mission. This significant payload is close to everyone's heart and especially to your country, Sweden. It is an honor to announce that the King of Sweden will venture into space. We will both fly the next shuttle mission. I am privileged to join His Royal Highness King Karl Ásgeirr XIII of Sweden in space."

The King handed Dalton his diploma and medal. After a moment of shock, the room exploded with applause; a buzz filled the auditorium. On December 10, he received the diploma with medicine engraved in red on the blue leather diploma cover made of the highest quality goatskin. Additionally, they monogrammed Dalton's initials (DM) in gold on the outside of the diploma.

I said, "Dalton, the whole ceremony is incredible. I have never seen such an impressive award, and you deserve such an honor. You are my hero, and I know you deserve this great tribute." Pride filled my universe. I remember thinking he was a great man and would soon be my husband.

## Chapter 16 – Surprise

When we returned to the Grand Hotel, Dalton stopped and kissed me repeatedly with a passion that engulfed my soul.

When we walked into our room, I noticed three boxes lying on the bed with my name on a card. The boxes were from Neiman Marcus. Excited, I ripped the first box apart. My face broke out in a smile. The package had a beautiful satin wedding dress, simple and sophisticated. I laughed. What a pleasant surprise!

I held the flowing white dress in front of the mirror and twirled like a child. It was perfect. I opened the second box, and it was my wedding headpiece. It was elegant. The third box was heavy. I tried to pick it up but decided to leave it on the bed to open. I couldn't open it up fast enough, throwing paper all around the room. My mouth gaped open. I was surprised to see a snow-white, soft, long white fox coat!

Now I didn't have to wear the simple dress I had brought with me. I would look like a beautiful bride. Yes, I was going to be a bride. I had never married, and now tomorrow was the day. I knew we would be happy. He was so gentle and considerate of my feelings. It is called respect.

I tossed and turned, thinking about the big day, my wedding day. Eventually, I fell asleep, and the dreaded nightmares began.

I was back at the Astronaut's cottage, drinking a hot cup of coffee in the kitchen, going over the plans outlining the King Karl Ásgeirr MECS experiment. The bright kitchen lights suddenly started flickering and eventually went completely off. The room was dark, but I could see the door moving. It swung back and forth, but no one else was in the kitchen. As I walked through the door, a plastic bag went over my head. The bag was taut, pressing against my face, making breathing impossible. I gasped, but the plastic got even tighter. Then, thrashing about, trying to scream, I heard this laughter. Who could it be?

A knife cut through the plastic bag, which allowed me to

breathe. Instead, my voice let out a blood-curdling scream, vibrating throughout the night.

Arms surrounded me as I lashed back and forth, fighting back with all the strength I could muster. I was fighting for my life.

A voice came from the darkness, "Wake up, Susan, wake up. I'm here with you."

My eyes barely opened, but I still could see the image of Dalton. He heard my screams.

"Susan, it was another bad dream. But don't worry; I'm here." He said as he gently soothed me, rubbing my head and kissing my face.

"Dalton, the dream was weird. I can't imagine why I keep having these nightmares. They are so real," I weakly said.

He said, "You know, Susan, you have been under a lot of stress lately. Stress can kill you, literally. I don't ever want anything to happen to my sweet, wonderful Susan."

"I will stay with you for the rest of the night. I'm not leaving you alone. I will be here to protect you."

"Thank you," I cuddled beside him, feeling his warmth.

He turned over, staring deep into my blue-green eyes. I felt he could see my insecurities creating turmoil inside me. I lived with the fear that he would know that I was not the strong, independent female I pretended to be.

"Turn over, Susan," Dalton demanded.

I turned onto my stomach, and he rubbed my shoulders, coaxing the tense muscles to relax. He ran his hands down my back until they touched my buttocks. His hands moved back and forth, squeezing the tense muscles. I felt a tingle inside me come alive, warmth intertwining our friendship's emotions. He turned me over and kissed me from my neck to my breasts. My heart warmed up as the bad dreams and feelings disappeared. I wanted him more than ever. He was my protector and soon to be my husband.

# Chapter 17 – Wedding Day

When I awoke early the next morning, Dalton had already left. The bright yellow sun shone through the window, blinding me with the reflection of the crisp white snow. The snow reminded me of delicate Brussels lace decorating the quaint Scandinavian buildings surrounding them as if with an expensive tablecloth.

Last night, the terrible dreams seemed real. Stress aggravated my subconscious with nightmares. I wondered if the dreams were a warning.

Nevertheless, today was our wedding day. I was going to marry the man I loved. How had life changed since I met Dalton? No longer was I alone, but I now had a sailing partner and a mate for life.

Never did I think I would be in a foreign country marrying the man of my dreams. He had arranged everything for the wedding. It was going to be a surprise wedding, and I couldn't wait to be surprised.

Someone knocked on the door. Frightened, I looked out the peephole, and there stood Pat, the store clerk from the mall. I unlocked the door, and to my amazement, Pat bustled into the room carrying several packages.

My mouth fell open, "Pat, what are you doing here?"

"Well, after our last encounter, I knew when you sent the packages back that you needed a whole new bridal outfit. Dalton called and sent the money with airline tickets. I know your size and have a perfect idea of what you like and want. This is like Christmas, except it is your wedding day. What a beautiful day to tie the knot. It's a little too cold for my blood, but I brought some clothes to keep you warm. It's going to be the best day ever." Pat rattled off.

"Pat, I don't know what to say except thank you. I didn't know what I was going to do. The wedding is at 1700. Look at me; I need all the help I can get," I said as I sat on the bed among the mounds of packages.

"Well, I made appointments for you, your nails, hair, and a

Swedish massage," Pat said, laughing.

"What else would you have in Sweden but a Swedish massage?" I joked; inside, I was thankful. My parents and siblings weren't there, but a stranger, a sales clerk, was there. The last time we were together was at the horrific bloody mall murders. After that, I didn't want to think about it.

She handed me the first package. I undid the ribbon and inside were delicate lace bikini underpants and a sexy bra. They were beautiful. I held them over my head and said, "Dalton will really like this. He will not know what to do. But, then again, he certainly will, and I want to make him happy."

I smiled, "Everything is so elegant. I feel like a Snow Queen getting married in a faraway land in the Ice Mountains. Now, what is this package you have for me?

It felt like Christmas; I told her, "You know this is my birthday, but don't tell anyone."

I opened the large package, which contained a snow-white full-length fur coat and white fur hat. I took the gifts out and gathered them around my face. The snow-white fur coat and hat felt so luxurious. Then, giggling, I opened another package. It was another delicate headdress with sequins on a satin cap with lace going around the edge.

I said, "Pat, you amaze me. I like everything you bought. I want to hug you." At that, I jumped up and gave her the biggest hug I could. Laughing, I knew this would be a day I would never forget. I didn't have the heart to tell Pat that Neiman Marcus had sent me a wedding trousseau gratis.

"Now it is time to go and make you beautiful," Pat teased. "Why don't you wear your new coat? It is so cold outside, and you look incredible in it."

I threw on some jeans and a cardigan sweater, forgetting to apply makeup, and ran a comb through my hair. "I'm ready, and here we go off to see miracle workers."

When we were walking through the lobby, I heard my name. "Susan, is that you, Susan?"

It was King Karl Ásgeirr XIII. Pat followed me over to his side, and I said, "Good morning."

King Karl said, "I was hoping to see you one last time before you become a wife."

I froze inside, I didn't know what to say, so I said nothing at all.

He said, "I am so attracted to you, and I know this puts you in an uncomfortable position, but I really would like to have lunch with you before your big night." He begged.

Pat looked at me, and I gazed back at her. What should I do? Did my eyes portray how I felt?

So, I finally whispered to Pat, "Do we have time for lunch?"

Including her in his invitation would work. It wouldn't look appropriate for me to have lunch with the sought-after King of Sweden alone before my wedding night. I took a deep breath.

Pat shouted, "We're available at 1200. Where would you like us to meet you?"

The King looked disappointed but said, "At the palace, of course. We will dine promptly at 12. I can't wait to see you, Susan; come casual."

I turned to walk out, saying, "It is a luncheon date." Then, all at once, a camera flash blinded my eyes. Oh no, not again; the paparazzi were encroaching on my space.

Will they make this into something it is not? I wondered if the King had planted them there so it would cause problems between Dalton and me. I just wanted to die.

Pat said, "Susan, is that King Ásgeirr? When did you meet him, and what was that all about"?

"Yes, it is! Well, I met the King at the Nobel Prize Ceremony of Medicine last night. Strange, isn't he? I don't know what to think of him, but Dalton is going into space with him, and the King will receive the lifesaving cancer treatment, Dalton's MECS Experiments. Dalton is so excited, and the King will go into space to receive the MECS experiment. Its medicine that grows in zero-gravity that encapsulates inoperable cancer."

I answered her questions. There was nothing to hide except I had an uncomfortable sensation in the back of my mind. Why did the King want me to come to the Palace? Did he have some devious plan?

We arrived at the spa, which had an ambiance of luxury that was fit for a princess. Pat joined me for an incredible pomegranate Swedish massage. It smelled fresh, clean, and refreshing. Afterward, the masseuse put hot stones on our backs, which miraculously made all my muscles loosen. After that, I felt like a limp rag doll. All my worries and cares seemed to disappear.

We were still in our robes when the masseuse led us into the beauty salon. All the hairdressers, makeup, and nail techs began fussing over us, chattering in English. I felt like a princess. Pat couldn't quit laughing and talking.

The salon hairdressers didn't ask what we wanted; they just began working on us from top to bottom.

While they did my hair, *I thought about my vows. I thought long and hard about how I could tell Dalton how I felt; no words came. I still had my luncheon at the Palace and needed to tell Dalton where I was going. How could I send a message?*

A phone booth was in the corner. I excused myself and called the hotel. I rang the room, but there was no answer. I waited until the phone would enable me to leave a message, "Dalton, darling, I'm getting beautiful, and thank you so much for my surprise. Thanks for sending Pat to accompany me. The King invited Pat and me to have lunch with him. It is my last luncheon as a single woman. Please join Pat and me at the Palace at noon sharp if you get this message in time. See you soon, sweetheart, and I hope you can make it."

After the entire makeover, I finally had a chance to peer into the mirror; I didn't recognize myself. I honestly looked like a princess.

Pat couldn't say enough, "Susan, wow, you look so beautiful. I'm a real princess; I can't believe the transformation."

I just stood before the mirror as if my dream came true. I felt like Cinderella, who had found her Prince Charming.

I needed to have something to settle my nerves. A chardonnay would do, but instead, I decided to compose wedding prose for Dalton. I found my composition notebook in my purse and wrote down the words for the ceremony. The words came naturally, as if I had written them in my mind a very long time ago. I would be his bride, but first, I was invited to have my last lunch as a single woman with a real king.

Pat and I were giggling as we flagged down a taxi. My

mouth dropped open when the taxicab stopped in front of the palace. I stood before the largest ornate building I had ever seen. It must be the world's most enormous palace. We stood staring at a man dressed in a crisp white shirt and a black tie and suit. He had dark sunglasses and looked like a secret serviceman. I knew the King had sent him.

He said politely, "Can I ask your names and what business you have here at the palace?"

I said immediately, "My name is Susan, and this is my friend, Pat. We are here to have lunch with King Ásgeirr. He invited us, but we didn't know where to find him. It is such a large building, and I don't know where to go?"

## Chapter 18 – Confused

Grinning, he said, "Let me escort you two charming ladies to the royal apartment, where the King awaits you. My name is Devon."

He took our arms, walking briskly down the street to an inconspicuous door. Security had hidden the entrance in the brick foundation disguised so no one would see it. He escorted us through a dark passageway. I began to feel uncomfortable; Pat was holding my hand very tightly.

She whispered, "Susan, we don't know this man. Where is he taking us?"

"I don't know," I whispered back.

"Don't worry, my pretty little birds; we are almost there." He said in a jolly manner. With that, he opened a door hidden behind the brick wall. I looked up, and there stood the magnificent king dressed in his most elegant gold and black ceremony attire. My mouth opened wide in amazement.

"Hi, I'm glad you two beautiful ladies could make it. Please sit and let me make you something to drink." He said, bowing to us.

I smiled, observing his outlandish outfit, and listening to his ascent, "I really would like a glass of champagne."

"Susan, I want to tell you I'm pleased you are here, especially on your wedding day. I won't keep you long, but I had to see you and tell you how much you brighten up my world. I know this is not the time to tell you, but I care for you. I wish we had met under different circumstances. I have been looking for you all my life, imprisoned in this huge building built on the original castle's site in the 13th century. I keep crowns, scept, orbs, regalia, and other crown jewels deep underneath the Royal Palace in the Treasure Chamber. They pale in comparison to you, and I would gladly give them to you if only you were mine. I will take you to the medieval vaults and shower you with all the royal jewels. It is an incredible sight. I feel wonderful when you're near, but you are the fiancée of the man who can give me life."

The suggestive lighting added to the atmosphere, and I knew I was in trouble. The King's attraction to me made me feel confused. I wished Dalton were beside me. The luncheon had been a big mistake, and I could not respond to his words. Instead, he kept staring at me.

Pat and the man hadn't heard the conversation since they were too busy talking to each other. I could see their mutual attraction. The King had taken the wind out of me. All I could think of was to leave immediately.

I said, "Pat, we have to leave now. Please tell your friend goodbye, and off we go back to the hotel to get ready."

Pat glanced at me with big eyes that said, "I don't want to go." She knew I had to get back immediately because Dalton was waiting for me. I couldn't wait to leave the largest palace in the world. I didn't want my relationship with Dalton to be in jeopardy. The King had put me in a very uncomfortable situation.

*I couldn't understand what he was doing. Dalton could save his life, and now the King was trying to kill my relationship with Dalton, but only I had the power to save my link. I'm afraid the King's behavior is too confusing for me.*

"Devon, would you please show us out? No time for lunch!" I appreciate your champagne, but now I have a wedding to attend," I said cheerfully, trying to pretend his previous comments never happened.

I took my glass and held it up to the King, Pat, and Devon, "I propose a toast. To my new friends, may the dreams hidden inside of you find a way to make you happy. But remember, the pursuit of happiness could be the source of your unhappiness. So, enjoy each day, each moment as it comes, because you will never see that moment again."

Pat held her glass and said, "Be happy."

The King said, "To everyone's happiness. Thank you, Susan, and Pat, for visiting the Palace."

Pat crossed the room and said, "Let's go, bride; time is running short. You look beautiful, but you have to put on your wedding dress and get more beautiful." She checked her watch, judging how much time we needed.

Pat looked at her new companion and asked, "Would you like to attend the wedding?"

"Yes, I would, and you can use the name Devon Borg as the name on the place card," he said, grinning at Pat.

"I want you to sit right next to me, my dear," Pat said.

I grabbed her hand and pulled her toward me. "Devon, would you please show us the way out?"

His Majesty moved forward, putting his arms around me. I froze. He said, "I know you can't love me, but I do want you to know if ever you need anything at all, I will be there. I do love you so much. It was love at first sight."

I was dumbfounded, and all I could say was, "Thank you for the champagne." I turned and left.

We made our way down the cold, empty corridors. The king was so attractive, but he wasn't my Dalton. How could anyone be so arrogant? To think he could take me away from the man who will possibly save his life. I asked myself how I could feel that twinge of excitement. Pat and I followed Devon through the maze until we found our way out into the sunshine. We were both blinded by the intensity of the sun.

Pat said, squinting, "Are you okay? Whoa, are all the men attracted to you? I'm surprised at King Ásgeirr's words. You have two men who are in love with you, and your wedding is at 1700. How confusing: a king and a renowned scientist that pursued me. Lady, we have to get back."

"Pat, don't ask me what is happening. I don't know; all I know is that I'm soon to be Dalton's wife. He is the one, and I don't care what the King of Sweden thinks. I have my wedding to attend." I said determinedly.

The brisk, cold air hit our faces with a vengeance. Nevertheless, it felt like the temperature had dropped significantly.

*I wanted to hurry back and get out of my clothes. It was time to begin dressing for the wedding and to get beautiful for my darling Dalton. But internally, I wondered why the King desired me so much. Was it the rivalry?*

As if reading my thoughts, Pat said, "It seems strange, but

maybe it is just a competition game between Dalton and the King. He could have any woman he wanted. So why would he play this game with you? Your fiancé is the one who may save his life."

"I know. I'm just as confused as you are. It was a mistake to meet with the King, a huge mistake," I said.

When we got back to the hotel, Dalton was in the lobby. I saw him and called out, "Dalton, we are back." I ran up to him and threw my arms around him.

His face glowed brightly in the room, and my heart swelled with love. It was already 1:30 p.m., and time was running out. I kissed Dalton passionately, feeling tingly with desire. I had to focus on my tight schedule.

It was time for me to get dressed for the most special day of my life. I turned around to see my Daddy. I gasped with excitement and surprise. What was he doing here?

Daddy said, "My little girl, do you think I would miss this special day?"

I began crying tears of joy, and then my mom appeared. How could I wish for anything else? The two people who cared for me the most were joining me on my big day. They both looked incredible; I couldn't believe they had made such a challenging journey. They wanted to be with me, and it caused my heart to swell with affection.

Mom laughed, "Susan, let's go get you dressed. The dressing up reminds me of your prom. Remember that sexy peach empire waist dress your grandmother made? You looked like a movie star. I want you to know tonight, you will look like a queen."

My back stiffened, thinking of the King and our almost luncheon. Finally, I got up enough courage and said, "I remembered my first prom date. Tall, lanky, red-headed Jonald came to the door with his hair slicked back, carrying an exotic lavender orchid. It was some night. It was the first time I had ever been to a fancy restaurant. In my naiveté', I ordered the beef stroganoff. The taste was unfamiliar, and I couldn't eat it. Jonald, being a good date, then ordered a filet mignon. It was a fantastic night and a learning experience for a young girl who had never experienced an expensive restaurant."

Going up in the elevator, I looked at my mom. *She still had the creamiest, young-looking skin that I had ever seen. How beautiful, I thought. It doesn't matter how old you are; beauty can remain for one's whole life. What makes you young? Is it creamy skin, sparkling eyes, bounce in the walk, or a beautiful soul? I hope I look like Mom at her age.*

"I need a hot, steamy bath."

I filled the tub almost to the top and turned on the Jacuzzi. I reflected on meeting Dalton and receiving that changing phone call.

*"Come to the Bahamas,"* he had said.

*"I did, and now look at me. We will be married and live as one the rest of our lives, our enduring commitment: forever and ever."* I said to myself.

I slipped into the warm, silky water, trying not to wet my hair. Suddenly, I felt a hand on my head, pushing me down under the water. I fought to get up, but the hand kept forcing me down. My nose and mouth began to fill with water. I wanted to scream but could not. Fear gripped me, but I managed to beat my hands against the water.

"Susan, tell me you are okay," I heard my mom's voice deep inside my head.

My eyes opened, and there stood the woman who had made me what I am today. My hair was still dry, and my makeup was still almost perfect.

My mother smiled and said, "Susan, are you having another nightmare? You always do when you are under stress. The wedding is going to be beautiful, and you are going to be a gorgeous bride. Susan, get ready; time's a-wasting."

My body and mind caught between a single girl's insecurities and my future as a married woman. I felt lost in a maze of nightmares. It was difficult for me to realize this would be for the rest of my life, married to the most intelligent man in the world. A man that is bigger than life, and I felt intimidated.

Taking a deep breath, I stood up in the bathtub. Water dripped from my shapely body. It felt warm from the hot, steamy water and soft from the silky oil. The towel's softness felt sumptuous, drying the water bubbles from my body.

*I looked in the mirror and noticed my hair was a little messy, and the makeup under my eyes was running. But I knew I could make myself presentable with a minor miracle.*

*I said to myself, "Breathe deeply. This is your wedding day."*

## Chapter 19–Church

Mom said frantically, "Susan, we have to hurry! There's so much to do. First, your Daddy wants to see you. Come on, little girl; you need to move your buns. Get dressed!"

I felt like I was in high school, once again, being late for school. Yes, me, the dreamer, who wanted to think about everything except what was going on.

I started humming the tune, "I'm getting married in the morning."

Mom broke in, "Yes, get the beautiful bride, Susan, to the church on time."

When I walked into the stateroom, there Pat stood with my trousseau. The wedding dress and accessories matched the whiteness of the snow outside. The delicate lace had the same pattern as the snow crystals.

I smiled from ear to ear. "It is my day."

I dressed as quickly as I could and redid my smudged makeup and messy hair. The full-length mirror reflected a sight I had never seen before. *For the first time in my life, I thought I looked beautiful.*

I wanted to show my mom how I looked, so I went to Mom and Daddy's room. The door was cracked open, and I saw Dalton and Daddy talking.

I was just out of sight, but I could hear them talking. Daddy had decided it was the time for the future son-in-law talk.

"Well, Dalton, I think this is a little fast. My daughter always said she would know her fiancé through four seasons. It has only been two. You must be a special man for her to marry you so soon. I hope Susan has used good judgment. I must remind you that if you hurt Susan, you don't want to know what would happen. She is my little girl and always will be my little girl. Do you understand?" He said harshly.

With those words, I slowly walked into the room, wearing my stunning wedding dress. Both Daddy and Dalton turned and smiled with their mouths gaping.

Daddy was the first to speak, "Susan, you are so beautiful.

Don't you know it is unlucky for the groom to see the bride before the wedding?"

Dalton piped in, "Wow, Susan, I wouldn't have it any other way. I'm the luckiest guy in the world, or should I say space or even universe." He placed his hand on my cheeks. "You look incredible and gorgeous. It is time to go to church. I have carriages waiting for everyone at the hotel entrance. Let's go."

I excitedly said, "Ok, I've got to put on my white fox coat and hat."

Everyone met in the lobby. Pat, Mom, and Daddy followed our white horse and white carriage.

As we rode through the streets, it began to snow. Soon, we could see no grey slush, no muddy roads, just a fairy tale world all covered in white. Finally, the carriages stopped in front of the church.

Dalton and I ran to the church entrance, holding hands like two little kids with the wedding party scrambling and trailing behind. Dalton opened the massive church doors while the wedding party entered. My nerves were flying between giddy and scared to death. Dalton stood beside me, soon to be my husband.

*Dalton is the best choice for a husband I could ever make in my lifetime. He is a good man, and he is my good man.*

I saw my Daddy waiting for his little girl in the narthex. I ran up to him, smiling as I had done as a child: my Daddy, the other man in my life, who could do no wrong.

He said, "Sweetie, you are stunning. I'm so proud of you. I love you so much but remember, you will always be my little girl."

Tears began flowing down my face. My makeup was running down my cheeks.

"Here, take this tissue and quit your crying. Your tears will ruin your wedding pictures." Pat said, laughing.

I smiled, and the sacred moment between my Daddy and me was gone forever.

It was time to get married. Pat, the only bridesmaid, walked before me. I watched as everyone admired her beauty and elegance. We heard about the beginning of the wedding in March. Daddy and I began walking down the aisle after Pat.

Goosebumps rose all over my body.  I could see Dalton at the altar waiting for me.  Mom intently watched as we strolled by her.  A magical harp played during the wedding.  It sounded like angels singing.

Dalton's eyes mirrored what he meant to me.  My heart was ready to burst.  Then, in a heavy Swedish accent, the minister said, "Susan, please recite your vows."

I responded, "It is easier to express myself in this poem,
**Forever**


I promise to take thee willfully
**Each Second**
Together, the consented journey
Along your side for eternity
**Each tomorrow**
Your sacred here with me
Creating a life at sea
**Each day**
Never to hide our loving
With the final breath lasting
**Each week**
Holding hands through life
As husband and wife
**Each year**
Together blessed by God to be
As life is always a mystery
**Forever My Love**


Dalton turned away.  I could see tears running down his face.

The Swedish minister said, "Dalton, please recite your vows."

Dalton said, "Susan, we had a chance meeting.  Neither of us was seeking a permanent relationship, but when I held you in my arms, I fell in love with you.  I never dreamed life could be so serene with my perfect Susan.  So, sail away with me through stormy and sunny days, and I promise I will hold you in my arms forever throughout time."

The ceremony went like a blur.  All I knew was that I said,

"I do."

My prince charming said, "I do," and we were married. We were now husband and wife.

Dalton passionately kissed me, sealing the bond of matrimony.

As we walked down the aisle, I noticed the King sitting in the back pew. He had tears in his eyes. Possibly, his life expectancy of perhaps dying of cancer was now a reality. Unfortunately, even a king can be lonely. I felt sad for him, but life shouldn't get this complicated. Now, I am Susan Masters, Mrs. Dalton Masters, and I'm proud of it.

## Chapter 20 – Reception

As we left the church, Dalton turned and kissed me again. His lips were inviting, tender, and soft. I felt a twinge of lust throughout my body. I wanted to escape to our room to consummate our marriage with passionate lovemaking. But, first, we had to go to the reception.

The white horse-drawn carriages took our small wedding party to the hotel's reception hall. We walked into the room, and the band began playing our song, "You Got It" by Roy Orbison. Dalton held my hand and led me to the dance floor. Everyone was watching as our bodies gracefully moved as one.

In the middle of our wedding dance, The King broke in. *It was so rude, and I wondered how he could do this to me on my wedding day.*

I could see the coldness in Dalton's eyes when he turned toward the King, and I could tell he didn't approve, either. But unfortunately, we were his guests, and, with a small bow, Dalton let him take my hand.

The music changed, and we were dancing to a waltz. We glided across the room with the lightness and smoothness of skilled dancers. He pressed his hand against my back and pushed me toward him, very close. As we circled the dance floor, the King put his cheek next to mine.

He whispered, "Susan, you are the most beautiful bride I have ever seen. I wish you had waited until after the Shuttle flight. You will see I will be a cancer survivor. You don't have to say a thing, but remember that I will be there if you need anything. I will always love you."

My heart and the music stopped at the same time. The King twirled me around, and I curtseyed. I didn't know what else I could do without making a scene.

Bewildered, I walked over to my new husband, who was grinning at me from ear to ear.

He said, "You looked beautiful dancing with the King. I'm not jealous since I am your husband and know who will take you home."

We had kept the paparazzi away from the wedding and the reception. Of course, we knew they were outside, but for that short time, we had peace.

The reception was perfect. Daddy danced with me next, proving he was an excellent dancer.

Daddy said, "My little girl, you have grown into a woman. I am so proud of all your accomplishments. How I love you, my daughter, my petite Susan."

I gave him a hug and a kiss on the cheek as his words made me float across the room. This is the happiest day of my life.

Pat was entertaining Devon and looking incredibly happy. They danced to the next song. Pat deserved the vacation of a lifetime. She had stayed by my side during the wedding formalities.

Suddenly, everything became chaotic. The paparazzi had found a way into the reception. First, I recognized Valerie, the cute news lady from Galveston and West Palm Beach. She stood across the room, hugging Dalton. I quit breathing. I felt as if someone stuck a knife in my lungs. I wanted to find a place to hide.

Dad pulled me over, "You will always be the center of attention now that you are married to a famous scientist. Susan, what is the problem?"

"It's nothing, Daddy. I need to leave. I don't like attention. So, I guess you can say the party is over." I sighed.

We both walked over to Dalton, with the bright camera lights blinding us. I hated it. It was as if the lights were a form of torture. My eyes watered from the intensity of the flashing lights.

I held onto Dalton's hand. Finally, he said, "Do you remember Valerie?"

I tried to be gracious and held my hand out, "It is nice to see you again."

"Congratulations. I must admit you got yourself a great catch. I would have married Dalton myself." She spoke. "I want you to know that he is the best man I have ever known."

I wondered what that meant.

"Dalton, it's time to leave. I want you all to myself," I said, giving Valerie a curt smile.

I hugged my parents, "Daddy and Mom, we will see you in the morning for breakfast."

With that, Dalton and I disappeared into the crowd. As we walked away, I noticed a mysterious man talking to Ken. They were deep in conversation. I started to ask Dalton about the secretive man, but he turned and smiled, distracting me from all the chaos in the room.

# Chapter 21 – Honeymoon

Dalton carried me effortlessly across the honeymoon suite threshold. He gently laid me down on rose petals spread across the soft silk bedspread. The sweet aroma surrounded us, which made my senses the most memorable moment in my life. Dalton gently undressed me. He took off one bra strap at a time, and slowly, he removed my underwear with his teeth. I giggled at his imagination.

I realized I was lying on the delicate wedding veil. I felt as fragile as the veil; how could this have happened so fast? All doubts disappeared when he kissed me. I fell into a bottomless pit as endless as space itself.

I closed my eyes as he held my long blond curly hair falling over the side of the bed. The incredible sensation made me feel as though I were in a trance.

The music in the background added to the evening's enchantment.

Dalton said, "Susan, you are a vision. In all my lifetime, I never dreamed I would find a woman like you."

His hands shook as they glided across my body, gently touching me.

I asked, "Dalton, are you okay?"

He answered as he massaged my head gently, causing chill bumps to rise over my body. "I haven't been married in such a long time. After I lost my wife and children, I believed I could not go on living. But I don't want ever to lose you. You are now a part of me."

I said, "You won't lose me, my darling. I'm yours forever. You are my king, and I will be together forever."

He faced me, bringing his lips only two inches away from mine. I wanted him so much, but I held back, waiting in anticipation. He softly kissed my face but not my lips. I could feel his hardness against me, but still, I didn't move. His lips moved down my body to my breasts as he cupped one breast and gently sucked the other. His lips moved from my breasts down my stomach, kissing my entire body. Eventually, he nibbled on my lips, but this was not a passionate kiss. Instead, he continued to please me unselfishly with an obsession, making me hard, just like a man. Desire engulfed my whole existence.

Uncontrollably, my body responded, shivering with excitement. I ran my hands across Dalton's body, feeling the strength of his muscles. He kissed me with all the passion of the world, leaving me breathless.

We made love all night long. He licked my salty flesh as sweat dripped from my body, and I opened myself up to him both emotionally and physically. Finally, I had found my soul mate.

The next thing I knew, it was morning, but still dark outside. I felt like Scarlet O'Hara waking up after Rhett Butler had made passionate love. I never believed I would ever find happiness and a man I could trust.

When Dalton awoke, he said, "You certainly look more beautiful in the morning than you did last night. Oh, what a lucky man I am."

I said, "No, I am the lucky woman."

I remembered, "Mom and Dad are probably waiting for us. They get up early. I'm hungry. Feed me; please feed me."

Dalton laughed, "Maybe I will keep you captive and make love to you all day."

"No, Dalton, I have to be the perfect daughter. But, of course, you know, I'm the perfect wife for you," I teased.

Our wedding night passed very quickly, like a movie one wished would never end. He slipped his hand around my waist. Again, I felt a twinge of excitement deep inside. At that moment, I wanted to leave as fast as I could and be far away from the palace and the paparazzi. I needed to be one with my husband, yes, with my wonderful husband.

Dalton called for room service and ordered breakfast. Afterward, I rang Daddy and Mom and invited them to our honeymoon suite for a champagne toast and breakfast.

We were safe in our room, away from the paparazzi. After my parents arrived, the hotel delivered a delicious Swedish breakfast of cheese, salmon, and eggs on an English muffin. The caviar tasted incredible.

Mom and Daddy were thrilled. They never believed I would get married. I was thankful they had made the long trip over for the ceremony.

Mom said, "We are staying in Stockholm for several days before heading home. It's such a long trip home, and I want to see the sights."

Daddy said, "Dalton, you know I wouldn't miss this occasion. I had to make sure you made an honest woman out of Susan."

Mom said, "Susan has always been honest. It is apparent in her work."

We all laughed.

Dalton said, "I have a surprise, Susan. Tell your parents. Goodbye."

I hugged and kissed Mom and Daddy goodbye. Then, Dalton led me happily from our suite to a luxurious limousine. I knew I was in heaven; my feet didn't touch the floor.

The sun was rising as the limo headed toward the shore. As we neared the port, I saw a barque square-rigger, majestic and stately in the morning sun. I was amazed to learn that she was our destination! The ship's captain stood on deck, waiting for us.

"Dr. Masters, good to see you again," said the charming Captain in a Swedish accent. "I have a honeymoon suite ready for you and a beautiful wife. Let me show you to the stateroom, the most romantic quarter. My name is Captain Erik."

I giggled, "I guess I'm in for a surprise."

Dalton said, "We are on the best-maintained ship-shape ship in the world. It's capable of sailing around the world."

I said, "This is a fairy tale. I'm just the most satisfied girl in the world. Yeah, how could a girl get this lucky?"

The captain opened the door to our cabin, and Dalton carried me across the threshold.

I said, "It's a perfect honeymoon. We're far away from the paparazzi. So now, my darling, we can have peace."

The captain said as he exited, "It is time for me to leave. I will see you two for dinner at 1800 sharp in the captain's dining quarter."

I turned to study the spot where the captain had stood, "Dalton, the captain, looks very experienced with his weathered face. His facial lines look like a nautical chart. I wonder where it would take us."

Dalton laughed, "Hopefully, to our destination."

Dalton lifted me onto the luxurious bed with a gold and navy duvet. He said, "This is the place we are spending our honeymoon for the coming week."

I tried to capture all the beautiful memories in my mind forever. *I studied Dalton's face, the wood-carved door, the intricate embroidery cover, and the ocean's movement out the portholes. My eyes watched the foam hitting the porthole as the boat moved us gracefully through the wind. My feelings consumed my body. Dalton leaned over and kissed me. Our motion felt as if we were one with the sea. My love of the ocean matched the love of my man. I didn't know how I could ever be more satisfied. So contented, I fell asleep in his arms.*

When I awoke, it was time for dinner. We quickly dressed and headed to the formal dining room.

There sat the friendly captain, who politely said, "I'm glad you joined me and first mate, Richard."

The aroma of the beef stew was incredible, and I starved from all the excitement. My adrenalin had been running high all day. We ate our hearty dinner without speaking.

The cook brought out a peach cobbler with strong hot coffee.

He asked, "Would you like some liqueur for your coffee?"

I immediately answered, "Do you have any Baileys?"

"Yes, we do; let me get it for you," the cook responded.

Dalton said, "I would like some also."

Captain Erik said, "We will be approaching rough seas. It will last approximately 10 hours. Be very careful not to fall and hold onto the boat at all times; one hand for the boat and one hand for you."

Dalton and I both nodded our heads in agreement. Then, Dalton asked, "How high will the seas be?"

Captain Erik answered, "Ten to twenty feet, but my ship can handle much more."

*I thought to myself, this is not good.* But that night, the ship tossed, turned, and rocked me to sleep like a baby in a cradle.

The following day, the sun warmed my face. Dalton said, "Let's take the wheel and show these sailors how to handle this amazing ship."

It was an ordeal to dress. My silk underwear felt smooth under my insulated bib coveralls. I put on a wool sweater, hoping it would keep me warm. Fortunately, I had packed my insulated wool gloves. The crew had suggested that we wear ski masks to keep from freezing outside on the deck.

I said, "Dalton, do you think we are crazy? Most people would. I know people generally go to the Bahamas for their honeymoon, but this is an incredible experience. We will have pictures and stories to tell for a very long time."

It was freezing on deck. The foul weather gear and the ski mask helped keep me warm but salt-soaked onto our faces. It was exhilarating.

Dalton said, "Susan, look at all the wonderful winter scenery. Who would have dreamed I would be in the inner archipelago islands? Luckily, the seas have not frozen over, or we would be behind an ice-breaking boat. Look at the beautiful island of Lidingö and the surrounding archipelago skerries. See **the Swedish-American Carl Milles' sculptures. It's an outdoor and indoor museum carved out from the steep cliffs of the Lidingö Island, high above Stockholm.** I want to stay here forever, but of course, I would rather be in the Caribbean."

I took the helm, fascinated by the vibrancy of this once tranquil and sedate Nordic city, "Dalton, Stockholm is one of the most beautiful cities in Europe."

The captain of the Swedish waters, Captain Erik, stood over us while we enjoyed the boat's strength. "Thank you, Captain Erik. It feels unbelievable. She is so easy to steer. When I see the beauty of the majestic sails filled with wind, I'm on top of the world."

I felt like I was being a helm hog and asked, "Dalton, do you want to take the helm?"

"Of course, I do, my sweet." Dalton gleamed. I noticed young Captain Erik make a scowl that sent chills up my spine. There was more going on here than appeared on the surface.

I tried to regain my composure and concentrate on my husband.

I said, "Dalton, you look like a teenage boy who just got his first shiny new car cruising the neighborhood for the first time. Could you take me to the drive-in theater so we can park? Just think, most kids today have never seen a drive-in, though I'm sure they still know how to park."

"Well, they don't know what they are missing. Where do you want me to park under the constellation Orion?" Of course, the Swedish crew had no idea what we were saying. Still, Captain Erik could understand, and he looked angrier and angrier. I wanted to tell him to get a life and be happy, but instead, I decided he was just not a happy person.

Suddenly, I got hungry. The pains struck my stomach, and I said, "Dalton, you are my star sailor. My darling, fly me to the moon."

Dalton laughed, "Captain Erik, I'm ready for some grub. Please take over. Thank you for allowing us to helm your beautiful ship. Maybe we can help out a little later."

Down below, the smell of bacon frying filled the cabins. My stomach growled, and Dalton said, "Sweetie, we need to take care of you."

I said, "Maybe the cook needs to read, The Care and Feeding of Sailing Crew by Lin Pardey with Larry Pardey."

Dalton laughed, "I will take care of you, but I'll let the cook take care of feeding you during our honeymoon. We would starve today if left up to me."

"Dalton, I thought you could do everything. Now I find out you are not the perfect man after we are married." I kidded.

"I am perfect for you," he kissed me passionately, taking me into his arms. The desire I felt was insatiable. I wanted the day never to end.

The dinner bell rang as we sat down at the table with Captain Erik. I noticed no other passengers came to breakfast. The crew had already eaten earlier.

The table had fresh fruit, hot buttery homemade biscuits, crispy bacon, and scrambled eggs. We immediately began eating with a vengeance. Finally, I noticed that Erik was enjoying his meal.

I said, "Captain Erik, this is a wonderful breakfast. You certainly hired a great cook."

"Thank you; I'll pass good words along." He said.

I asked, "When do we get to the next port?"

"Well, ma'am, this is a cruise to nowhere. We will make our way around the islands and enjoy the view for the next five days, and then we will head back to port. It's a special honeymoon cruise. You two are our only passengers. I hope you find everything comfortable and satisfactory." He said.

I smiled, "It's perfect; I have never been sailing in such a winter wonderland. It's an impeccable ship, which handles beautifully. I can see how sailors get mesmerized by the blueness and the serenity of the ocean. The sea gets into your blood. Maybe I was a pirate in another lifetime?"

"Remember, Susan, the Vikings came from this area, and they were stalwart sailors, warriors, and looters. In other words, they were the pirates. The Norse raided the coasts, rivers, and inland cities of all Western Europe in 844. Vikings even attacked the coasts of North Africa and Italy. They plundered all the coasts of the Baltic Sea. No one could do anything about it because of the lack of centralized powers. Pirates had the advantage, the life of a pirate," Dalton explained.

Captain Erik laughed, menacing, "You know, pirates still exist today."

Chills ran up my back, "My captain, you will keep us safe. Won't you?"

Captain Erik's eyes cut through me, "Of course, of course." With those words, he left the table.

A crusty old sailor started cleaning the table, and we left for our quarters.

When we entered, I noticed someone had gone through our belongings.

"Dalton, do you have anything missing? It looks like someone was looking for something. Who would do such a thing?" I inquired.

"I don't know, but maybe it's your imagination," he said.

I sneaked up behind him and said, "Take my mind off such things." I purred.

The wind picked up, and all I wanted was to have Dalton's arms around me. The coziness of the small cabin felt comfortable. The spray of the ocean caked salt on our faces. I began licking the salt off his cleanly shaven cheeks. I licked down his neck and around his nipples, which stood up in excitement like two little soldiers. My tongue made its way down and circled his sensitive area. Dalton groaned in pleasure. He gently pulled me up into his arms and kissed me passionately. He picked me up and placed me on the bed. I fell into a trance as our lovemaking matched the rhythm of the boat. The vessel rose and fell with each peak and valley in the waves.

Afterward, we drifted into a deep sleep on the calm royal blue sea.

## Chapter 22 – Terror

I jolted awake, engulfed by a sense of dread. Oh, no, I thought, another nightmare. Again, only the demons returned in vengeance, but this time the nightmare was real.

I opened my eyes to see my terror imprinted reflected on Dalton's face. I shivered; my body shivered, and I realized the floor had water.

"Get dressed and put on your foul weather gear quickly, or you will freeze," he screamed.

I said, "How could this happen on our honeymoon? Why didn't the crew alert us? Dalton, let's get to the lifeboats on deck. We need one now!"

The roiling sea crashed against the side of the boat, which sounded like a locomotive.

I couldn't see for the ocean spray. I broke out in a sweat even though I screamed, "We've been in a storm, and the ship is taking on water! Get dressed now. It's going to be a rough landing. We must have headed into a storm. Let's get topside as soon as possible."

I followed his orders as quickly as possible, hampered by the boat's pitching and the sloshing of icy water on the cabin floor. I could tell he was just as scared as I was. My stomach churned.

I said, "How could I be freezing inside? I screamed as loud as my voice was heard above the roar. "I'm afraid. Dalton, we may die."

I heard Dalton's voice. "Susan, the sea is ice cold. We won't last long in the freezing water."

I tried to be brave, saying, "I know."

*I thought the only thing about life was death, and it was lurking on this ship. The dark figure of death was waiting for Dalton and me. It is certain that our lives could end on our honeymoon.*

Once on deck, we both didn't expect to see what we saw or, rather, what we didn't see. *No captain! No crew! No lifeboats!*

"Dalton, what are we going to do? I want to spend the rest of my life with you, not dead, but alive." Then, hysterically, I screamed over the roaring sea.

"This is the plan. Let's stay on the boat if we can. We will not survive in the icy sea. I'm going to look for the radio for help." He yelled.

My heart sank; the freezing water was rising fast.

*I thought of climbing onto the furled sails and hoping they would be the last to go down, but I waited for Dalton. I wondered to myself, where did everyone go? Why did they desert us, their passengers? Did Dalton's experiment have anything to do with our situation? Could the crew abandon us on purpose? Why would anyone want to hurt us? The anger bubbled inside of me; I felt like I was going to burst.*

Dalton came up from below, "I radioed SOS for help but received no answer. We must decide on our next step. We can only climb up the mast and pray the ship doesn't broach before being rescued. I don't know what else to do. I didn't see any more lifeboats. Here, put on this life jacket. It will keep us afloat but not warm. I'm afraid we won't live five minutes in that cold frigid sea. I hope you can forgive me for getting you into this. I thought this would be the perfect honeymoon. I'm so sorry, Susan."

"Dalton, at least I will die with my soul mate." Tears poured into my mouth as I tried to talk.

Dalton kissed the frozen tears on my cheeks and held me close. "Susan, from the moment you walked down my pier to go sailing on my sailboat, the Naia, I've loved you. Yes, you are my life. Thanks for sharing all the excitement."

In the distance, I heard a faint noise. It sounded like another vessel coming toward us. The waves hid the vessel's view. I didn't know if I'm hearing things. "Dalton, do you hear what I hear?"

"Not sure; it could be the noise of the sea. I pray to God; it is a rescue boat. Maybe they heard the SOS I sent out." So, he said as the icy water nipped at our feet.

"I pray they get here soon. We don't have much time left. I want to spend more time as husband and wife." I said.

We both began climbing up the mast steps. They were

slippery from the water. My foot slipped on the icy step, and Dalton effortlessly pulled me back up. A rumbling motor faded in and out with the roar of the waves. In the distance, we saw a tugboat coming toward us. The tugboat's view became lost in the thrashing of the waves. It would magically appear on a 30-foot crest.

I prayed, "Please, God, let them see us and rescue us."

Suddenly, the tugboat turned away. I started to cry as my teeth chattered, "Oh no, don't leave. Maybe they think no one is on the boat, or it's too dangerous."

My heart sank. The turbulent winds must have been twenty to thirty knots with gusts up to forty knots. I could barely hold onto the mast, but Dalton kept me from falling. My body froze inside and out. My chilled hands barely gripped onto the mast.

"Susan, do you hear a helicopter?" Dalton shouted.

"Yes, I do," I said with hope. I knew if someone didn't get to us soon, we would die. The helicopter flew over the sinking crippled ship. Survival was hovering over our heads. In several minutes, I saw a steady light on the water heading toward us again. The tugboat and the helicopter pilots pointed the light on us, guiding the way for the tugboat.

I said in terror, "Dalton, look, they are lowering a man unto the tugboat. Can't they just come and get us? I want them to come now."

The ship made an incredible moan. Dalton screamed, "The ship is about to broach. If that happens, we will not survive the icy water."

"Dalton, I see a flare on the tugboat and a man hanging from a helicopter. He's boarding the tugboat in the darkness. He's on board the tugboat. Please, God, I hope they have a plan," I pleaded.

The tugboat approached the sinking ship on the leeward side, and the stranger jumped from the tugboat to us as the seas tossed each vessel in rhythm. *I thought of the Blue Danube waltz as the miraculous dance took place.* Dalton held onto me as we clung to the lines.

The man's shadow fell in our direction as he said in a composed voice, "Remain calm. We have a lot to do in a short time. I believe we only have ten minutes left before the ship goes down." He screamed as he handed us a survivor's suit and security lines.

We put on the survivor's suit. He wrapped the guidelines around us as he threw it over to the men on board the tugboat. The strength of the stranger was incredible. He led me onto the deck, and I jumped into the tugboat. My knees hit the side of the boat and buckled underneath me, feeling as if my knees broke. I screamed in anguish while the sea saviors pulled me on board.

I watched my husband stand on the side of the sinking ship. The boat began to toss angrily, and my heart stopped. Dalton fell, but the line kept him from falling off the ship. I wanted to reach over and keep him safe. The stranger pulled him back up. I knew the boat was ready to have the last pocket of air filled with water. I felt helpless. Dalton jumped too early and fell into the icy, dark, deep navy-blue water. He didn't zip his survivor's suit all the way.

The men pulled him up as fast as they could but ice covered his body. It was cracking off his survivor suit, and he was fighting hypothermia. Immediately, they pulled him inside the warm cabin. His frozen clothes were removed and replaced with warm wool blankets.

He looked up at me, and he said through chattering teeth, "Susan, I bet you can't top that for a honeymoon. I can't believe I've put you in danger once more. I'm so sorry."

I took my clothes off and put my arms around him. The warmth of my body under the wool blankets began thawing him. "It's over. You had no control over what happened. We are safe now".

I wanted to crawl inside of him and stay safe. I needed to go back to the States.

The man who had saved us came into the cabin. Tears started flowing down my face, "Thank you so much for coming to rescue us. How did you know to come?"

The strong, silent type said in a heavy Swedish accent, "I'm Bjorn from the Swedish Coastguard from Skavsta at your service. The ship's crew radioed for help. They apparently forgot about their passengers until they were all on the life rafts. They could not make it back to the sinking ship. We picked them up earlier. The crew, all accounted for, survived. It surprises me that they made such a huge mistake, leaving you behind. I can't imagine how that could happen, but I will be traveling back to port with you on the tugboat". He nodded once, turned, and left the cabin.

"Dalton, were we set up?" I asked.

Dalton answered, "That's hard to imagine. No one in their right mind would allow the destruction of such a beautiful ship".

Secretly, I believed it was a planned execution. We had been the targets. I started to cry, thinking we were still in danger. Confused, I didn't know if it was from relief or anger at the crew. We had entrusted them with our lives. I clung to Dalton even more. His body extremities were getting warmer, and the closeness made me feel safe. Once again, he had still saved my life. I would have fallen off the ratlines if it weren't for him holding onto me.

*A loud growling noise vibrated in our ears, "We both made our way to the porthole. The magnificent ship had broken apart. The square-rigger sank into the dark, icy-cold grave, lost and gone forever.*

The tugboat moved away from the ship as fast as the motors would go. I saw the tall wooden mast falling toward us. We weren't exactly away from imminent danger.

I heard a loud pounding thump; a piece of the mast hit the tugboat. The porthole cracked but didn't break off.

The brave captain maneuvered the boat away from the sinking ship. I knew it was time for us to go back home, not as two but as one, Dr. and Mrs. Masters.

I knew the emotional effects of escaping from a dark, icy death would last for a very long time. But we had survived; we were still alive.

It felt good to return to the hotel. I took a long hot bath, washing the crusted salt away, causing my skin to turn a deep rose. The warm water stung, making my skin feel prickly. I had bruises on my hips and arms from banging against the mast. I gently washed myself as if I were a baby. I hurt, and I could only imagine how Dalton felt after falling into the icy water.

"Brrrrr Rabbit," I said.

Dalton walked into the bathroom and asked, "What is Brrrrr Rabbit?"

"I'm cold. I've always said that. Silly of me." I explained.

"No, it's not. Scoot over; I'm coming in," I said.

I looked him over. "Dalton, look at your bruises. Your skin is purple."

"I know. This water is stinging my skin. Ouch," Dalton complained.

"It will go away once your body gets accustomed to the temperature," I said.

He put his arms around me and held me for a very long time until the water began getting cold.

"I need to get out," I said.

"I'll just stay in a little longer," he said.

"I'm going to bed. I'm exhausted," I said as I crawled between the sheets. I was asleep before my head hit the pillow.

## Chapter 23 - Home

The next day, we couldn't pack fast enough. We both wanted to leave the frozen country forever. It had almost taken our lives.

Ken met us in the lobby. He was smiling and sincerely happy to see us. It was good to see him again.

We all got the first flight back to the States. Unfortunately, the trip back to the States was not as much fun as the flight over had been. I was acutely aware of each bruise. It even hurt to breathe. I decided to take some Benadryl and sleep my way back to the States. It worked. As I fell asleep, the airline attendant recognized Dalton and began talking to him.

As I fell into a deep sleep, I heard her say, "Tell me about your cancer experiment."

When I awoke, she was still asking questions. Finally, Dalton said, "I'm tired." He put his arms around me. "I thought you would never wake up. I have answered too many questions."

"You need to get some rest, darling. Go ahead and close your eyes," I said.

As I watched him sleep, my mind replayed the events of the last week. My life would never be the same. Was it only a short time ago that I was the Shuttle Flight Software Quality Assurance Engineer? My life had gotten so complicated since meeting the most intelligent man in the world. Now, he received one of the highest honors anyone could achieve, the Nobel Prize in Medicine.

I closed my eyes and saw the sinking ship. On the ship's deck stood Congressman Dan Fletcher. He was smiling, waving at me. He faded into the sky as if he were ascending into the heavens. My hero was giving me comfort. It was a sign to focus on Dalton's aerospace mission to rid the world of one of the cruelest diseases, cancer.

As we landed, Dalton awakened. He gently kissed my lips. The airline attendant ran up to Dalton, handed him a card, and said, "If I could ever have a personal tour of NASA, please let me know. I will be there in a flash."

My mouth dropped open, but Dalton handled it very smoothly. "I will gladly pass it along to the Space Center in Houston. They will contact you for the next event."

You could see the disappointment in her eyes, but she managed to say, "Thank you."

I smiled and stared directly into her eyes.

We both moved slowly, holding onto each other while working our way through the various airport procedures on our way back to our car. Ken had gone on ahead.

I wanted to tell everyone, "Look at us; we survived our honeymoon, barely." The cameras flashed in my face from out of nowhere, making me feel like I was back in the eighties with strobe lights dancing to Bee Gees' "Stayin' Alive." The sounds went through my head. I wanted to forget and hide, but there was no place to hide.

The constant questions began, and I recognized the voice. It was from Valerie again. Valerie asked the first question, "Dalton, tell us about your honeymoon and the legendary rescue."

I stood stationary while the tune exploded in my head: *Stayin' Alive, Stayin' Alive.*

Dalton answered, "It was an unbelievable, terrifying experience. Yes, the legendary rescue, as you call it, was incredible. We thought we were going to die, but Susan gave me hope. I wanted us to be together forever, alive, not deep in the cold blue sea. The whole rescue was a miracle."

Valerie quizzed, "Up until the near-death experience, how was the honeymoon?

*In my head, the song kept on playing,*
*Life goin' nowhere, somebody help me.*
*Somebody help me, yeah, stayin' alive.*

Dalton smiled, "Have you ever sailed a square-rigger in deep cobalt blue water while the brisk cold air hits your face? It was invigorating, and the cabin was cozy. We had an incredible honeymoon until the sinking of the ship."
*And we're stayin' alive, stayin' alive.*

Another reporter asked Dalton, "Did the crew abandon you?"

He continued, "Yes, the crew abandoned us without life rafts. They said they forgot us, and I wish I could believe them, but I'm not sure. I feel we are so fortunate that we survived the incident."

Another reporter said, "Susan, how did you feel?"

I wanted to scream but calmly said, "Dalton made me feel secure even as the ship went down. I'll never forget our honeymoon. It is a tale we can tell our grandchildren and their children. From now on, I prefer tropical breezes and sailing in the Caribbean."

I noticed Valerie staring at Dalton, but it didn't bother me. I knew he was mine now since we were married, especially not Valerie.

Finally, I said, "I don't ever want to be cold again."

Dalton added, "We are exhausted, everyone. The interview is over. We have to go home."

"Dalton, I can't hold my eyes open." With my last comment, I turned and took Dalton's hand. I was going home with my husband and to bad Leona's trial.

## Chapter 24– Leona's Trial

After a week, I was still trying to recuperate from our nautical nightmare honeymoon. We had rested and took it easy each day. On the morning of Leona's trial, I awoke early, and the birds sang outside the window. I felt as good as new or as new as good gets.

Ever since I had met Dalton, my life was full of peril. It certainly has been interesting, to say the least. *Suspiciously, I wondered what would be next. I shuddered, knowing I would have to appear in court for Leona's trial. I didn't want to go under interrogation, but the State court system required my presence as a witness and victim. I thought they should copy the NASA videos and let them watch firsthand the awful occurrence.*

I got dressed slowly in a navy-blue dress with a jacket. I didn't want to go to court. I felt like I was going to a funeral. I was reliving the death of my hero when Leona attacked me. I held my hands to my neck. The bruises healed slowly, but the dark memory will stay forever.

Dalton walked into the room and said, "Let's get going."

We left our home and walked out into the sunshine. Dalton said, "Look, I know this isn't going to be any fun, but it will be over fast."

A dark cloud covered us, as I said. "I hope you are right. Make it all disappear and have everyone leave us alone. Regardless, I will keep positive thoughts until it is over and Leona is locked up forever."

*Deep down inside my head, the nightmares were reappearing. The ominous voice replayed like a broken recorder, "I'm going to kill you if it is the last thing I do."*

When we arrived at the courthouse, we walked hand in hand into the massive doors of justice. Ken had saved us two vacant seats near the front of the courtroom. The district attorney motioned us to come over to him. He was a blustery older man with whiskers. The district attorney held his hand out to Dalton and me, saying. "It is a pleasure to meet both of you. I will be calling Susan to the stand first, and then you, Dalton. The questions will be to the point. Answer them honestly, and don't be intimidated by anyone in the courtroom, including Leona."

Not knowing anything else to say, I said. "I have not seen Leona since the night she tried to kill me. I am not looking forward to seeing her again."

Leona walked in. I froze; she looked wild, with her eyes blazing with hatred. Her hair was in disarray, frizzy, and not blond, but red. She had dyed her hair red, bright orange-red.

We both looked at each other in surprise. The defense attorney began his speech, "We have crucial evidence that will show Leona's innocence."

I said, "What and how could that be?"

"This trial will step you through the events that led to Leona's irrational behavior."

"Let me call my first witness." He gruffly said. "Will Susan take the stand?"

My heart stopped as I got up without making eye contact with Leona. I couldn't look at her. The anger and the hurt still weighed on my shoulders. I sat on the witness stand. It was hard and cold, like Leona's blazing eyes.

When the bailiff brought the Bible, I placed my hand on the top. "Do you swear to tell the truth, nothing but the truth?" He asked.

"Yes, I do," I said.

Her defense lawyer approached me. "How do you know the defendant?"

"The first time I met her, she was on Dalton's boat, S/V Naia. We went sailing in Galveston Bay." I stated.

"Did you find her behavior strange?" He asked.

"Not at the time, but she did seem secretive," I said.

"What do you mean, secretive?" He said.

"She kept watching Ken and making gestures to him," I explained.

"I don't know what it was all about, but she kept trying to keep me away from Dalton. It seemed that she disliked me from the beginning." I said.

Suddenly, Leona stood up, screaming, "I didn't do a thing."

The courtroom began whispering about her outrageous behavior.

The judge immediately said, "Order in the court, the order in the court."

"Please sit down, Leona. It's not your time to speak." Her lawyer advised.

He continued, "Being secretive is not a crime or strange behavior. You were a guest on Dr. Masters' boat, just like Leona. Was there any other evidence of strange behavior?"

"She tried to choke me to death," I said.

"Strike that comment from the records. That is circumstantial evidence." The lawyer bantered.

I began to tremble as I looked around the court in disbelief.

I began speaking, "I don't believe that occurrence is circumstantial evidence. Look at my neck; I still have bruises from Leona's hands. Is this circumstantial evidence? I don't think so.

"She also tried to incriminate me in the software incident. Looking back, I believe Leona changed the Software Quality Defect program, causing a misreading of the MECS data."

"We are not trying her for changing a software program but trying her for attacking you. This trial is to prove she was an accomplice in the death of Congressman Astronaut Fletcher. Dr. McKnight is now deceased, and he is linked romantically to Leona. They were having an affair. It's the strings of the heart and not a murder of the heart." He said.

I spoke, "Also, the red dot. She was the only one who could have applied the red dot on the MECS formula with the chemical warfare medicine." I said urgently, thinking about how badly I wanted her locked up.

He continued, "No one proved that. This unpleasant incident was just that, and Leona was a victim. Dr. McKnight, the NASA Astronaut physician, used and controlled her with drugs and a microchip device the size of a tip of a pencil. It can control a person's brain waves and alter people's behavior and actions. Even to the degree a person will perform acts against their basic moral values. This experimental device works. They removed the microchip."

The prosecutor said, "Did NASA scientists analyze the

microchip device?"

"Yes, they did. I want to present it as exhibit number one." He rebuffed.

The prosecutor turned to the jury, "This is farfetched., and I can't imagine that this is even plausible. It sounds like science fiction. This whole theory is inconceivable, and we will have it thrown out of court. Leona should pay for her heinous crime. The court is responsible for ensuring Leona pays for her crime. It was a cold-blooded murder. Not only did her actions cause the murder of the astronaut congressman representative Dan Fletcher, but the severe emotional and physical damage to Susan Masters."

"I object." The defense attorney barked out. "I will prove beyond a shadow of a doubt Leona was not responsible for her actions. Judge, can I call for a recess."

"We, the people, will be in recess and reconvene until tomorrow at ten AM." The judge announced.

Leona turned toward Dalton, "Dalton, you know I would never hurt anyone. All my life, we have been friends."

The police carried her away.

"Dalton, I'm so confused. I don't understand." I inquired.

"Research demonstrates a manipulation of the brain waves by having a microcapsule implanted into the portion of the brain that controls behavior. You insert a small needle with an automatic shot, like a hypodermic gun, which can feel like a small prick. The needle implants the microcapsule in you. You might not even notice it if you have had a couple of glasses of wine," Dalton explained.

"I wonder who would have done that to her? What proximity would someone be to alter Leona's brain waves? Could it be Dr. McKnight? Did he have the technology to do such a thing? He may have programmed her, not her grandfather. Should they do an autopsy to see if he had this done to him?" I asked.

"Leona's behavior was not controlled by someone near, but by the microcapsule. Leona was pre-programmed. It's almost as though her grandfather programmed her since she was a little girl." Dalton continued.

I gasped, "Who would believe this? She tried to kill me. I

still have the remnants of bruises on my neck. She was completely out of control."

We went back to our home in complete disarray. I couldn't believe the turn of events, and I wanted to scream. It was inconceivable she was going to get off free.

That night, the nightmares returned in spades. The faceless man kept coming at me with a chip embedded into a gadget that would control my brain.

I screamed, "Leave me alone. No, don't touch me!

I tossed and turned with sweat dripping from my body.

Dalton heard me screaming when he was in the other room, working on the MECS Experiment. He rushed from the room and held me firmly.

Dalton said, "This will soon be over. Please don't fret."

In the morning, I moved very slowly, thinking about the turn of events. It was like a slow-motion movie in black and white. Leona kept on laughing at me. She turned into the faceless man haunting me in my dreams. I could not escape the nightmare even while I was awake.

We re-entered the courtroom and sat in the same two vacant seats next to Ken. I felt like death warmed over.

"Let me call my second witness." The prosecuting attorney gruffly said. "Will Dalton Masters take the stand?"

Dalton got up from his seat slowly, making his way to the stand. He shook his head, looking toward Leona. I didn't know what to think of his actions.

The bailiff brought the Bible, and Dalton placed his hand on the top. "Do you solemnly tell the truth, nothing but the truth?" He asked.

"Yes, I do," Dalton said.

Dalton sat down as the jury watched the famous doctor. The questioning began. "How long have you known the defendant, Leona?"

He stated, "Well, I've known her most of her life. She lost her family, and my family adopted her. It was unfortunate."

"Your family took her in. What was her behavior at that time?" He inquired.

"Leona was always lovely. She wanted more from me than I could offer. She's like a little sister, and that is all," he said.

I knew Dalton wanted to ask his own questions, but he couldn't. The prosecuting attorney began asking Dalton questions: describe what happened the murderous night of our honorable Astronaut Congressman Fletcher."

Dalton began, "It was the most miserable night I had ever spent. The whole night was like a nightmare. After Dr. McKnight died, I went to find Susan. Everything was crazy. I entered the door to her room, and I found Leona choking Susan. Her voice was shrill, screaming; she was going to kill everyone. Her lover, Dr. Daryl McKnight, had died, and she wanted revenge. She was not rational."

"Was the defendant trying to kill you and Susan?" He questioned.

"Yes, she was; Susan would be dead if I hadn't shown up. If she were stronger, I would be dead. I fought as hard as I could. It's as though an unknown spirit possessed Leona, and her strength felt like a man. I couldn't believe her endurance." Dalton explained.

"But Leona is a small framed woman with not much power. I didn't think but just reacted. At that moment, it was me against her," he said.

"I understand, but you are a man, and she is a woman. Would you call Dalton's actions an act of brutality? Ladies and Gentlemen, look at this petite woman. She doesn't look like a murderer," the defense attorney explained.

Immediately, the Prosecutor said, "I object. The size of Dalton is of no subsequence. He was protecting Susan from being murdered and strangled to death. Leona attacked Susan. Take a good look at Susan's neck. The bruises are still apparent from the ghastly assault. Dalton, you may return to your seat, and I would like to recall Susan."

I knew the time was coming, and I dreaded being on the stand again. It was a horrible feeling. I gradually made my way up to the stand. It seemed as if I was going into slow-motion. I looked around the courtroom. Mrs. Dan Fletcher sat very solemnly with sorrow in her eyes. Her children sat next to her, holding onto their mother, or was their mother holding onto them?

The prosecutor asked, "Susan, did you ever notice any

peculiar behavior in Leona?"

I took a deep breath and said. "Yes, Leona never rested, and her actions were irrational at times. She was unreasonable about her Russian Grandfather being her hero."

Leona stood up, "My grandfather is the greatest scientist that has ever lived. He worked for the Germans."

The judge slammed the gavel on the bench. It vibrated through my body, and all the hairs on my neck stood up. I was afraid and knew deep inside that she was evil. I put my hands around my neck, protecting it from another attack.

"Order in the court, order in the court; may I have silence, now? Leona, you will be in contempt of the court if there are more outbursts."

The court became quiet, and everyone silently looked at each other. The outburst came as a shock. The jurors began looking at each other in surprise.

The defense attorney called his expert witness, "Leona, you may return to your seat.

"This is my expert witness, Dr. Kirk Kovey. Please take the stand. Can you state your name?"

"Dr. Kirk Kovey." The bailiff swore in the doctor to answer the questions.

The questioning continued after he sat down, "Can you tell me about the technology on the mind-controlling microchip technology?"

Dr. Kovey began speaking deliberately. "I have been studying this technology for ten years. I performed a CT scan of her brain, and it appears a tiny array of microelectrodes were in her brain, which picked up the din of her neural activity. The microelectrodes change the signals found inside a connector in Leona's scalp. These signals control behavior and actions.

"The question I have is who was doing the controlling. It seems Leona doesn't remember submitting to any tests or surgeries, but it was likely she didn't know when it happened. The microelectrodes were possibly implanted when she gave blood or even in a dentist's office. I can't tell you when it happened, but the procedure took place."

The prosecuting attorney said, "Object, you are leading the

jury with the last statement."

The judge said, "Strike the last comment. Continue with your questioning."

The defense attorney continued, "Before dealing with the business at hand, could you tell the court your credentials and how you came up with such an unbelievable conclusion?"

The man squirmed back and forth in the bench chair, turning toward the jury box, "I was the leading scientist at the Research Technical Institute. We performed mind-controlling experiments on guinea pigs. Three hundred guinea pigs were used in a controlled environment that provided insurmountable findings. The results conclusively showed all the guinea pigs ran through the maze correctly before the implants. Then, the scientists implanted microelectrodes in 150 guinea pigs. It reminded me of a video joystick that commanded them to go backward in the maze. Guinea pigs could not control their actions. They followed each command using the joystick.

They then took it to a higher level for the next step to implant the microelectrodes into a well-known criminal's brain on death row. He volunteered for the experiment, which took him off death row. This one act of kindness extended his life and modified his behavior forever. In return, he will spend the rest of his life in prison but now can associate with the other prisoners. He is no longer a threat to society and fellow inmates."

A strong, muscular man walked very slowly and deliberately into the courtroom. Two police officers escorted him to the bench. He didn't look like a criminal but a tall, good-looking, and rugged model. All the women gasped as he walked toward the stand.

"I would like to introduce you to Mr. Bill Chavez."

"Mr. Chavez, you may take a seat on the witness stand."

The bailiff swore him in, "Do you tell the truth nothing but the truth."

He responded, "I do."

I suddenly got chills down my back. The total mind control was unbelievable. It was undoubtedly a three-ring circus.

The prosecutor led the examination. "Will you state your

name?"

"Bill Chavez." He said in a proper midwestern ascent. Bill's eyes met Leona, locking them together as chills ran up my back.

Dalton stared at me, recognizing their familiarity. We both shook our heads.

The cross-examiner began questioning Mr. Chavez. "Sir, can you tell me about the experiment."

The criminal said, "The experiment has caused an extremely significant change in my life. The wonderful thing about this whole ordeal is that I have never felt better in my life. It was a simple operation, and after the operation, I have not had the neurosis that caused my violent behavior as a hardened criminal."

The defense attorney stated, "I heard it is a dangerous operation, and yet you volunteered for this surgery. Why would you do such a thing?"

"Well, Sir, it was a win-win situation. You see, the death chamber had my name on it. I would have died within the year with no chance of parole. I am not ready to die. When they told me, a small transistor could control my behavior. I was fascinated and excited.

"As you know, I have not been a perfect citizen. All my life, I wanted to be better and show everyone I wasn't a demon. I couldn't make myself be what the rest of the world expected, but the microelectrodes did the trick." He calmly said.

The defense attorney told him, "You may take your seat. He has just told you about the dramatic difference in personality. How did it happen? A tiny microelectrode implanted in his brain changed his life. You see him. He functions now as a model citizen in the penal system. It is amazing."

As the man, Bill, sat down, he had a smirk on his face, literally a crooked smile. He looked straight at Dalton and me. I had an uneasy feeling about the man. He had evil in my eyes, but no one else could see it.

*I didn't know what to think. It had to consider who else was close enough that could have programmed Leona. Could it be Ken? I didn't know, but maybe someone else was in the background. My head was reeling. It is beyond what I ever thought would happen.*

I looked at Dalton, and he at me. We were speechless. The courtroom buzzed with tension.

The defense attorney called Dalton to the stand. Dalton walked again to the bench and sat down.

The first question asked, "Sir, what is your relationship with the defendant?"

Dalton answered, "Leona has worked in the aerospace program for her adult life. She performs quality control for hardware payload experiments."

He asked, "Was her work satisfactory?"

Dalton said, "Her work was superior. I never had one complaint until the mishap with Congressman Fletcher."

Another question, "Do you think her actions were of her own free will?"

"Objection, the defense is leading the client." The prosecuting lawyer said.

The judge said, "Over-ruled. You may answer the question."

Dalton paused, "Well, her behavior was not normal, but she seemed to be acting not of her own free will."

Everyone in the courtroom began talking. Dalton's statement could change the outcome of the jury. Silently, I died. How could he make such a statement? She knew what she was doing.

The judge cried, "Silence in the court. Silence in the court; we will reconvene tomorrow at 1000." Everyone became quiet. The jury went out to deliberate.

*That night, I felt my world crashing around me. Why had Dalton given the courts a way to release Leona? I knew he was telling the truth, but she had tried to kill me!*

The following day, the judge ruled, "I would like to remind everyone in attendance how important it is to respect the decorum of the court. Please remain quiet while we render the verdict.

The honorable judge said, "Prosecutor, please argue your summation."

"Ladies and Gentlemen, in the jury before you release a

dangerous woman back into society."

"I object. The prosecutor is leading the jury." The defendant said.

"Let me rephrase the opening. Leona is sitting before you, a woman who attacked the plaintiff, Susan Masters. She marked the MECS capsules with a red dot, which identified the capsules filled with chemical warfare solutions, killing Congressman Fletcher. Jury, I know the story told across the nation. I don't believe that mind control could manipulate another human action. Leona Sharply is an accomplice to Congressman Fletcher's death. His death was an atrocity. The court's verdict to protect the innocent and allow Leona the freedom to hurt someone else would cause an injustice to my clients. My client would be in danger. Don't give this person the freedom to kill again or attack Susan Masters or Dr. Dalton Masters." He eloquently said and sat down.

"Will the defendant give their summation?" The Judge stated.

The defendant's lawyer stood up. Leona's eyes followed him as he began speaking. She looked like a wounded animal. For a moment, I felt sorry for her and hoped the jury didn't.

The defendant's lawyer began speaking slowly and deliberately. He walks over to Leona, who looks like a small little girl, frail and scared. "Here sits before you, a child who, beyond the tortures of society, manipulated her. However, she was controlled without her consent and knowledge. Dr. McKnight controlled her with his good looks and manipulation. Her grandfather controlled her with the microchip implanted into her brain. He was ahead of his time. Leona is still a child in so many ways. She has worked as a woman and has been a productive adult in society. The implant manipulated her to become an accomplice in the murder of Congressman Fletcher and a conspirator against the Space Program. Yes, she acted as such but controlled not by herself. You heard Dr. Dalton Master say her behavior was always exemplary. She is a textbook employee and model citizen. The evidence of mind control is absolute. "

He picked up the microelectrodes in a plastic bag tagged as evidence. He held it up and began speaking, "Leona is innocent. She didn't know what she was doing and didn't remember attacking Susan or putting chemicals into the MECS formula. I want you to search in your heart and come back with a verdict of innocence because she is innocent. Leona Sharply is Not Guilty."

He sat down beside her and held Leona in his arms while she shook uncontrollably with tears running down her face.

The judge said, "These are the last arguments. May the jury take an adjournment and return with the verdict."

The lead juror stood and said, "Yes, sir, honorable judge."

They left solemnly from the courtroom in a single file into a room. The jurors had a big decision: whether Leona would be free or locked up forever. The courtroom scenario all seemed as if it were a masquerade.

The judge said, "Court will reconvene in two days at 1000."

## Chapter 25 - Verdict

*We were silent all the way home. I was furious at Dalton for giving her a way out. I knew he wasn't lying, but I didn't want to be looking over my shoulder for Leona for the rest of my life. I decided not to say anything. I didn't want to think about it. I thought the morning would never come as I tossed and turned all night. I suspected Leona had once been his lover, but I didn't know.*

As we walked into the courtroom, I finally broke the silence, "Dalton, I know you will protect me from Leona."

"Susan, until my last dying breath," he said as we sat down.

The judge called the room to order and asked the court to give the verdict.

The jury bailiff said, "The State versus Leona Sharply; may the verdict be known?"

The lead juror stood up and said, "The jury finds the defendant not guilty."

The judge stated over the roar of the courtroom, "The evidence of mind control is permissible. Leona is not responsible for her actions. The State ruled that her actions weren't of her own free will. She is free to go. Dismiss this case."

Everyone in the courtroom was pale from the verdict, including Congressman Fletcher's family. They were anxious to have Leona put away for life to have closure for his death. It didn't happen. Tears of injustice flowed down everyone's face.

Dalton, "This is ridiculous. Even though a trial is a formal examination of the facts, but these facts are farfetched. How could the court free Leona when she was an accomplice to the death of Congressman Fletcher? She almost killed me."

The courtroom buzzed with the shock of the verdict. My head hurt from the rumblings and grumblings in the courtroom.

Dalton said, "This was not a fair trial."

I said, "Don't they know she's crazy? We're in danger,

Dalton. Now, the enemy is free. I don't believe she is the innocent one with mind-controlled mumbo jumbo. She hates me. I can't have her free. She will soon come to kill me. My dreams are a sign."

"I will protect you, Susan. I'm not comforted to know the burden of the consequences of the courtroom is on the judge. I wonder what his motivation is to allow mind control as an alibi. I can't believe he let Leona go free." Dalton said.

"I think we need to look at Bill Chavez. What is their relationship?" I said.

"Don't know, but I'm going to find out. Bill Chavez is on death row. I want to make sure he stays there. Now, so many sympathizers will advocate his freedom. I want to contact an investigator who can find out more information about Leona's supporters. Oh yeah, I remember a private detective I met at one of Jackson's parties." Dalton said.

"I'll call Karen and find out his number. She should be with Jackson." I said.

I dialed her number as fast as I could. She answered. "Hello."

"Susan, I've been watching the news about the trial. I can't believe they let that maniac free," she commented.

"Neither can I. Dalton and I want more information about this culprit, Bill. Somehow, there is a connection between Leona and him. I just know it." Karen said.

"Karen, Jackson has a friend who is a private detective. I think his name is Mike." Susan said.

"Yeah, let me get his number from Jackson. Until then, please be safe. I don't like Leona. I never did. She is a dangerous woman." Karen said.

"Karen, I've had nightmares about her. She is scary." I said. "You know you have that sense — more than once, you have predicted the future. Just keep your eyes open, and don't be alone. She is now out of prison, and I truly believe she will be after you, mind control or no mind control."

My friend said, "I know. I'm not going to take any chances. Soon, we will be going to Kennedy Space Center to begin the experiment. I'm now the project manager since Dalton will be in space with the King." I said.

"Tell me about King Karl Ásgeirr XIII." She asked.

I started laughing. "The King is an incredible man, or should I say, playboy. What a flirt. Actually, he makes me uncomfortable. I want this experiment to be over and life to be normal. I want to keep Dalton to myself. I hope we can return to the Bahamas or the Caribbean. I need a sailing fix."

"Well, when you head out, Jackson and I would like to go with you," Karen chirped in.

"It's a deal. Let's get that number and put the man to work. The more I find out about Bill, the safer I will feel." I said.

She gave me the number and his full name, Mike Cook.

Talk to you later, girlfriend." Karen said.

"Goodbye, Mama," I said.

Out of the corner of my eye, I saw Dalton talking with that news reporter, Valerie. She was getting too cozy.

I interrupted, "Hi, how are you, Valerie?"

"I'm doing just fine, but I'm sure you're not. It looks like Leona got off scot-free. I don't know about our judicial system. As a newspaper reporter, I should say this is big news. It will be all over the networks. Can you tell me how you feel about the outcome, Susan?" Valerie prodded.

"Valerie, I can't describe the emotion I am feeling. It is as though someone knocked the wind out of me.

"Do you have anything to say, Dalton?" She quizzed.

"Misery surrounds all of us: Dr. McKnight, Congressman Dan Fletcher, my friend, and partner Dr. Jon Keller. He wrote the infamous note, and his beautiful family was destroyed in a house fire mysteriously. All are gone. A jury of her peers will try Leona and possibly acquit Leona. I want to have this over for my wife and me to have a normal life." Dalton eloquently said.

Inside, I was screaming. How do I feel? Scared, awful, and I wanted to have Leona disappear. Now that Dalton is going into space, I will be alone to defend myself. I am alone, with Leona lurking in every corner.

Dalton said as Ken walked up, "Let's go get a drink."

Ken said, "I thought you would never ask with everything that's happened. I wish we could sail with the wind on our faces on Galveston Bay or take off on my Scarab. I would never have thought Leona was a psychopath."

We walked away with despair written on our faces like three sad musketeers.

## Chapter 26–MECS Experiment

On the way home, I could not comprehend what happened in the courtroom. Nevertheless, it was time to get to work since I had a job to do. It was the most challenging job I'd ever undertaken. My husband's career and the King's life depended on how well I performed the MECS responsibilities. We made our way back home in the dark. When Dalton opened the door, I heard something moving inside.

"Dalton, did you hear that noise?" I whispered.

"Yes, you stay here, and I will go investigate." He said.

"No, I will go with you. I don't want to stay here alone." I said.

I gasped when we walked into the house. Someone turned everything inside out, with broken furniture and debris everywhere. The fractured pieces crunched as I walked behind Dalton.

Suddenly, a person dressed in black with a mask knocked me over. My face began bleeding from the broken glass on the floor.

Dalton screamed as he ran after the intruder, "Are you okay?"

I cried, "Yes, I think so." Everything became a blur as I passed out. The next thing I knew, I was lying on our bed with Dalton standing over me.

"Sweetie, you took a hard fall. Your cut is just superficial, but the bruise on your head got the best of you," Dalton said lovingly.

"Will I be, okay? Did you get the intruder?"

"The answers to your questions in order are yes and, unfortunately, no; I'm afraid he or she got away. I really couldn't tell if the person was female or male. By the time I got out the door, the person had disappeared." He said.

"What do you think they were after?" I inquired.

"I don't know, but I do have the MECS journals safely locked away in our safe," Dalton stated.

"I want this to end." My heart stopped. Tears ran down my

face, and I began shivering. "Do you think?" I asked.

Dalton's face dropped. "Could it be Leona? She just got out of jail. What would she gain by destroying our home? Could she be looking for the MECS formula?"

"Yes, yes, yes," I said. I wanted to believe the nightmare ended, but it hadn't.

"I'm going to stop her if it is the last thing I do. I still can't believe they let her go," Dalton said.

"Neither can I., and we won't be safe until she is behind bars again. That's a bunch of garbage about her being under mind control. She knew what she was doing, and she will do it again. I believe she will not stop until she has the formula," I said.

It hit me when Dalton was up in space; I would be alone with no protection. Of course, she couldn't get onto the KSC campus, so I should be safe. I didn't like to think about our last encounter, and I automatically put my hands on my neck. My neck was sore and bruised.

"Dalton, can we just go to bed and forget this ever happened?" I asked.

"Of course, we don't have time to waste on Leona. We must start concentrating on the MECS Experiment. You must run the experiment from the ground, and I must administer the MECS drug delivery in space. In the morning, I'm going to go over the MECS process with you. You must know I'm so proud of you for taking on this project. Let's clean up your cuts," he touched my face where the abrasions throbbed.

I couldn't help myself; the tears ran down my cheeks, burning the cuts. I wanted to find out why Leona continued to pursue the MECS Experiment. Had she and Dr. McKnight acted alone in Congressman Fletcher's death? I didn't think so.

He tenderly cleaned my face with witch hazel and picked out little pieces of glass with squeezers. I put on my best grown-up face and didn't cry even though hot, salty tears ran down my face.

Dalton held me all night. He didn't let me go, not once during our sleep. I felt safe; he was my teddy bear. His affection took me to places I never knew existed. It was more than just sex; it was a bond between two people who would always be together. I knew this relationship would last forever. He is my husband, soul mate, and the one I want to be with for the rest of my life because he kissed my soul. * 5

I was exhausted and fell into bed. Dalton and I held each other all night since we knew that we would soon work day and night. We had to rest when we had the opportunity.

In the morning, Dalton said over breakfast, "I'm ready to teach you about the prostate research procedure. We will process the microcapsules formula in a zero-gravity environment. Still, first, you and your team will formulate a test MECS formula in the NASA laboratory. I already have a team in place. I will introduce them to you as their leader."

The responsibility of developing the MECS formula weighed heavily on my heart. The last MECS payload, Leona, helped me. She had done the MEC's formula many times before. I wished she hadn't become a crazed woman. The event was on my shoulders with a team of strangers.

"Dalton, are you sure you want me to run the MECS Experiment?"

"Who else could I trust? I have all the confidence in the world in you," he said adamantly.

"I guess you are right," I said as I lifted my lips. *At that moment, I remembered our lovemaking in the Bahamas, the warm breezes, his soft touch, and the wonderful endless days. My thoughts turned to space. I could imagine making love in a blanket of stars.* * 6

"Susan, where are you? Here you are, daydreaming again; come back to me. Everything will be fine," he said.

"Yes, I am, but I'm daydreaming about us and our vacation time in the Bahamas," I said.

"I wish for those times again, and we will have them. Now, on to a more serious issue about the changes to the MECS experiment. The formula is the same, but I want to change the process of the formulation. I have been doing clinical studies perfecting the microcapsules, which use ultrasound imaging,

5 The poem "Kiss My Soul" is in the Poetry Section.
6 The poem "Blanket of Stars" is in the Poetry Section.

releasing real-time formula using a 25-gauge needle to insert into the prostate tumor. I can control the amount of MECS formula without opening the capsule. This procedure will keep contamination down. If the first dosage doesn't work, then we will increase the quantity to 30-gauge."

I asked, "When do I need to begin mixing the formula?"

He said, "The last time we ran short of time. I want to begin the mixture four days before launch. I will be in quarantine at that time, so you will be in charge."

"Dalton, I'm apprehensive about the experiment because of the deaths during the last MECS mission."

"We have to move on from the past. It is gone, and now the future of humanity is in our hands. The King will be dead in two months if this procedure doesn't work. Life as we know it is about to change," he said.

"Timing is everything," I said.

"I never imagined we would have a King's Payload," Dalton said.

"I know, but as you said, he will die without treatment. He has a death sentence, and you are the only one who can give him a space pardon," I said.

"A space pardon from death. Never heard it stated that way." Dalton said.

"I'm tired and need rest before we meet our team tomorrow," I said.

Dalton said, "I will be happy to tuck you into bed, my dear."

The following day, I woke up early. The events of last night faded. I just didn't want to think about all the work ahead of me anymore. Dalton turned to me as we lay in bed. The smell of jasmine came through the window. The fragrance permeated throughout the room. It was fresh. He smiled and pulled me over toward him, making my whole world light up. His kisses were making my body shiver. He brought me to ecstasy, kissing my breasts and touching my skin gently as he ran his hands down my legs. My eyes closed, and yesterday's events were gone.

Afterward, I looked at him and said, "We have work to do. Let's go out for breakfast."

"Sounds good," he responded.

When I walked into the living room, I saw a mess of broken vases, papers, and drawers thrown on the floor.

I screamed, "Oh, Dalton, what are we going to do?" I felt violated all over again as I sat down and cried.

Dalton sat down, "Don't worry about this mess. I will hire a cleaning service to come while we are at work. It will be okay."

"Shouldn't we call Ed Davis, the detective, and report this incident?" I inquired.

"I will call Ed at breakfast. I can't stay in the house. We don't have much to say except someone broke into our home and ransacked it. I will wait to call the cleaning service after he permits me to do so. We have so much work to accomplish today. He already has a key to the house, so it shouldn't be a problem." Dalton said.

"That sounds like a plan. Let's go to Skippers. It's my favorite breakfast place," I said, agreeing.

On the way to Skippers, our focus turned to the work at hand. Dalton started.

"I'm excited about the upgrade to the capsule and performing my first spacewalk," Dalton said enthusiastically.

"It must be an incredible feeling of weightlessness and buoyancy. I can't imagine, but I would think the nearest sensation would be scuba diving. The water has the same freeness. It's exhilarating floating in warm water being light as a feather. The suits are so heavy on Earth, but they don't weigh a thing out in space. It would be wonderful to walk in the dark blue space surrounded by stars." I said.

"Also, I guess I will automatically lose weight, with bone loss and lack of taste. When I get back, you will have to fatten me with a lot of good cooking." Dalton said.

"Of course, I will. Please don't lose weight. I like you the way you are. Unfortunately, most people don't know about all the inventions that have come from the space program. Just think what life would be like without diapers, Velcro, and not to mention Lasik surgery." I said.*7

"Yeah, Lasik technology comes from the satellite deep

7 Chapter 58 – NASA Spinoffs

space Hubble telescope. I wish the public would understand how many things came from the aerospace industry," Dalton explained.

"Oh, you forgot about the most important technology, the MECS Experiment. It's a cure for cancer. The King will be the first to receive the MECS prostate intervention. I still don't understand how it works." I said excitedly.

Dr. Dalton Masters, Ph.D., explained, "Susan, what I'm going to tell you is Top Secret. Since you will be managing the MECS Experiment from the Ground, you need to know I will be in space. Listen carefully; I need to explain precisely how the MECS formula works.

I listened carefully to his very technical description, taking many notes.

"Dalton, your explanation is intriguing. It is your life's work and will change cancer treatment forever. Think of the King and his prostate cancer. I can't imagine how a man would feel. His manhood threatened. I guess you could compare it to women having breast cancer." I said.

He continued, "Yes, but there is more. The microcapsules are a drug delivery system to administer the highest concentration of the drug crystals. You cannot inject imperfect drug crystals into the bloodstream. The sharp edges will damage the arteries or veins. However, the microcapsules protect the blood vessels from damaging crystals. I will use "focal chemotherapy microcapsules" strategies to localize the chemo-drug inside the target tumor rather than traditional therapy where the drugs affect the whole body. The MECS will keep everything else healthy in his body except for the cancerous tumor.

We finally arrived at Skippers. I said, "I'm hungry. Dalton, I didn't understand everything you were saying. If you have additional information, I could study so that it may make more sense to me."

"I have a training manual I can give you, which will help," he said.

We walked into the room and continued.

"I'm hopeful the microcapsules, developed in space, will stop cancer growth for human prostate and lung tumors. The microcapsules should inhibit cancer growth and destroy deadly cancer. I cannot tell you the secret component, but it's time to release. I will inject the crystals into the King while he is in the capsule since it is a clean white environment. The oxygen will activate the MECS drug. I believe the formula is what they want. They want to know the ingredients of MECS, but I will never tell the enemy." * 8

"It's incredible the results of the microcapsules made in space and think of the additional advantages for chemotherapy applications. I'm getting excited about being part of the program. I'm up for the challenge," I said.

"Well, you can't do this alone. Ken will work with you as your assistant. He knows the process and can assist you in any capacity. Ken's finally excited about being your right-hand man. We will be getting together with him for lunch at Franca's. I need an Italian fix." He grinned.

"I'm so glad you picked Ken. I feel less nervous about managing the MECS Experiment." I said, even though I still worried about Ken's true intentions.

8 Ref. - Le Pivert, P., Haddad, R., Aller, A., Titus, K., Doulat, J., Renard, M., Morrison, D.R.. "Ultrasound Guided, Combined Cryoablation and Microencapsulated 5-Fluorouracil, Inhibits Growth of Human Prostate Tumors in Xenogenic Mouse Model Assessed by Luminescence Imaging, *Technology in Cancer Research & Treatment*, 3 (2), 135-142, (2004)

When we arrived at NASA, we immediately went to the MECS laboratory. The MECS project team was waiting in the conference room. I was comforted to see Patti, David, and Connie on my team. I trust them. They are the best of the best.

Dalton called the meeting to order and introduced me to the team, and then he left.

I stated, "First, I want to introduce Ken, who is the MECS hardware developer. Please introduce yourself, your line of expertise, and what organization you represent."

One at a time, they introduced themselves: Patty, the quality technician/technician; Connie, the quality engineer; David, the technician/engineer; and Ken, the hardware expert.

I continued, "MECS is an acronym for **Micro Encapsulation Crystallization System**. It is the most important project in your career. We will be responsible for formulating the MECS formula. Your selection is critical since you have TOP SECRET CLEARANCE, and you are the best of the best. I want to thank you for accepting this challenge. I will give everyone a list of procedures based on their expertise. No one has a full set of procedures due to security. Our MECS team is critical to a successful mission and the life of the King Ásgeirr of Sweden. He has prostate cancer, and the formula will save his life. I am going to draw an outline on the whiteboard and assign your area of responsibility."

The day was very tiring, but we had managed to understand what was required by the end of the day. I felt we would handle the MECS formulation to perfection, or should I say to the requirements.

Dalton said, "Here are the MECS procedures for you to study. We will review them tomorrow after you have had time to familiarize yourself. Ken or I can answer any questions. We will meet tomorrow morning at 1000 in this conference room, but please don't share it with anyone. You have signed a confidential agreement and punishment by the federal government. Do you have any questions?"

Patti questioned, "Will we be going to KSC?"

"Good question, yes, we will. The final formation takes place in the KSC astronaut laboratory. You will be staying at a local hotel one week before the flight and will be attending the VIP launch," I said.

Everyone in the room became very excited since some of the team had never seen a launch, even though they had worked on the space program their entire career.

Patti said, "I've never gone to a launch, and I've been working for the space program for twenty-five years. It's difficult to find the time and money to attend a launch at the Cape from Houston. Thank you for the invite."

# Chapter 28 – Flight Space Equipment Building

Early the next day, Dalton had an appointment to visit the Flight Space Equipment (FSE) building at JSC NASA. Since the meeting was at 7:30 AM, I decided to visit the facility before meeting with the MECS team. FSE personnel make, ship, or process the astronaut's equipment needed in space. The most important was the food.

A very friendly receptionist/security guard met us with a smile, "Please sign in and show me your NASA badges."

She very carefully inspected our badges with an intense look.

"Who is going to be your escort today?" She said swiftly. I noticed her name badge said, Linda.

I said, "Doc Doolittle." Before I could utter another word, she was paging him.

"Doc Doolittle, please come to the front desk. You have guests in the lobby."

A short, attractive, white-haired man with a gentle manner appeared. It was Doc who escorted us on a VIP tour. He was a local star and an engineer who processed equipment daily. His well-known expertise in the space program has been a legend for a very long time.

Introductions were in order; Dalton said, "Hi. I'm Dr. Dalton Masters, and this is my wife, Susan. She will accompany me throughout the tour and into the Food Lab for my preview of the menu selection."

Doc shook his hand and turned to me, "It is so nice to meet you, Susan. We have all heard about the quality program you developed for Flight Software. It has kept the onboard software safe with a Six Sigma (.000067 per million) error ratio."

"She certainly is amazing," Dalton said.

I blushed, "You guys are too much."

"Follow me," Doc said as we turned the corner, "In this area is where we package and inventory all the space hardware, including any bags. It's where you will take inventory of everything you take into space with you."

We peered through the looking glass.

I said, "This reminds me of a hospital's maternity ward window with all the delicate equipment."

Doc laughed, "That's a good comparison; in the Bench Review laboratory, every piece of equipment everyone treats like a newborn baby."

We turned the corner, and I saw what was behind in the next window. It looked like a department store. It had watches, gloves, socks, and even diapers.

Dalton piped in, "I guess I will be a baby again wearing a diaper."

Doc said, "Yes, on the launch, you will be wearing a reinforced diaper. It is a necessity. Sometimes, the delay in launch makes it impossible to go to a restroom facility. I have heard tales that the smell can get quite disgusting."

"Yuk, that is too much information. I see you even have makeup, my favorite Clinique. Why do you use that product?" I asked.

"In space, you don't want any smells, contaminants, or particles floating around. It happens this product is space friendly so that the female astronauts can look pretty in the cameras. Dalton, you have a choice of watches, iPads, gloves, and much more.

Your fitting schedule for your flight crew equipment is our next stop. Just make sure once you are fitted for the flight suits, not to gain too much weight. If this happens, we will start all over again, causing a delay in the flight. We are going into another building for you to have a fit check," Dalton said.

We walked outside, seeing beautiful pink azaleas blooming. Squirrels were running across the sidewalk. They were a little too friendly, acting as if I should stop and feed them. I wondered if the employees had been feeding the squirrels, which wouldn't surprise me since they had benches and tables to have lunch in the courtyard. The squirrels looked very well fed.

When we entered the adjoining building, there were astronauts' photographs lining the wall. I stopped at a section with the Space Shuttle Columbia astronauts who died entering the earth's atmosphere. The foam compromised the shuttle structure. The repeated news and reminders of flowers and American flags in front of the JSC NASA Campus kept the whole NASA family and community in mourning.

Also, businesses wrote thoughts of sympathy for the community and the names of families of lost ones on their billboards. I drove to work, not looking at the signs, wishing it were all a dream. It was disheartening, and I never want to go through that again. I stood in front of their pictures and could not move.

Dalton said, "Honey, I know how you feel. Remember, every astronaut knew the risks; they chose this vocation and enjoyed every moment. It is their life; astronauts are risk-takers."

I said, "I know, but it still doesn't make it easier. You will be going into space, and I understand the risk. I don't want you to go."

Dalton responded, "I know, but I have to go. It is also my way of life, and I understand the risks."

Doc escorted us into the Food laboratory, which is a white room. We dressed in caps and hairnets covering our heads and necks. We covered ourselves from head to toe after putting on gloves, gowns, and shoe covers, which protected our bodies.

We entered the Food laboratory and saw the table displaying all the dehydrated food in their plastic bags."

Doc introduced us to the food engineer, "This is Nani. I will leave you in her capable hands."

She asked us to sit down, "Hi, I'm Nani. You must be Dalton, and you must be his new bride, Susan. I'm your nutritionist and food engineer for this flight. I will help you develop a menu with the appropriate caloric intake for a man your size in space based on your food selection."

Dalton grinned, "I've needed a stringent diet for years. How do you do it?"

She surveyed his physique; "We calculate the average caloric amount required for survival in space based on your body weight. The biggest difference between activities on Earth compared to activity in space is man's energy without gravity. Movement is effortless in space, and your muscle elasticity reduces significantly."

He laughed joyfully, nudging me, "Well, that settles it. I guess I can't go if I can't eat all I want. Nani, I know you will let me eat all the food I want."

Nani laughed, "No, I will not. Here is a list of all the foods. It has 1,500 items. Why don't you select your food for the long journey in space? We have a menu available, which will help put the right foods together."

I said in surprise, "The selection of food is unbelievable. You can have M&Ms, oatmeal, peaches, tacos, and much more, which surpasses most restaurant menus; wow."

He asked Nani, "How is the shrimp? I heard it is the best."

"I have to be modest since the scrumptious shrimp is my creation, but if I say so myself, it is delicious. The shrimp is very spicy. Your taste buds in space are weak. The food is generally tasteless, so the spicy shrimp is the most popular selection," Nani said.

Dalton began laughing, "Look, Susan. Can you believe Tang is still on the list? I guess you can say we have tang and tail."

Nani giggled, "Yes, it is the astronauts' drink of choice, so to speak."

He began filling out his menu list, and he chose his favorite foods. "I can't believe I have 1500 items on the menu. It is great!"

Nani said, "Please don't forget the liquid salt and pepper. The spices are wonderful in space. Since we are here, why don't you two have a taste test? Let me go get some ice cream."

To my surprise, she brought out dehydrated ice cream. I opened the package and placed it in my mouth.

I said, "The ice cream melts in my mouth. It's like cotton candy consistency. It's incredible and delicious."

Next, she presented cauliflower with cheese. She added hot water through a faucet on the oven. "Why don't you try some vegetables?"

This time, we both made faces. "It's awful. No offense." I couldn't get the orange concoction called cauliflower out of my mouth fast enough. I took another ice cream package and devoured it to disguise the disgusting flavor.

"Yuk, I have never tasted something so bad," I complained.

Dalton said, "That is not going to be on my list. Could I take an Elvis peanut butter and banana sandwich?"

"I'm sorry, bananas are not an available food choice in space. Everyone is in a small, enclosed environment, and the intense aroma of bananas permeates throughout the station. Everyone would get sick from the smell. I like bananas, but not in space."

"The formula for all recipes is almost neutral, and this keeps the offensive odors to a minimum." the beautiful food engineer said.

Dalton watched her every move. Who wouldn't? She was a lovely woman with exotic features.

"I have a question?" I broke the trance, "How do you eat in zero-gravity? The food must float away."

"Well, the function of the food containers is designed with flaps. The flaps simultaneously wipe the spoon or fork clean as you eat your food," Nani explained.

"You guys have thought of everything," I said.

Dalton put his arms around me, "It may not be like my wife's home cooking, but I certainly won't starve. It will be inconvenient when I can't go down to the local grocery store and buy more food. We are so used to the simple conveniences, which are not so simple far, far away in space. It is like going to a foreign country with a limited number of supplies like The Bahamas."

Nani said, "Well, don't order everything on the menu like most of the astronauts. I'm afraid everyone has the same feeling. They don't want to go hungry. Also, make sure you keep an eye on your supplies. Food disappears in space. It is a mystery, you know."

I snickered, "It not only melts in your mouth but in the food container."

Dalton said thoughtfully, "Let's hope my food doesn't disappear. In space, those would be fighting words, an out-of-space incident. Hope you packed a suitcase because you are going to the moon, Alice."

I laughed, "Of course, it would be called an international food fight."

Nani chirped in and said, "All I can think of is the movie *Animal House* and the notorious food fight with John Belushi."

Nani said, "Remember we have a meeting at 1600 to go over all the food with the entire astronaut flight team. Please be there promptly."

Dalton said, "I will complete my food menu with the astronaut team at 1600."

Everyone removed their protective clothing in the locker room and put it in a disposable container. We both thanked Nani as we left the building.

Dalton laughed, "Well, where are you going next, my dear?"

I said, "I have to meet with the MECS team at 1000, but since we have been talking about food, I'm hungry. How about I meet you for lunch at around twelve?"

"Well, young lady, let me take you to the Classic Café again. It will tantalize your taste buds without you eating out of a tube. Now that's international."

I laughed, "Take me somewhere international, Thai Seafood, Signature Bistros, Francas, or La Brisas, or even to the International House of Pancakes."

Dalton said, "You know, I don't think I will get that type of food in the Food Laboratory, so I must pick my menu carefully. Do you have time to go back to the Food Laboratory with me at four?"

"Of course, I do," I said, "Just don't make me too hungry."

"Well, it's going to be a treat to taste more food," Dalton replied.

I said, "Choose wisely. See you later, darling; I have work to do."

# Chapter 29 – MECS Formula

As I walked toward Building One, I felt chills crawl up my spine as if someone were watching me. Turning, I saw a man on a bicycle about 20 yards behind me, pedaling slowly and keeping pace with me. The hooded sweatshirt and dark sunglasses made it hard to tell who it was, but I felt sure he was watching and following me. I quickened my pace, and the last few yards seemed to take forever, but soon, I was in the building, standing next to the security guard. I watched the cyclist as he slowly pedaled out of sight. I tried to bring my breathing back under control, telling myself that this was the JSC campus and that I shouldn't feel I was in danger. It's getting close to launch, and I had so much to do before the MECS formula would be ready. I almost panicked, just thinking of all my duties and responsibilities. I had to concentrate and not be suspicious of everybody who passed me on the street, but I knew I had to be careful in the back of my mind.

I went up to the NASA conference room, and there sat the MECS team. Everyone had signed the Meeting Attendance Sheet; no one was missing. First, Pat and Connie stated they had reviewed the procedures and had a couple of questions.

I almost froze, wondering if I would know the answers.

I responded, "If I can't answer any of your questions, then I will get an answer for tomorrow's meeting."

Pat asked, "We would like to have a simulation of manufacturing the formula before the actual occurrence."

I said, "That is a great plan. I will set it up for tomorrow, and we can go through it. Anyone else has any requests?"

David said, "I would like to meet with management and double the security when we perform the simulation."

I said, "Yes, I will set it up. We will perform the MECS simulation tomorrow at 1300. Our team will complete five capsules. I will request that Dalton attend our simulation to ensure we have Six Sigma. Six Sigma is a process that must not produce more than 3.4 errors per million opportunities. It is performance perfection.

David, please make sure the equipment is in the MECS Laboratory. Connie, have you reviewed the procedures and schematic charts for quality sign-off? If so, get together with David. I will ensure the inclusion of the formula's safety requirements and the latest configuration. It will be a test of an authentic simulation of the MECS formula.

Ken, you will be the third set of eyes to watch the quality technicians perform the formulation. Does anyone have any other suggestions?"

No one said a word. I handed out a small test and said, "I will not grade this test, and the answers are on the back for your review. I don't want anyone to guess the answers. Hopefully, it will bring everyone up to speed on the process. We will go over the test in the morning, and I will have security management in attendance."

I continued, "Well, you have a lot of work to perform. Tomorrow, I will check with you at 1000 to check the MECS simulation setup is ready for 1300 trial testing."

It was now noon, and I called Dalton. I asked, "Where are you taking me for lunch, Darling?"

He said, "Let's go to Franca's Italian Restaurant in fifteen minutes."

"Franca's sounds GREAT to me," I said. *I thought about how Papa Franco had made all the restaurant statues to inspire Italy's atmosphere. I adored the ambiance. His daughter, Franca, was the new owner since Franco had passed.*

Dalton said, "I always get special lunches at Francas for my teams. I particularly enjoy the lasagna!"

When we arrived, Franca greeted us at the door. I was so surprised to see her hug and kiss Dalton on the cheek as though he were family.

Dalton said, "Let me introduce Susan, my new bride."

I smiled and said, "I'm happy to meet the Italian side of the family."

We all laughed. The lunch was incredible. I over ate, but I didn't know when I would have time to eat again.

When we left the restaurant, I kissed Dalton quickly on the

lips and headed to my office. I needed to catch up on email updates, the MECS charts, metrics, and project plans. I would present the information to Dalton first to ensure the timeliness of the formulation of the MECS formula at our daily meeting, starting tomorrow with the MECS Team at 1000. I worked very fast and completed my work at 1545. I sent the updated charts and metrics to the printer team and the MECS team.

# Chapter 30– Food Laboratory

I met Dalton back at the Food Laboratory conference room promptly at 1600.  As we walked into the food conference room, we met a whole host of people.

Introductions were first by Nani.  She instructed everyone to sign the Meeting Sign-in Log sheet.  I recognized Nani and some of the food technicians and their managers.

The exotic Nani smiled at everyone.  She began her presentation.  "Here is a copy of all the foods available for selection.  Let's go over the categories.  Remember, when you are in space, your taste buds become deadened.  I suggest selecting spicier foods.  We do have a spicy shrimp cocktail, which is the astronauts' favorite and, of course, mine since I made the recipe."

Nani continued, "Go over the list.  Select any items you have not tried before and let me know so I can get you additional samples."

Dalton said, "I enjoyed trying the shrimp this morning.  It is spicy, but it has great flavor."

Nani said, "Select any foods that you would like to try the most.  We can accommodate whatever is on your menu within the criteria.  Some of your choices are peach ambrosia, cream of mushroom soup, scrambled eggs, green beans, and mushrooms, which are re-hydrated, freeze-dried foods. You may be familiar with the following Meals Ready to Eat (MREs).  These formulations are even provided to the military by the Texas A&M Retort facilities: beef tips and mushrooms, chicken strips, salsa, blueberry, and raspberry yogurt. Another tip is that the food will be thermal stabilized.  Freeze-dried or thermo-stabilized foods can last three years, while regular foods only last two years.  There is only so much room aboard the ISS to resupply the missions; thus, the long shelf life can last from one mission to the next."

She kidded, "If you want to change your menu, you can do so, of course, for an extra fee.  It is expensive to design, develop, and produce space food.  It will be an upcharge, so to speak."

Everyone laughed.

Nani continued, "You should select items, making sure your caloric intake corresponds to your weight and your activity level. On Earth, if you take in 1,500 calories a day, but in space, you will require 3,000 calories."

I said, "Now I want to go into space. That way, I wouldn't be breaking my diet."

Everyone agreed.

Nani said thoughtfully, "Remember: food is always important to everyone. Countries fight wars over food. Don't take anyone else's food or switch color code identifiers because somebody packed more M&Ms or what we call candy-coated chocolates than you did."

Dalton said, "I guess you can't just run over to the corner store for a snack. Is there a limit on how much food you can pick?"

Nani answered, "The limiting factor is the container in which we package the food. I assure you that you will not go hungry in space. You learn how to stow during the Bench Review, and if you have any questions, we will address them at that time."

Dalton asked, "We know about the food, but how about our beverages?"

Nani explained, "Our favorite is Tang, but we have orange-pineapple drinks, teas w/lemon and sugar, and coffee. We don't offer carbonated drinks since they would explode into a million bubbles. Can you imagine how hard it would be to contain the bubbles and fluids? They would scatter throughout the cabin, float into all the corners, and even get into the machinery. The sugar would cause problems with the equipment. The sugar would be dangerous for everyone."

Astronaut Dr. Greg Hart said, "I'm not in for clean up."

We all looked at him, and I noticed how very handsome he was. What an incredible specimen, *I thought to myself, just gorgeous. This guy exuded masculinity.*

Nani responded, "Well, that's why it's not allowed."

Dr. Greg asked another question, "Where will the silverware be located?"

Nani answered, "Of course you would want to know that. You can locate the silverware in the pantry with all the accessories. Let's talk now about re-entry. The pantry also contains the re-entry kits. This kit is fluid loading and will replenish your electrolytes upon a delay re-entry or what we call a wave-off delay."

Dalton asked, "What happens if you have to wave-off? I mean, if you think you are going to land, and it doesn't take place?"

Nani said, "If you have too many wave-off delays and you run out of kits, you have to use an alternate food, which the flight surgeon will give you. He may suggest chicken consommé artificially sweetened drinks, orangeade, lemonade, or limeade."

Dr. Greg smiled, "I'll take a little chicken consommé with my orangeade."

Nani laughed and said, "Only if they are left over from the flight. I know this is a lot of information, but we need to discuss how we stow (store) or allocate food. If straws are needed, they come attached to the packet. If a crewmember stays at the ISS or has a change crew member, the food is re-allocated or replaced. Remember, food is available at ISS to eat on day four after docking with the station. The station crew member doesn't select soup until the last few days. After 15 days, the descending crewmember will begin eating out of the shuttle kitchen. Commander Mike West makes sure no one eats another's food, so beware of the consequences."

Dr. Greg said, "How about fresh fruit? I need my bananas. They give me potassium."

Nani explained again, "Bananas are not allowed. The banana aroma is too strong. You can have only two or three trays of fresh fruits: apples, oranges, or grapes."

Dalton said, "I like sweets."

"Well, you are in luck. I can serve candy apples, maple candy, or chocolate cake. If it is your birthday, we can provide a non-crumble cake. You can imagine what the crumbs would do in space," she said.

"Well, it is going to be my birthday. Can I have candles?" Dalton inquired.

Nani said, "No, it is too dangerous."

I said, "Let's have a party before you go into space."

Dr. Greg said, "How about having a Pre-Shuttle Birthday Party and inviting all the Apollo and Mercury astronauts? Then, I can begin inviting them."

"Sounds like a plan," I said.

Nani interrupted and said, "Let's get back to the program. Begin to think about what kind of foods you want in your trays that go into the food locker. It's important to consider the items you cannot live without. We have had coffee beans from Costa Rica, refried beans, curry, and wasabi from Japan. Once, we had a reindeer request, but it wasn't politically correct since it was Christmas. Besides, the Canadians wanted moose pâté, and the Texas cowboys requested beef jerky."

I giggled like a little girl during Christmas, "If you eat Rudolph, who would guide the sleigh for Santa? That could be a problem. I guess we could use the Shuttle." I could see Santa Claus pulled by the Space Shuttle. What a sight.

Everyone laughed, including Kati-Linda, who had just walked into the meeting.

Nani told everyone. "Okay, guys and girls, I have one last thing I need to go over. The Bench Review ensures your food's correct packaging and any personal items you are taking into space. I will explain how to assemble the tray nets so your trays are not stuck. Also, we have included trash bags integrated into the food lockers as dividers.

Furthermore, you will have a unique color code that will identify your food. Make sure you verify your color code. Each person will have their tray on day one for breakfast, lunch, and dinner. Your commander, Mike West, can decide to allocate the food by flight, by day, or by the crew member."

Dalton said, "How do they allocate alcoholic beverages?"

Nani said, "I can't say, but I've heard they drink vodka and whiskey in moderation."

Greg said, "NASA shot me into space with the largest bomb in the world, but I really could use a shot, I mean a drink."

I said, "That's when I would ask for a Cosmo."

Dalton said, "For me, I would just like a Silver Bullet beer."

Nani finally interrupted, "Ladies and gentlemen, you can

never pack any alcohol in the food lockers, so figure it out."

I knew it wasn't a joke but a serious discussion on how to relax in space. *My thoughts turned to other ways you could relax in space, and I smiled inwardly. Sex would be relaxing, right? Would the positions by weightlessness lead to an incredible sexual experience? Where would one have enough privacy on the shuttle and station? Humans are innovative creatures. The sex drive is so strong that I knew they would find a way. I remembered the husband and wife team who went into space together and wondered if they found a way to relax together, so to speak — what a rush.*

I couldn't resist asking the question. "Nani, I have to know. I may sound out of line, but do you know if anyone has had sex in space?"

Nani started laughing. "I can't believe you asked, but yes, I do believe it has happened. You know NASA has what I call watchers, who keep an eye on everything that happens in space. They are like private eyes, always watching."

I laughed. "I guess watchers get to see or hear more than they expected." Both Dalton and Nani laughed with me.

"Well, honey, I guess that won't happen without you, but maybe I can convince them to let you go, and we could join the Space Shuttle fly high club," he kidded.

"Flying high would be my theme," I said. "My imagination is running wild. I can imagine the scene in *The Postman Runs Wild*. The 1981 movie where Jack Nicholson makes love to Jessica Lange on the kitchen table after clearing the table of food in one clean swipe with his masculine hands."

"Susan, I believe the movie is named *The Postman Always Rings Twice*," Dalton said.

"I can't imagine. First, could you wait until I add water to hydrate the food? Then, you would have to squeeze the food out of the little lip. It would almost be like stripes on your body," Nani kidded.

"Nani, you take all the fun out of my fantasies." I grimaced. "Maybe, I'll just think about it with real food and a real kitchen table."

Dalton said, "Let's go practice at home."

Nani laughed, "Too much information."

We left the building, and I was flying high into the skies, thinking of floating in zero-gravity, holding the man I adore. When we got home, I put my arms around Dalton and held him very close. His hands moved over my body, making me feel very sensual. Dalton lifted me onto the table, and we recreated the scene from *The Postman Always Rings Twice*. His tender love caused tears of joy to stream down my face as I had an incredible orgasm.

# Chapter 31 - Space Suit Fittings

The following day, we met a well-seasoned female spacesuit technician, Shirley, who smiled at Dalton. Shirley had an excellent reputation. I knew when the astronaut's suits were ready for space, Shirley was the last person to touch them. She had a final signoff on each flight suit. This signoff means they meet all the requirements for their spacewalk. Shirley packs each suit very carefully when they are ready to ship into space for their mission.

She said, "You know the last thing I do before a flight? When I pack the astronaut's suit in the container for space, I pat everyone on their sweet little butt, I mean on their suit's butt, and wish them a safe flight."

She laughed, "I mean your space suit's butt. It is my tradition, and now, I am superstitious about not doing it."

She pretended to pat Dalton on the butt with that statement, and then she patted the suit. I laughed hysterically.

"Don't get too excited. Dalton does have a cute butt," I said.

Shirley said, "Dalton, let's take your measurements to pick out the right fit for you. You know. Reuse is the name of the game. These flight equipment suits are costly and not replaceable. We use them in space until downgraded for training."

"Well, I didn't know you were going to a resale shop, Shirley. I do enjoy shopping for a bargain," I said.

"This resale shop would cost over two million dollars if Dalton paid for it," Shirley responded.

"Honey, it is not in our budget," I said.

"Well, I don't think we need one for our use anytime soon," Dalton chuckled.

Dalton put on the layers of space clothing, and then the extravehicular suit looked very uncomfortable. I saw sweat beading on his forehead.

He said, "Let's turn on the air ventilator carrier in the suit."

Shirley turned on the air ventilator carrier, which gave

Dalton extra relief. The hoses running through the suit will keep him cool.

She said, "I'm going to leave you some extra space in your flight suit, so if you eat more food than usual, you will still have room to put it on. However, weight gain is a common occurrence, and we don't want to change suits at the last minute.

"First, we have a limited number of suits, and second, the configuration management team tracks and follows all the associated components. The situation itself is a feat."

"Well, you make it look easy. I can't wait until I get to pick my watch, CDs, and the infamous astronaut diapers." Dalton said.

Shirley replied, "My expertise does not include diapers. Diapers do work, but we sew extra material in the commercial diaper products to wick the liquid away from you."

I said, "I just want to know if you can use baby powder?" Shirley responded, "It's not approved, but you can request it. I'm afraid they would say "No" because the powder might get into the Shuttle filtering systems or the Space Station. We can't afford to lose any oxygen capability in space."

"I vote for that. However, I do want to be able to breathe in space." Dalton grinned.

Shirley finished fitting him and said, "Once, when I fitted an astronaut, he suddenly jumped to the ground and began doing pushups. It surprised the mud out of me! I had never seen anything like it."

I asked, "Why did he do that?"

She laughed, "The astronaut said he wanted to make sure he could still move in his suit, or if he gained weight, he could get back up."

Dalton laughed, "What a character."

"I have seen lots of characters with big egos. But, of course, you are different; you are a scientist and not a hotshot pilot with a big ego," Shirley said.

I said, "Might you be talking about Humongous Greg or Dr. Greg?"

"I can't disclose that information. It would be unethical, and I would get fired," Shirley explained.

"I understand," we both said simultaneously.

I laughed, "Well, you don't have to tell me, I know. Dr. Greg's ego is as wide as the sky, but you must adore him. He is an oncologist on staff at MD Anderson. I wonder how an astronaut has time to become an oncologist. It's awe-inspiring, and he's so cute."

Shirley agreed, "It's time for business. I need to begin your flight fit. First, let's measure you and fit you into a flight suit. You see, we have to choose a suit for the closest fit so we can do alterations to a perfect fit."

Shirley measured Dalton's shoulders, waist, arms, and legs. I remember my grandmother meticulously placing the tape around my body and making beautiful dresses for me. You could tell she took the same pride in her work.

"Well, Shirley, is Dalton the typical size?" I inquired.

Shirley explained, "Typical is in the eyes of the beholder. Female and male astronauts can sometimes gain up to 20 pounds, depending on how the stress hits. It can be awful. They look composed, but deep inside, they are not."

Dalton said, "I'm just a man who is going into space to find the resolution to cancer. I want to take the pain away from the unfortunate who have cancer."

Shirley grimaced, "My daughter fights that ugly disease every day. I will take special care of my disease fighter. You may be her salvation."

Shirley continued to work with him like a proud mother tending to her baby.

After so many years of service, she had perfected her craft. I studied the lines on her face and noticed tears streaming down her face. I touched her arm and said, "What's the matter? Is Dalton giving you a hard time?"

She said, "No, Ma'am, I was just thinking about the Shuttle Program ending."

Before now, no one had mentioned the end of the program. It was just too painful. Tears came to my eyes, also. I couldn't think about the retirement of the Space Shuttle. It was just an awful thought.

Dalton spoke, "I certainly don't understand. NASA built the Space Shuttles to launch 100 times. The shuttles have only flown approximately 30 times each. NASA needs to keep the Space Shuttle Program until the United States can launch its space rocket to the Space Station or even to the moon. If we lose our edge, our economy will suffer. That's what happened to the Russians when they lost the race to the moon."

I said, "Not only that, but it will affect the dreams and hopes of our children. They will lose their desire to be astronauts, scientists, mathematicians, and aerospace engineers. Where will the technical inspiration come from?"

Shirley said, "I don't know. I think it is a shame. Shame on our Government, Congress, the Senate, and the President! All are contributing to the loss of our technological edge."

Shirley stomped her feet and shook her head, "Let's get back to work. I want to do my job - while I still have one."

# Chapter 32 – MECS Simulation

Later that day, Dalton and I met at the Astronaut Laboratory, where the MECS simulation would occur. I went to my office to put the presentation together. Connie brought me the MECS Test Preparation Sheet for approval, which provided a detailed simulation test. I approved it, noticing David, the MECS Engineer, had already approved the test.

I said, "Connie, if the test is successful, please have Dalton, the owner, approve it. If not, have him sign the unapproved line."

Connie responded, "I will take care of it. Do you want me to present the metrics at the meeting?

"Sure, let me give you a copy to review. Then, I will put together the metrics overview for the opening presentation. After that, we will work as a team."

At 1230, I entered the Astronaut Laboratory to present to the astronauts and Dalton. I noticed many people attending the meeting whom I hadn't invited. Some I didn't even recognize. People were completing the Meeting Attendance Sheet. I asked Connie to make sure I got a copy before the meeting started. I wanted to review the attendees.

When she handed me the sheet, I looked directly into her eyes, pointed at a group of attendees, and whispered, "These people didn't have an invite, and they must leave. They will be a distraction to my team and a possible security threat. I won't take the risk!"

Connie asked approximately ten attendees to leave, and each gave me a menacing grimace as they passed. I didn't care. It was my meeting and my responsibility.

I said, when the last uninvited person left, "Let's get on with the simulation."

Connie passed out copies of the MECS Test Preparation Sheet, and we began. It took all afternoon to get the five MECS formulations into the capsules. Everyone worked efficiently and professionally. Inside, I wanted to explode with pride, but I was a professional.

As a professional, I said, "Thanks for attending this important component of the MECS simulation. It is a successful simulation, and I know we will be able to formulate the MECS formula before the next flight."

Connie presented the metrics overview, and I gave the MECS management overview. I was thrilled with the success of the simulation.

Afterward, I proudly said, "The MECS formula is ready for flight. Tomorrow, we will go over the results."

# Chapter 33– Vacuum Chamber

Each day, he brought me fresh, new experiences. The next day, Dalton entered the Vacuum Chamber to train in his extravehicular spacesuit.

When we arrived at the NASA gate, the guards treated Dalton as royalty when displaying our NASA badges.

I said, concerned, "Dalton, I'm scared that the Vacuum Chamber is too dangerous. If something goes wrong, you could die. I don't want anything to happen to you."

He said, "I know you are concerned, and so am I, but many other astronauts have gone into the Vacuum Chamber for training. I am just one of many. I would rather know everything is okay than not."

We entered the building and proceeded to the Vacuum Chamber testing area for the extravehicular (flight) suits.

"Hi, I'm Dr. Jim Logan; it's so nice meeting you," he said.

Dalton said, "This is my wife, Susan; she will observe the Vacuum Chamber test activities." Dalton went to put on his suit.

I asked, "Dr. Logan, please tell me more about the Vacuum Chamber test. I'm so interested and concerned about my husband's safety."

"It's all about pressure, and testing the suit is to ensure it is reliable in space. Yes, the test is dangerous, but no one has ever gotten hurt so far. I don't believe Dalton will be the first. The air is less dense in space, so we vacuum the chamber to simulate the lack of atmosphere or pressure. On Earth, normal atmospheric pressure is 14.7 Pounds per Square Inch or PSI. In space, there is no such thing as a perfect vacuum with 100 percent oxygen. So, we try to evacuate as much air as possible. The test feeds in 100% oxygen and prays there is no serious leak in his spacesuit. We test if the microphone works and the pump works for the cooling system in the suit. The suit cools the water flowing through microscopic pores through the suit. Since it is so cold in space, the water circulates through the ice on the surface of the suit down to 15 Pounds per Square Inch

(PSI)), then it warms up. As it gets closer to the body temperature of 100 degrees, the water temperature keeps it from turning into solid ice. The pump has a magnet, which turns the pump with a small motor, and thus the water spins. If the little motor stops, the magnet stops, and the pump will no longer work. You will turn to ice," he said.

I said, "I hope it doesn't stop working. It would be a disaster."

Dr. Logan reassured me, "We tested the equipment for safety, and we haven't lost an astronaut yet."

Dalton said, "Not all astronauts have performed spacewalks, and this test is so important to simulate how it feels in space. I feel so fortunate to have the opportunity to travel into space and update the MECS capsule. Not many astronauts ever get this opportunity. It's my turn, and I'm thrilled."

I tried to smile, even with all their assurances. I had concerns about Dalton's safety. I had become used to expecting the worst with everything that had happened.

After Dalton dressed in the proper attire, the technicians hooked up the medical monitors. I tried to believe Dalton would be safe, but the thought of him being in the Vacuum Chamber made me uncomfortable. I had heard of the Vacuum Chamber, or some called it the Foot Chamber. I guess the correlation would be Dalton would be walking the whole time and moving toward zero-gravity with his feet, thus the Foot Chamber. I didn't know the connection, but that analogy made sense.

I did want to watch his long day of training in the Vacuum Chamber, or should I say Foot Chamber.

Dalton's challenge is the gradual adaptation to zero atmospheres.

The extra-shuttle engineer asked Dalton, "What movie would you like to watch while your body acclimates to zero atmosphere? You will have about two hours before that happens, and we will test your suit to ensure the suit and the atmosphere are in sync."

Dalton thought for a second and said, "I would like to watch *Fifty First Dates*. It reminds me of my wife, Susan. She looks like the movie star Drew Barrymore."

I smiled, "Of course, I could be her mother."

Everyone laughed, and the Mission Manager said, "You know that's not so. If I may say so, you are incredible and just as cute as Drew Barrymore."

I thought for a second, he was out of line, but I said, "Thank you."

I was flattered since he was a handsome young man.

They began dressing Dalton in his spacesuit, and I couldn't see him even though I wanted to. It was an extraordinary opportunity. He alone had to do this. As he walked out, he had support lines holding up his 400-pound suit weight so it wouldn't crush his body. He looked like a marionette with a puppeteer, making him move.

I laughed and blew him a kiss. He turned but could barely wave back. I knew he was looking at me, so I decided to go to the observation room to see him.

Dalton entered the Vacuum Chamber.

Dr. Jim Logan gave him several things to test while he was in the vacuum chamber. First, he handed him a piece of Mylar cloth, a woodblock, and a bowl of water.

He said, "I want you to perform several tests with these objects. First, you will drop the cloth and wood at the same time. Then, the test will show you how to in space objects fall. Next, you will watch what happens to the water and report it to us. I'm not going to tell you the results, but let you find out for yourself."

Dalton responded, "I think I know what will happen."

"Do I?" I said.

Dalton entered the Vacuum Chamber. It was 11.0 feet x 19.0 feet with dual airlock compartments for human testing in a vacuum environment and Space Suit development. The technicians began pressurizing the chamber.

*I could see the movie Fifty First Dates start on the Vacuum Chamber monitor. The movie made me feel very warm inside, thinking about how someone could love another person so much; he made the woman he wanted to fall in love with him again each day. But, of course, the best part was sailing and living his dream. He made it work. He didn't lose focus. I*

*don't think many people would have that much perseverance.
It warmed my heart.*

Dr. Logan said, "We will adjust the pressure, increasing it from 3.6 to 3.7 to the maximum of 4.3 PSI. Susan, stabilize the pressure at 4.3 PSI. If it goes beyond 4.3 PSI, he will pass out or even die."

I closed my eyes, and my mind became frantic. We had been in so much danger throughout our short and turbulent affair. Please, Lord, don't let any harm happen to my husband. I cringed, thinking what would happen to someone in zero-gravity if the suit malfunctioned.

I knew the Extravehicular Activity (EVA) technicians diligently followed the stringent quality requirements to repair and test the spacesuits. Their dedication made me feel better.

Dalton waved to me, and I smiled, knowing he was safe.

Dr. Logan asked, "Susan, are you okay?"

I said, "I'm afraid; I just want everything to be okay."

Dr. Logan said, "Everything will be okay. Dalton has the best hardware specialist in the world working with him. In addition, he has the Space Exploration Corporation expertise protecting him."

I wanted the test to be over. But, as I investigated the window, Dalton moved slowly around. I could see he was a little uncomfortable with the heavy suit and the change in pressure.

"You know, Susan, the motor is very loud when it is circulating the water inside the suit. However, in the vacuum chamber, as in space, it's completely silent, as everything in space has no sound," he explained.

Eventually, Dalton walked out of the chamber, assisted by the technicians. It was as if he had been to a resort. He looked so excited, "Susan, you will never guess what happened. The bowl of water first turned to ice and then vaporized."

Dr. Logan said, "I've always wanted to see that, but as you know, it is impossible to see from my vantage point."

Dalton said, "Also, the Mylar cloth and block of wood fell at the same rate. Well, Dr. Logan, I'm tired. This test took a lot out of me. Susan, let's leave as soon as I can get out of this 400-pound suit."

The technicians helped Dalton remove the spacesuit. It was very cumbersome and hot in Earth's atmosphere. We walked out of the building, and Dalton turned to me, "I admire all the astronauts who have come and gone. Training is not easy."

I smiled jokingly, "I know, but I never thought you were trainable; maybe you are just problematic – Not."

He lifted my head, laughed, and gave me a tender kiss. "This is why I adore you so much. You make me laugh."

# Chapter 34 - Neutral Buoyancy Lab

Dalton said, "Once I asked Alan Shepherd how he felt to be the first man to travel into space.

"His answer was, 'Well, how would you feel if you were the replacement of a monkey?'

"I told him he should be glad that at least it was a monkey and not a parrot. NASA might have said, *this is Houston. Polly want a cracker?*"

We both laughed when we entered the Sonny Carter Training Center, the most extensive training swimming pool in the world used for research. Not every astronaut gets to do the training, just the thrill-seekers who walk in space. *I thought, yes, Dalton was a thrill seeker. Dalton was going to update the MECS module while in space. I knew they used the Neutral Buoyancy Laboratory (NBL) test flight suits, which are not space ready but are simulated use in space. These were efficient but didn't meet all the space requirements after being in the water environment.*

I watched from a viewing room that was above the NBL pool. It had multiple televisions, which monitor every movement in the pool area. The NBL technicians attached Dalton and Dr. Greg to the yellow cranes, which lined the pool.

Slowly, the yellow cranes took them into the NBL pool to the Space Station modules' giant mockup.

The yellow crane reminded me of dinghy davits on a boat, which lifts the dinghy into the water using a block and tackle (pulley systems) and out of the water onto the back of the boat. Likewise, the crane has a pulley system that lowers the astronaut in and out of the pool with safety assistance.

I watched Dalton's blue tether tube move very slowly under the water. In contrast, two safety divers and a mission specialist diver moved along his side.

Dalton moved sluggishly through the water and stopped at a space station module. A mission specialist, the diver, handed him a tool. The tool was a simulated welder, which works in space. The only difference is the welder will not get hot in the water. He worked on welding the MECS module parts together. I watched his bubbles as he worked diligently as his bubbles were his life force to earth. The primary life backpack supplied the mixture of oxygen and nitrogen used in his spacewalk. His tasks were to maneuver the MECS capsule into direct sunlight.

Yes, Dalton would be going out into the dark, empty vacuum of space. He would be a spacewalker. I kept staring at the bubbles, and I noticed the bubbles abruptly stopped. He was in distress! I ran to the window, trying to get a better view.

I heard over the PA, "**Dock crews meet immediately on the deck to remove Dr. Masters' suit! There is a medical emergency – Egress!**"

My first guess was he had the bends, which occur when a diver surfaces before the body's nitrogen dissolves. As a result, bubbles form in the blood and tissues, causing severe joint pain, paralysis, and even death. I was in shock. I had to find out if it was the bends or something else.

Several technicians got Dalton out of the water as quickly as possible. Meanwhile, I was panicking. My eyes began burning as the tears flowed down my face. I watched and waited as they laid him horizontally on the side of the pool and removed the space-life suit.

I heard over the PA, "The medical staff diagnosed Dalton with the bends."

I watched as they gave him high-flow oxygen as transported him horizontally to the hyperbaric chamber.

I ran down to the chamber, which I had passed when we walked into the building.

He was in danger. What had happened? How did it happen so quickly? I looked into the hyperbaric chamber and saw Dalton.

A muscle-bound rugged-looking man with sandy blond hair diver was standing at the chamber. He introduced himself, "Hi, I'm Nick. You must be Susan. Everyone remembers the person who straightened up the Neutral Buoyancy Lab and Tool Laboratory processes with your infamous audits."

I couldn't believe he was talking about me and not Dalton, the astronaut. Ignoring the comment, I said, "Could you please tell me what happened to Dalton?"

He talked slowly, "Well, I guess he got too much nitrogen in his blood. If that occurs, your body goes into the bends. Yep, that's what happened. He went into the bends. It can be excruciating with all that nitrogen released into the joints. Too bad; he'll be in there for a while."

I was right in my diagnosis. I peered into the chamber window, which separated us from each other. Pain emanated from all the lines on his face. The bends must be causing the joint pain in his arms to be excruciating.

I could read Dalton's lips through the porthole in the hyperbaric chamber, "I'm itching. Boy, this is driving me crazy."

The Neutral Buoyancy Laboratory (NBL) Manager approached me outside the hyperbaric chamber. It was a familiar face. I had audited Pam's organization before and respected her judgment and character.

Pam said, "Susan, I have a request. Would I like you to do an NBL Mishap Investigation to find the underlying cause and write an Incident Report? The mishap should have never happened. I don't understand what happened."

I said, "Pam, I guess I could be objective in discovering what happened. That would be very important."

She responded, "I want you to do this, Susan. It is imperative; that the NBL has never had an incident like this before. Just tell me what you need, and I will get it."

I responded, "I need an organization chart, and please highlight all the personnel involved in this event along with their job responsibilities. In addition, I will need a conference room so I can interview the personnel. Oh yeah, I need a list of all the procedures associated with the event."

"I'll have everything you requested in Room 208. I will also alert all the personnel involved that you may be calling on them," Pam said.

"Great, I'll report to your office the day after tomorrow at 1:00 P.M. You know Pam, auditing is 90 percent listening to the answers," I said.

"That is what makes you the right person to perform the Mishap Investigation. Thanks; I appreciate your performing this task. I know this will take away from your other tasks. Still, if you can give me three days to complete the Incident Report, I would certainly appreciate your auditing expertise. I know you can find the source of the problem." Pam said.

"I'll do my best. But, Pam, I need to keep watch over Dalton. I know he'll be out soon." I said.

"Yes, he will, and he will be okay," Pam said as she walked across the vast room.

The pool's chlorine smell surrounded me as I watched through the chamber's portholes. I wanted Dalton out now.

The NASA Medical Doctor, Dr. Jim Logan, came over to me, "His oxygen level is going up, and he should be fine in two hours. So, after he leaves, he will be back to his old self."

"Thank you, Doctor. Do you know what caused this?" I inquired.

Dr. Logan explained, "Some individuals are more sensitive to the mixture of oxygen and nitrogen. This combination must have gotten out of balance. The chemical makeup of their system calculates the precise mixture. Dalton's oxygen mixture must have gotten unbalanced somehow. It happens occasionally and generally; this situation is only temporary. Dalton's case is more severe than I have seen in the past."

I said, "Thank you for taking good care of him."

They released him, and I took Dalton home immediately. He was exhausted, so I held him in my arms, as a mother would a child. I wanted to defend him and wondered if this was an accident or maybe even sabotage. The Mishap Investigation will lead us through the events to possibly the responsible party.

We stayed in bed the next day, just resting. I promised myself I wouldn't leave him alone. I desired to caress him. I couldn't believe how much my heart felt for him when he was hurt. I wasn't his mother, but I felt the pain of a mother, helpless. I wanted to make everything all right. I felt like a mother bear protecting her cub. I would find out who tried to hurt my Dalton, and I would defend him with my life.

Joking around, I threw a pillow at him.

"Watch it, Dalton. You can't dodge this bullet," we laughed.

"But you can't." He grabbed me and pulled me to the sofa, kissing my belly and making me laugh even more.

During the laughter, I heard his cell phone ring. Dalton answered the phone, trying to regain his composure, "Hello."

I could tell from his side of the conversation that Dalton was assuring someone that he recovered. He got very animated about something before he rang off.

When Dalton got off the phone, he told me he had some good news.

"That was Dr. Jim Logan, Flight Surgeon. He wanted to know how I was feeling. After I told him, I had recovered fully. He said that Richard Harvey, NASA's Reduced Gravity Program Director, asked me to ride in the KC135A, the Vomit Comet. Susan, he requested that you ride along. We need to be at Ellington Airport tomorrow morning at 0700 sharp. Do you want to go?"

I had always wanted to ride the Vomit Comet, the Boeing 707, that simulates zero-gravity. Wow, what a thrill!

I screeched in excitement, "Dalton, everyone knows it's the best ride of a lifetime. What a high! I feel like a little kid going to the State Fair for the first time or like Christmas morning. I can't believe I'll get to feel what it's like to be weightless."

Dalton said excitedly, "This isn't my first time since I went through astronaut training. I got to ride the Vomit Comet before. I can't wait to see your face when you float effortlessly in space."

"Now we have one more thing to celebrate about, yeah," I said, throwing another pillow at him. He ducked, and we both giggled like two little kids.

The smell of Dalton's body made me feel so warm and safe inside. Darkness surrounded me as I fell into a deep sleep. We were asleep in each other's arms. 9

I felt myself floating in the nothingness of space without a spacesuit. Something brushed against me. It was cold and clammy. Suddenly, bright lights were blinding me. It seemed like an eternity before I could focus. There before me was the

9 The poem "Safe Inside" is in the Poetry Section

repulsive corpse of a ghastly disfigured man. In my panic, I screamed and tried to free myself from the cold body. The harder I tried, the more entangled we became. I pushed it away, but the hideous dead body kept returning. Zero-gravity wouldn't free me. I couldn't catch my breath or stop screaming.

The nightmares had returned, but this time, the backdrop was space.

Dalton woke me up, saying, "Wake up, Susan, you had another bad dream. It's time for us to take the aerial thrill ride of our lives. Are you ready?"

Groggily, I said, "Oh, yes, I am. I'm okay. I'll get up now, Darling."

I jumped up and made my way to the shower. I moved very fast. The excitement filled the air, just thinking about the significant event. The song _Born to be Wild_ from _Top Gun_ movie kept running through my head as Tom Cruise rode his motorcycle racing a jet. Astronauts are thrill-seekers, and now I would be one of them, racing with the jet plane!

## Chapter 35 – Vomit Comet

We left early in the morning for Ellington Airport to ride the "Vomit Comet," sometimes called the "Weightless Wonder," over the Gulf of Mexico. Later, I agreed to meet with Pam, the manager at the NBL, at 1300.

We arrived at Ellington Field fifteen minutes before, and I began looking around the giant hangar. Everyone seemed to have a mission watching several men performing maintenance on a standalone engine.

Dalton pointed to the T-38 Talons lined up on the field. The jets were NASA blue and white, waiting for the astronauts to fly for their mandatory training.

He said, "I wish I could fly one. It's like soaring on the pointed end of a Roman candle, fast but very maneuverable."

I said, "Yes, it's just you, two engines and fuel. What a rush, just like the firelight inside of me."

A tall, lanky man with silver hair and a chiseled face approached us. He held out his hand, and Dalton began shaking it.

The stranger said, "You must be Dalton and Susan Masters. I'm Dan Womack, your Test Director."

Both Dalton and I said, "Nice to meet you."

He began, "Let me tell you about your upcoming adventure. Riding on the microgravity flight lasts two to three hours. After that, the plane will make 30 to 40 parabolic maneuvers."

I asked, "What is a parabolic maneuver?"

"It's a descending arc that generates negative G's, which simulates weightlessness for about 30 seconds at a time," he explained.

Dalton popped in and said, "You want to make sure when you are doing this that you know where you will fall when the gravity-pull returns."

He started laughing, "You know I've hurt myself by having too much fun. It is a real trip, so to speak."

Dalton and I laughed, feeling exhilarated. What a chance

in a lifetime.

Dan asked, "Do you like roller coasters or amusement rides?"

I said immediately, "I like them all. I can ride forever. The scarier, the better."

Dalton said, "Maybe not as much as Susan, but I will go on an amusement ride, possibly the Ferris wheel. I don't like the jerking around."

Dan grinned, "I don't like any amusement ride, roller coaster, or even going to buy cotton candy. Just ask my family. On the other hand, I enjoy riding the Vomit Comet all the time. I do it at least two or three times a week. As the lead test director, I ensure the experiments carried out aboard the aircraft are safe. The personnel flying with them are medically qualified and trained. So, wherever the plane goes, I go with it."

Dalton said, "I'm impressed. You certainly have an interesting position. It sounds like a great job."

Dan said, "You know, every mission is different around here. It's exhilarating to meet new people worldwide and work with them and their experiments. It flies various missions about 33 weeks per year."

I said, "Did you get to work with Good Morning America?"

"Yes, I did. It was so much fun. Diane Sawyer is such an elegant lady." He said.

"You have such an exciting position to meet so many different people," I said.

"Yes, I do. So now I get to meet the famous Dr. Dalton Masters, who received the Nobel Medical Prize, and his beautiful wife Susan," he graciously said.

He said, "Let's get this puppy on the road and see what it will do."

"I'm ready!" I exclaimed.

Dalton said, "You look like a little girl going on her first amusement park ride. We should do this more often, but I don't think I could afford it if I were paying the bill."

"This is great, Darling. Once is enough, but you know I'm worth the money," I said.

"You certainly are," He took my hand and squeezed it as

we entered the plane door.

Dan said, "Susan, since you have never done this before, please take a seat and observe."

I grimaced a little but followed his instructions. I found a jump seat on the side and watched the other astronaut crew members. The plane took off, and the test began. The first parabolic maneuver took me by surprise. My stomach flipped. It reminded me of when I was a little girl, and my father would go over a hill quickly. All three children would fly off the seat, and I had the same sensation. It was incredible. I watched everyone float in space with great big smiles on their faces.

I couldn't stand it anymore and moved out of my seat. Dan nodded and said it was okay. The pilot performed another parabolic maneuver, and this time, I felt how it would feel in space. Surprisingly, it felt effortless. Being weightless, if only for 30 seconds, was incredible.

Suddenly, I got hot, my forehead began to sweat, and my stomach churned. *I thought to myself, oh no, please don't let me get space sick now.* Incredibly, I have never been seasick or carsick. I reached for a vomit bag, but not soon enough. My morning breakfast was soon floating by me. Mortified with embarrassment, I tried to gather up the vomit floating in tiny balls like mercury, which didn't work so well. Finally, after our 29 seconds of zero-gravity, the flight went back to normal gravity, and my breakfast plopped down onto the deck. Dan threw me a towel, and I cleaned it up as fast as I could. I certainly didn't want anyone to slip on the disgusting mess. Yes, this is the Vomit Comet, and now I understand why all too well.

My stomach began to feel better, and I realized I had another pressing need. Why me, Lord? I asked, "Dan, where is the restroom?"

"It's over here." He said.

By this time, the KC135 plane was performing another parabolic maneuver. Finally, we floated over to a door near the pilot's cockpit.

Dan opened the door and handed me a tube with an elliptical cup attached to it, "This is suction at the end. Just flip this switch, and it will do its thing, so to speak."

"Sure will, thank you," I said, embarrassed, as I closed the door in the limited space.

Everyone must go to the bathroom, but still, it is uncomfortable to discuss. My shoulders felt the sides of the small room. I placed the oblong cup into position and thought, "I wondered how a man could fit into this small area."

Soon, I was back floating around with Dalton and the other crew members. Dalton and I held hands and turned flips. It was the most fantastic trip, and it was so much fun.

Now Dalton would be going up in space and performing a spacewalk.

All I could say was, "Awesome." Finally, I couldn't say it anymore.

There were impressive riders on the passenger list. Of course, the astronauts were along for the ride. Mike West, the commander, Kati-Linda Mission Specialist, and Dr. Greg Hart, the Astronaut's physician, and payload specialist, were the primary passengers.

I was so excited about being with these amazing heroes. I wished my parents could see me. I grabbed my cell phone and took pictures of everyone. I floated gracefully, laughing with everyone. Thank you, Lord, for all you have done for me.

I said, "Dalton, pinch me, please; I must be dreaming.

We did another parabolic maneuver. Again, Dalton pinched me on the butt as I went by.

I turned and laughed as my blonde curly hair floated straight up, "This is an experience of a lifetime. How exhilarating. I wish I could stay up here forever. Or better, travel into space."

I remembered I had to start the Mishap Investigation early in the morning."

# Chapter 36 – Mishap Investigation

At 1000, I stopped at the gate that controlled the Neutral Buoyancy Laboratory (NBL). The security guard met me with a bright smile. I tried to smile even though it was dawn and I was still sleepy.

He said, "Hello, may I see your badge?"

I smiled and said, "Here's my badge. I hope you have a wonderful day."

He touched it with his right hand and read my name. Suddenly, his smile turned into a frown. He paused and motioned me to go inside the gate.

Maybe it was just too early in the morning for him. I didn't need a frown. I noticed the security sign color-coding was orange, which meant terrorist alerts, reporting anyone who caused suspicion. I often wondered who decided to change the security colors. It was probably a military intelligence reading all the news and interpreting what could happen in the country's different areas.

For the first time, in the front row at the NBL Lab, I parked, which housed the largest swimming pool in the world. Unfortunately, it was too early for everyone else.

Inside the door, the second layer of security checked my purse and scanned my badge. Finally, four security guards operated cameras and watched for any intruders.

A female guard said in a high-pitched voice, "The EMU lab manager, Lou, is waiting for you in Room 208. Do you need directions?"

I quickly said, "I'm familiar with the building. I believe I know where it is. Thank you anyway."

I proceeded to walk into a colossal staging section. Beyond this area was the largest swimming pool in the world, which housed the Space Station simulator. My heart sank. Dalton had almost died in this same area.

I headed toward the hyperbaric chamber, which had saved

Dalton's life. I was staring into the hyperbaric chamber when a cheerful, pleasant man marched up beside me.

He said, "Hi, I'm Lou. You must be Susan."

"Yes, I am," I said.

He continued, "Let me show you to your office so that you will have privacy for your interviews."

He escorted me into an office. I placed my briefcase on the desk and powered up the computer. An astronaut poster displaying the current astronauts and pictures of past heroes and heroisms wallpapered the walls. It looked like a memorial to the Challenger and Columbia deceased crew.

I saw Astronaut Fletcher's picture, and tears came to my eyes. The wall displayed lost heroes, women, and men who had given their lives to further space travel and humankind.

Lou looked at me as if reading my mind. "I'm sorry about your loss. Everyone at the NBL felt the loss. He had trained here four times; now, he's passed. But he was also our friend."

"I know," That's all I could say as a big lump came into my throat. Finally, I cleared my throat and my head to begin the tedious task of auditing.

"Do you have the list of the involved employees and the procedures used to process the equipment and tools for the Neutral Buoyancy training?" I asked, *thinking I needed to take one step at a time to figure out what exactly happened to Dalton during his training. I didn't understand why anyone would want him dead. He was on the verge of ending the vicious disease, cancer.*

*I thought of all my dear friends, whom the ugly beast had destroyed before their life expectancy.*

"Yes, I do," He removed an employee list from his pocket and handed it to me.

I said, "I will need the rest of the day to perform an investigation and research the problem. Then, I'll begin calling individuals for interviews tomorrow."

First, I had to write the problem statement and list topics for study. Someone had tampered with Dalton's air supply. What caused Dalton's air supply to deplete? Why, who? Who had access to the air supply? When did the air change? Each question had to have an answer. I needed to take one question at a time and break it down. I needed to use these questions as a basis for the interviews and accumulate more answers. I will use these as a base and use the procedures to address each question. Plus, I needed security questions. I wonder if it was someone who was not a NASA or subcontractor employee who forged their credentials and gained access to the facility."

Very methodically, I read all the procedures and developed my checklist. I had to keep my emotions independent from the Mishap Incident, which caused Dalton's near-death experience. I took a deep breath. It is a job that pays for my living. Emotions had no place in being an investigator. I kept telling myself to be professional.

I made a list of questions from the procedures for each interviewee, depending on their expertise.

Late into the night, I was completing my last question. I hoped this would work. I had to find out who put Dalton's life in jeopardy. It could be someone else's life next time. I needed answers.

It was time for me to go home. I soon realized it would be daylight outside. A twinge of fear ran up my spine. Then, I calmed myself, thinking the NBL was on NASA property, which backs up to Ellington Airforce Base. It is secure and safe, but the person is still at large who tried to kill Dalton. This person could be in the building.

Why had I stayed so late? Dalton must be worried. I walked out into the hall carrying all my paperwork. I didn't want to leave any data out for someone to see or confiscate. Then, I heard voices at the end of the hall. It must be the third shift Extravehicular Modular Unit lab technicians working on the mission training suits.

The NBL staging area seemed to be much longer than I remembered. As I turned the corner, I heard muffled voices around the pool. Finally, I passed the hyperbaric chamber.

A shadow passed behind the chamber, and my heart stopped. I screamed shrilly inside for help. I had no voice. I tried it again. I knew I was only a hundred yards away from the door, and there would be guards. I would be safe. My pace turned into a trot, and I couldn't get to the door fast enough. Sweat dripped onto my forehead, making it difficult to see the door. I felt I was in slow-motion.

I heard a loud noise and looked up at the 20-ton hook to lift the Space Station equipment into the pool. Another crash resounded through the large room. The giant hook began swinging back and forth, threatening my life. Before I could move, the hook grazed the side of my face. I felt blood streaming down my face.

Frantically, I moved sideways, almost falling onto the floor. The hook swung toward me, and I stumbled out of its reach. The colossal hook oscillated erratically. Someone, but *who* worked the crane? Once again, someone was trying to kill me and trying to destroy my life with my Dalton. Why didn't they want Dalton to continue his experiment?

The menacing hook continued to swing, dropping toward my every move. I felt like I was in that Edgar Allan Poe story with the swinging pendulum. So far, I have been able to dodge the large hook. Then, breathlessly, I fell flat against the floor. I turned over in time to see a figure disappear down the hall. I could not determine whether it was a man or a woman. Sweat was pouring from my forehead.

I crawled slowly on my back to the door, looking upward at the hook. My cheeks burned from the narrow escape of that menacing hook. Finally, I made it to the door, sitting very still, watching the hook move back and forth until, mercifully, it stopped.

I sat motionless against the security door. It was probably only for a few minutes, but it seemed like an eternity. Nevertheless, it gave me comfort to be next to the security area.

"Why hadn't security come to my rescue?" I asked myself.

Suddenly, the large hook swung so hard it embedded itself into the wall.

Finally, I could leave, knowing the hook wouldn't move. With shaky legs, I stood up. When I entered the security area, I must have looked like a ghost.

The guard asked, "Are you okay? You look like you have had the fright of your life."

I said hysterically, "No, I'm not okay. Did you see what happened in the staging area?"

He said, "I don't understand what you are talking about."

"The hook in the staging area came right at me and almost killed me," I cried.

He retorted, "I have full surveillance of all the NBL. I didn't see or hear anything. Let's look at the security cameras."

He rewound the video taken by the security camera, and we saw absolutely nothing.

I stammered with tears in my eyes, "Someone almost killed me. See the blood on my face where the hook almost pierced me! It's stuck in the wall."

"Let's go look and see." He said.

We walked into the Neutral Buoyancy Lab's staging area, and the hook was in its place, with no hole in the wall.

The guard looked at me as if I had gone crazy and said, "Well, ma'am, I don't know what happened, but I didn't see anything, and the staging area looked normal. So, I think you need to go home and get some rest."

With that comment, I said, "Please walk me to the car."

The security guard stated very firmly, "I cannot leave my post. If I do, I will lose my job."

I let out a great, big sigh and hurried to the door. I ran frantically to my car, seeing threatening shadows in every area of the parking lot.

# Chapter 37 - Interviews, AKA the Mishap Interrogation

The following day, I felt like death. I had only a few hours to sleep but could not stop thinking of the incident. I tossed and turned. I felt awful. I know I'm not crazy. But it did happen, and I kept saying to myself.

Dalton said, "Honey, are you okay?"

I didn't want to tell Dalton what happened last night, so I said, "Oh yes, darling, I just had a rough night. It was a long day's night at the office, and today shall be even worse. Sometimes, it is difficult to be an auditor. It's a lonely job, and it's a fine line of finding out the real information compared to what people know. But I must find out the culprit who almost killed you. I must!"

As I was leaving our home, Dalton stopped me at the door. He put his arms around me, "Please, Susan, be safe. I know whoever is doing all this destructive behavior must be a dangerous individual. They will not stop until I'm out of the picture. I believe it is someone who doesn't want cancer eliminated from society."

I looked deep into his eyes and breathed deeply, "I agree. It is someone who probably has a huge investment in one of the largest money makers' enterprises, the cancer business."

Dalton responded, "Probably so; just come home to me."

He took me into his arms and kissed me passionately. I tingled from the bottom of my toes to the tip of my nose.

I arrived at the Neutral Buoyancy Lab, and I stopped at the security station. A heavyset woman took my badge and looked at it very carefully. Then, she made a phone call and finally, allowed me to proceed through the gate.

I entered the security station, where I displayed my badge, and the guards inspected my purse and attaché case. The first person on the auditee list was one of the divers who had helped rescue Dalton. His name was Diver Dan. Diver Dan walked into the room wearing his sunglasses. You could tell he thought he was cool. I couldn't believe my eyes. *My inter-*

*wishing told me he didn't want me to see his eyes. What was he hiding?*

He slumped over in the chair and waited for me to speak.

I cheerfully said, "Hi, how are you doing?"

Pausing, Diver Dan answered, "Ask your questions so I can get back to work. I'm a busy man and don't have any patience for this inquisition."

I responded, "You know I'm not here to waste your time or have an inquisition. I'm here to correct the mishap. Let's begin with you telling me what you do. Please start with your process."

He finally looked up and removed his sunglasses, "I make sure the astronauts are safe under 6.2 million gallons of water at 85 degrees."

I asked, "Do you have all your certifications?"

He opened his wallet and said, "Yes, here are my certifications."

I checked the certifications to ensure they were current to perform his job responsibilities. They were.

I asked, "Tell me about the safety requirements."

Diver Dan responded, "Safety is of the utmost importance. I'm alongside the astronauts, watching them work on the mock space station in the NBL."

I asked, "What are you watching?"

He said, "Well, I have a requirements checklist. I observe the use and comfort of the tools and tool applications underwater. Yes, some observations are from my checklist, but also my years of experience. The astronauts get a sense of spacewalking, just as if they would be in space without gravity. The water is so clear it shows their every move. Crew aids and tools make it easier for the astronauts, but they need practice, and I mean lots of practice."

"Did you complete a requirements checklist on the day of the accident," I asked.

"Yes, I did. Let me find it. I stay very organized and keep all my paperwork in a central location," Diver Dan said.

He walked over to a filing cabinet. Look under the STS-999 Task Preparation Sheet (TPS), which has all the instructions or what you call a requirement checklist for dive technicians.

He turned his back, looking for the file, "I can't find it. It is not in the files. So, someone must have checked it out."

He went to the database and looked under TPS-999, "The TPS didn't get checked out! So, there is no entry."

My heart stopped, and I slowly stated, "We have a security compromise."

Diver Dan shook his head, not believing that the TPS was missing.

I said, "I have to write a nonconformance and alert NASA of the occurrence. Tell me more about your observations on the day of the incident." So, I made notes to write the nonconformance later.

Diver Dan paused and began sputtering, "The space environment is very harsh. It goes from extremely hot to extremely cold. The NBL space water environment is a simulator, making our mini power tools easy. It is a cool tool. The astronauts use repetitive training to ensure it becomes instinctive."

"That's very interesting. Thank you for the education, but which procedure do you use?" I asked, trying to get the audit back on target.

He quickly responded, "Oh yeah, the NASA AQG Astronaut Training Guideline, OP1055, our living astronaut bible."

"Can you tell me about it?" I asked.

"The tools are described, including their application. It even explains their best function, and if there is an emergency, how can it be used," Diver Dan said seriously.

I thought this information was not anything of interest to what happened to Dalton.

I said, "Can you tell me about the day Dalton developed the bends? Did you see anything unusual?"

"Now that you mention it, a stranger was working on replacing a piece of the simulated space station. It was a big man. I didn't know him, but sometimes they bring in new people to catch up on the work since we are shorthanded. It's called outsourcing." Dan smirked.

I questioned, "Do you remember what he was doing?"

Slowly, he answered, "He was untangling the underwater air tubes. We do it all the time. First, we have to make sure the air passages are clear."

I hesitated and questioned, "First, can you get his name? Second, can we look at the airlines?"

"Slow down, young lady; I'm just Diver Dan and not a manager. The manager will have the name. I didn't look at his badge. No one is allowed on the flight training poolside unless they have permission," he said.

"Well, who can give me this information?" I asked.

"Let's go visit Lou. He's the manager with the ticket," he said as he walked out the door.

I obediently followed.

We walked through two large white doors into a tool room. I noticed five technicians busy working on tools. We turned to the right side of the room to locate his office. He sat behind the closed door.

Diver Dan knocked on the door, and a voice said, "Please enter."

We entered, and a fair-skinned black man with a giant smile turned and greeted us, "Diver Dan, it is so good to see you again. I guess this must be Susan, who is performing the Mishap Investigation. How can I help you guys?"

I shook his hand. I froze; this was not the same man who showed me into the NBL the other night.

Keeping my composure, I said, "It's so nice meeting you, Lou. Dan said you could help us. You had new personnel on the simulator deck. He was working on the breathing airlines. Do you know his name? Also, I would like to interview him."

Lou looked surprised and said, "My personnel had called in sick, and so I was shorthanded. Therefore, I didn't assign anyone to the poolside."

I shook my head in disbelief, "Where is security for the pool area?"

Before anyone could answer my question, I asked, "Doesn't security have an electronic video of the pool?"

Lou's smile turned into a frown, and he said, "Yes, we do have security. I will get you the names and request the electronic video. It will take a few days, but I will contact you when I receive it. Have you found any non-conformances?"

I nodded, "Yes, unfortunately, the TPS 999 is missing, which I will document in a nonconformance. This TPS was used on the day of the mishap. So now I must write another nonconformance documenting an unauthorized person on deck. So far, it doesn't look good."

Diver Dan wrote down the TPS number and said, "I will begin looking for the missing TPS. Sometimes, people forget to check them out. I will check with Quality Records, who keep the TPS in their files. I will also investigate if anyone knows the man on the poolside deck the day of the incident."

Lou left Dan and me sitting in his office.

I observed Dan and said, "Next, I want to inspect the breathing airlines at the pool."

Diver Dan said, "As you wish." I followed him silently up to the pool deck. All kinds of unanswered questions began forming in my head for the analysis. Usually, I don't take the answers personally, but I needed to know the details this time. So, I write up the nonconformance(s), and the auditee fixes the problem.

I asked him, "How do the hoses work?"

He explained, "Well, a perfect mixture of oxygen and nitrogen is mixed in tanks and mated with the hoses. The divers monitor the flow to ensure the astronauts are not in any trouble. I was on duty, and everything was going to plan. Unfortunately, someone had to interrupt the airflow, which caused Dalton's injury. Let's look at the connections and follow the hose to see if there was any disturbance."

I picked up the hose, checking for any breaks in the material. It was heavier than I expected.

Diver Dan helped me, "Well, you are a persistent little lady. These hoses weigh a ton." So, he said, as we inspected every inch of the hose until we reached the side of the pool.

The hose was in perfect condition.

"I guess that means I have to go in the water and check the lines," Diver Dan said.

"Please do," I requested.

He had already begun putting on his tank and adjusting the regulator. He jumped backward into the Neutral Buoyancy

Laboratory swimming pool, holding his mouthpiece so it wouldn't dislodge.

I took out a copy of his requirement checklist and began observing his actions.

The first question is to observe astronauts and ensure hose lines don't cross.

Looking deep into the pool, I followed the hose he was using. I saw a strange attachment to one of the breathing hoses. I motioned to Diver Dan at my finding, and he swam toward the attachment.

He began removing the part. I tried to get his attention to leave the attachment alone. It was not on the checklist. He didn't see me. I called out to the NBL deck lead when an explosion occurred, breaking the part into pieces.

Dan's mask exploded into a million bits. I could see the fragments falling to the bottom of the pool as Dan frantically swam to the top of the water. His face was bleeding profusely.

Emergency technicians jumped into the water, another rescue. The same emergency technicians surrounded Diver Dan, retrieving him from the water. I froze in disbelief as I watched his blood turn the water crimson red.

My pounding head kept repeating, "My whole life was sabotaged; someone or something is trying to kill Dalton and me. This whole bloody mess is a cover-up."

Tears ran down my face. I felt unprofessional, and I wanted to run away but couldn't. I still had to complete the investigation. "Be the expert," I said to myself. Then, discreetly, I dried the tears from my eyes.

I stated emphatically, "Retrieve all the fragments. The incriminating piece of evidence could tell a bomb specialist who constructed the bomb. I have to find the perpetrator!"

*I thought, who would do this? Someone is trying to undermine and destroy Dalton's efforts and achievements. I had to find out who this menacing person could be.*

The emergency technicians brought Dan up to the NBL Deck. He was holding a towel against his bleeding face. "Dan, I'm so sorry," I said, watching them wrap his eyes while the blood ran down his cheeks. I wanted to make the bleeding stop. The technicians instructed him not to rub his face so the fragments wouldn't go into his face deeper.

I put my hand on his shoulder, "Oh Dan, what can I do?"

"It's okay, Susan," Dan said.

"What happened? I saw an explosion," I asked.

"It looks like someone had set a booby trap for your Dalton. Unfortunately, he missed that explosion, so instead, they got to his oxygen mixture," he explained as the blood dripped down his face.

"We do have clues. We need to get all the exploded parts from the water," I turned to the NBL technician lead and asked the other divers to get into the water and retrieve the pieces.

He looked at me and said, "NASA regulation 101 requires to shut down the pool. No one can get into the water, no astronauts, not anyone. There may be another booby trap."

I said, "I agree. We will wait until the proper bomb security arrives. I summarized, "There would be no traces of fingerprints since the device was in the water, but the device has evidence: I know it. We must find out who built the device. I will write another nonconformance documenting the incident. The mishap categorization is against safety, possibly espionage, or even a terrorist attack. The nonconformance's now added up to three or more."

Pam stood next to me in disbelief, "Susan, you have to find this person."

I said, "This has to be more than one person since the man working with the hoses could not have been the man who installed the bomb in the water. Have you ever thought it could be an inside job?"

Pam said, "This is a possibility, but I wouldn't want to think someone working for me could have had such a horrible experience."

The ambulance arrived, and they took Diver Dan to the hospital. I stood in shock, watching as they removed him from the same door I had escaped from the menacing hook. So, the hook incident was the perpetrators scaring me away from the NBL. What will happen next?

I went back to my office and sat before the computer. I laid my head on the keyboard. I felt helpless. Deep inside of me, a voice spoke, "Don't give up. You must find out who is doing this, or your life with Dalton will never be normal. Now someone injured Diver Dan."

The voice was right. I sat down and began performing an analysis of the problem and the five Ws. It was a place to start why, when, who, where, and what.

Why would anyone want to kill Dalton?

When would be the most convenient time?

Who could get into the NBL?

Where would be the best place for another occurrence?

What time did they have access to the explosives?

Why? Why? Why? Why? Why?

I pulled up the events file showing the NBL schedule. It had the names of the mission personnel responsible for each event.

I pulled out an organization chart and started comparing the mission personnel with the events' personnel. The comparison must be a clue to show authorization for the NBL pool deck. I took a yellow highlighter and began marking the names off. After completion, two names were outstanding. These people are assigned to be available for any assistance."

I said, "Were they responsible for these horrific accidents? First, I must interview the names listed. They were Brooks and Shannon."

I began doing background checks and found that they were subcontractors from Research Underwriters for Specialty Hospitals, RUSH.

I said to myself, "Interesting. RUSH was the same organization Ken wanted Dalton to have an interview session. I wonder how their company became a subcontractor. What services do they provide? I must investigate this even more.

I contacted Pam to schedule Shannon and Brooks. I scheduled them individually, at least two hours apart. The hair on the back of my head rose when Brooks entered the office. He was a large-framed male with tattoos on his arm. The prominent tattoo covering his forearm was a bright color emblem of the doctor's Hippocratic Oath.

I smiled, "Please have a seat."

He grimaced and looked very uncomfortable.

I needed to make him feel relaxed so that he would give me details of the incident.

I asked, "Can you tell me about your job?"

He began speaking with pride with intelligent and articulate words, "I am a subcontractor to Research Underwriters for Specialty Hospitals, called RUSH for short. My job is training doctors to use cancer specialty tools in space. I am the lead technician and know the tools like the back of my hand."

I smiled, "Were you at the pool for assistance the day of the incident?"

He said, "Yes."

I asked, "Tell me about the day of the incident."

He continued, "I am on call if any problems exist. You know I'm studying to become a doctor specializing in oncology. That's the reason I work for them. I'm very excited about working on the Space Program and RUSH."

I asked, "Do you remember what took place the day Dr. Dalton Masters went into the bends?"

He answered, "I was watching his performance on the monitors. I observed him losing his grip on the riveting equipment. I thought the tool had malfunctioned. The next thing I knew, Diver Dan was bringing Dalton to the surface and rushing him to the chamber."

"Did you notice anyone suspicious at the pool deck?" I inquired.

"No, not while I'm working; I only have one thing on my mind, and that is the performance of the tools, which is my responsibility. Otherwise, no one or nothing else exists. You know I have a TPS, which tells me exactly what to do," he stated as he flexed his tattoo on his forearm.

I continued to smile, thinking that the space culture allows only the technician to perform the TPS tasks. The Space Program wouldn't allow any changes at random and absolutely no freethinking and no innovation. The engineers were the experts and required perfection as the paper writers and technicians explicitly followed their directions.

I asked, "Can I see the TPS and your certification cards."

He handed me the TPS and his up-to-date certification cards. I briefly looked at the proper signatures and asked for a copy of the TPS. He made copies, stamping COPY in bright red.

I took the copy and said, "If you remember any more information than you just told me, please let me know."

"I will. Maybe Shannon can add to what I said. She is a management favorite." He said inappropriately.

I had thirty minutes before Shannon arrived. *I thought about what he had just told me. He was correct about the culture. You stay within the guidelines, or you don't work in this environment. I couldn't put my finger on it, but something didn't add up. I need more information. This Mishap Investigation was far more complicated than I've ever done. I made a fishbone diagram to break down the complexity of what happened. When finished, it will look like the skeleton of a fish.*

I began writing on the whiteboard, documenting the happenings. It showed Dalton's day in time, schedule, and tasks. The main points were his tasks performed and the people involved.

I dove into my work when a beautiful young lady entered the room.

Shannon arrived; she had long, brown, shiny hair, large blue eyes, and a beautiful smile. Her skin was flawless, and she dressed differently than most of the employees. Shannon was an engineer, young, and full of life who wore professional clothes.

She walked toward the whiteboard, looking very intently at the fishbone diagram section describing Brooks' duties.

She shook my hand in an aggressive manner, which surprised me. She had a presence, and my hand hurt from her firm grip.

Shannon was the first to speak, "Hi, I'm Shannon."

I stopped what I was doing and asked her to take a seat. She interjected, "Can I look at your fishbone diagram?"

I didn't want to discuss my findings with her, but the way she said it made me reconsider. In addition, she could add additional information to the fishbone diagram, which I may not know.

Air mixture tampered

Who had assessed? Subcontractor

Why would anyone want to kill Dalton?

Destruction of the experiment
Who saved Dalton?
Safety Divers
What benefit of Daltons' death is to the MECS program?
No more cancer experiments
Would the King of Sweden, Karl Ásgeirr XIII, die without Cancer Cure?
When did this incident happen?
During training
Who knew about the Training Schedule?

- Everyone in the Shuttle training organization, NASA, Subcontractors and News Media

Who had access to the Test Preparation Sheet?
Bomb Explosion?
Who had access to the NBL?
Who was the unknown big man on the NBL deck working on the hoses?
Who built the bomb?
Who was new to the program?
Who has the expertise?
Who has a grudge against the aerospace program?
Hurt the program.
Hurt someone.)
Would it take one person or many people?
Unauthorized Personnel
Who had access to the NBL deck?
Who could get into the water without authorization?
Was this an inside job?

She went over to the explosion leg of the fishbone diagram and said, "You know Brooks is a diver. He vacations in Belize every year. I hear he is an expert diver. His father owns a sailboat, and he has been on the water since he was a child."

I entered onto the diagram leg, Brooks' diving expertise, and said, "Shannon, are you a diver?"

She laughed and stated, "I don't even get into the water. I don't know how to swim, nor do I like the water."

*I thought it very interesting she worked at the NBL but didn't know how to swim or even like the water.*

She seemed to be reading my mind and said, "It's just when

I was little, I wouldn't wear a bathing suit. It was just awkward. This embarrassment kept me out of the water, and besides, I don't like getting my hair wet."

"I see," I said knowingly, "Well, do you have anything else to add?"

"Not really. I think you are going to have a tough time finding out who did it. It just seems unbelievable that anyone could get into a secure facility like the NBL, plant a bomb, and tamper with the oxygen mixture. Top it off, no one knows who did it. My company, RUSH, would never be so careless. They don't leave any rock unturned," Shannon said arrogantly.

I asked, "Can you help me understand RUSH?"

Shannon answered, "During our orientation, we have to complete 150 hours of security training. We keep alert to all of our surroundings and the people with whom we come into contact. We must keep a journal every day, describing what we have done and how it affects the job we have done."

I requested, "May I see your journal?"

She quickly answered, "Oh, I left my journal at home. I will bring it tomorrow."

I asked, "Can we go to your house now and let me review your journal?"

Shannon said, "I'm sorry, but that's against my rights. You will have to get a search warrant from the police to enter my home."

Every hair on the back of my head turned up. I knew I was on to something, but all I could do was get the police to request a search warrant. Of course, I couldn't make that request unless I got NASA permission. With the government policies, it would take until next week to gain access to her home. It is always complicated.

I smiled and said, "If you could, please bring it in tomorrow."

Instinctively, I knew RUSH might change everything written today.

I said, "I'll see you at 0900 tomorrow in my office. Have a wonderful evening."

When she left the room, I called Brooks. He didn't answer

the phone. So, I decided to walk over to his desk to see if he was in the area.

Everyone was leaving the building, and I thought I saw him at the end of the hallway. When I got there, no one was around. My head was aching. I had never done a Mishap Investigation on something of this magnitude. I needed to talk to someone who could help me. I worked long into the night. Each lead on the fishbone diagram came to a dead end. The next day, I had to have a second interview with Brooks and Shannon.

*What was I going to put on the report? I have three nonconformance(s) to write.*

I said to myself, "Just the facts, lady, just the facts."

Before I left the building, a Spanish woman came into my office.

"Hi, my name is Brenda Cortez. I've come to discuss your Mishap Investigation," she said.

I sat back in my seat, looking at the woman who had just entered my workspace. She had dark, long, curly hair. Her petite body was well-dressed very professionally, and her skin was pale next to her dark, long curly, hair.

She smiled and said, "I am the Quality Director of RUSH. NASA has asked me to take over the Mishap Investigation."

My heart stopped. I felt my face get hot with anger. I couldn't understand how this could happen when I got close to finding out who had done it.

She seemed to take enjoyment in seeing my face fall. She stared at me like a snake, which had just eaten a helpless rat, caged with nowhere to run. I didn't like her body language, and I had to think fast. This woman had taken me by surprise. Was she part of the conspiracy? Could RUSH enterprise facilitate my demise?

I immediately said, "Can I see your badge?"

She handed me her badge and continued to give me a blank gaze. I felt a coldness go over my body as I looked at the badge with her name on it.

I said, "I cannot give you the data without permission from my management."

She didn't even budge. Instead, she retrieved a letter from

her attaché case and handed it to me.

It was from the NASA Director, Head of Quality, Safety, and Mission Assurance.

I read aloud, "Research Underwriters for Specialty Hospitals (RUSH) are now investigating the NBL Mishap Investigation. This investigation involves Dalton Masters and Dan Clark (Diver Dan), who sustained injuries at the Neutral Buoyancy Laboratory. The Federal Government has appointed a liaison, Brenda Cortez, Quality Director of RUSH, to investigate these two incidents. Brenda Cortez will continue with the investigation and use Susan Masters as a consultant when necessary. It is a conflict of interest for Susan Masters, who is married to Astronaut Dr. Dalton Master, to lead the investigation. Effective immediately, Susan Masters is to turn over all her evidence and pertinent information to Brenda Cortez, RUSH Quality Director,, signed by Cody McNeil, the NASA Director, Quality, and Safety & Mission Assurance (QSMA)."

My face dropped. I could tell Brenda took enjoyment in taking over my project. I just sat there in shock. I wanted to scream at the smirk on her face. It was awful. I knew I could not fight her and, especially, NASA.

I said, to ensure the legitimacy of the request, "I need to make one call."

I picked up the phone and called Pam, "Hi Pam, and I have Brenda Cortez in my office. Could you come to my office?"

"Sure, I'll be right over," Pam said.

As Pam walked into my office, I could tell she didn't like the woman sitting across from me.

Brenda gave her a smile, which made us cringe.

Pam assured me, "The management team alerted me of the change. It explicitly states the information and the NBL Mishap Investigation would be turned over to RUSH representing NASA, and not to involve you unless for consulting or as a witness." Pam didn't look at Brenda but directly at me.

I retrieved all the data, including the interviews, and handed Brenda all the notes and the fishbone diagram.

Brenda quickly left.

Pam and I sat in shock. Pam was the first to talk, "Susan, I can't get over what just happened. It doesn't make sense. First, they assign you to perform the investigation, and now they remove you from the investigation. They knew you were married to Dalton when they assigned you to the mishap."

I said, "I guess they didn't think it through."

Pam said, "Can I trust you? I want to speak openly with you."

I said, "Of course."

"Well, I don't like this woman, and neither does anyone else. We all feel there is something about her that is not right. She has a reputation for being crazy. She just can't be trusted. So why can't management see it," Pam said.

I said, "I don't know. I didn't get a warm feeling about Brenda. On the other hand, I am generally astute to crazy people, and I think she made be just that. I know this is not professional, but please keep an eye on her and let me know how the investigation progresses."

Pam said, "I will. First, we must capture the bad guys."

I said, "Thank you, Pam. We will be talking."

After Pam left, I looked at the whiteboard information. I decided that I should keep my fishbone diagram information. So, I captured the data on my iPod before erasing the whiteboard.

The phone rang. I jumped, "Hello, this is Susan Fletcher. I mean, Susan Masters."

Dalton said, "Honey, don't you know your new name? Kidding aside, I've been waiting for you. Can you come home? I need my baby."

"Of course, I just got caught up trying to figure this problem out. Honey, I miss you too. I'll be right home. I need to have some pillow talk." I said.

"I'm here for you," he said.

"I'm on my way home," I said, relieved that I wouldn't have to do the NBL Mishap Investigation. I needed to focus on the MECS Experiment. Unfortunately, I felt responsible for sending another person into the pool, injured, and almost killed. I knew the rules, but emotion had taken over. I wanted to find the person responsible for all the heinous incidents. I couldn't stop thinking of the fishbone diagram and the personnel involved. It was no accident.

When I got home, I immediately began making Dalton's favorite dish, lasagna. I turned on the cable music channel, which played the old romantic classics. Then, I poured myself a glass of Cabernet Sauvignon. I needed to relax, and the wine did the trick. I could feel the wine taking hold of my anxiety.

Dalton walked into the kitchen as I put the lasagna in the oven. Sauce decorated my face, which looked like an Italian pizza. He laughed and licked my nose.

He said, "How is my Italian Mamma Mia?"

I kidded, "I'm just your hot tamale; I mean your hot tomato."

Dalton began licking my whole face, cleaning the tomato sauce off.

"Stop, stop," I called out, laughing as I fell to the floor in tears.

He picked me up, rubbing my breasts next to him. He held me close, kissing me as if he had never kissed me before.

All the anxiety transferred into a passion. I lost control as Dalton led me to the kitchen table. We will have dessert first.

The lasagna was the last on my mind, even though the smell permeated my nostrils. I was hungry but hungrier for Dalton's body.

Dalton whispered, "Susan, you are a temptress. You are the most beautiful woman inside and out."

I said, "I do like the inside."

He moved below me, and I gasped with joy. I didn't want the moment to end; the oven buzzer went off, and we both looked at each other.

Dalton laughed, "I'm hungry."

"So am I!" I met his passion and kissed him.

Afterward, we both hurried to dress. I put the salad and bread on the table and served the lasagna. The garlic, sauce, and fresh bread aromas infiltrated the kitchen.

We both had worked up a tremendous appetite. Dalton opened another bottle of Cabernet Sauvignon and poured a large glass. I swirled the wine to let it breathe, removing the tart vinegar taste.

We clicked our glasses together as a toast to our marriage.

Dalton was the first to speak, "You know Susan, you're preoccupied, and I think it is time you told me what has been on your mind."

I turned away from him. Tears started going down my eyes. He got up from the table and wrapped his arms around me, comforting my wounded wounds. I didn't want to spoil our dinner, so I composed myself and said, "Let's eat, and afterward, I'll share the details of today."

Dalton said, "Dinner can wait."

"No," I said.

We sat in silence. Dalton knew I was upset.

I raised my wine glass to his. "You know the clinking noise sounds like bells. Actually, the clinking noise is supposed to drive away the devils."

He said as my glass clinked, "I will drive away the devils that are bothering you. If it is the last thing I do."

I smiled to agree. Didn't Dalton know the devils were also his demons? I served the hot steaming dish with a salad and hot Italian bread.

We ate very quickly, as if it was our last meal together. I knew Dalton would be asking me questions, and I tried so very desperately to formulate the answers in my head. But my mind kept on saying, "Nothing but the facts."

After dinner, we sat on the patio. The moon was full. The moonlight danced on our bodies to sprinkle us with imaginary moon dust. *I thought soon my Dalton would be in space, away from me.*

Finally, he said, "Spill the beans, Susan. You have been as nervous as a cat."

I started to cry, explaining what happened at the NBL with the hook. Then, I described the incident with Diver Dan. Last, I told him about Brenda Cortez from RUSH, the infamous hatchet woman who took my project away.

Dalton took me into his arms, "Susan, it is a conflict of interest. I am glad you are off the NBL Mishap Investigation. Unfortunately, your life is in danger at the NBL. Why didn't you tell me what was going on?"

I said, "It's my job, and I wanted to find out who was trying to kill us. So, we do have a vested interest."

"But you have to know if anything ever happened to you," he paused, "life wouldn't be the same, and I don't know what I would do."

I said, "I feel the same way. What do you know about Brenda Cortez?"

Dalton grimaced, "This is weird. She was Leona's quality mentor at NASA. They worked on several projects together. Leona used to enjoy her so much, and they bonded."

I felt shocked and confused, "Strange, really strange. I wished I had known this. I would have asked more questions. I need to tell Pam, the NBL manager, about Brenda."

Dalton said, "It's out of your hands. The less you are involved, the better. Don't worry; Brenda is supposed to be an expert. I was friends with Leona, too, and didn't know what she was doing. It is a small quality world. Sweetie, let's get some sleep. Tomorrow is another day of training for you and me. You know I'm going into the deep space brine."

*Chills ran down my spine.*

# Chapter 38– Building 99

As we walked into the simulation building the following day, there were mock-ups of the Space Shuttle everywhere. I felt like I was on a movie set with real-size replicas of the shuttle, vacuum chambers, and some of the Apollo equipment.

My mouth opened in amazement. I couldn't believe I was now part of space history. Groups of astronauts were in training in areas specific to their mission. I wanted to climb and investigate the hardware. Unfortunately, I knew security would escort me out of the building if I did. A childlike emotion grew within me, thinking, "No birthday had ever been this special. It was extraordinary knowing Dalton would go through the necessary training."

Dalton saw a Flight Crew Lead (FCL) and smiled. Drew, the FCL, grinned back and motioned Dalton into a dressing room. Drew asked me to stay outside with an escort.

Dalton came back suited in his orange flight suit. Drew, the FCL suit technician, adjusted the sleeves very meticulously. I saw pride in Drew's eyes.

Dalton caught my eye with a sheepish grin. I knew the training event thrilled every part of his body and soul. I could feel the adrenalin pumping rapidly in both our veins. It was electrifying just watching the performance. He confidently climbed into the mock shuttle. The other members of his crew followed him. They were going to perform the escape exercises.

My thoughts began analyzing if this situation happened. If there was a disastrous situation, I didn't think anyone could escape from a Space Shuttle catastrophe. Everyone would die. Everyone knew that every astronaut is a risk-taker. It's just a reality check.

After the Challenger, they designed the orange flight suits to be fireproof to protect the astronauts against fire during re-entry. The extra protection gave the public a warm and fuzzy, but the astronauts knew they risked their lives every time they flew. Their family knew life had no guarantee in the astronaut's world. The chances are slim if the shuttle has a disaster that anyone would survive. Ironically, it is their home away, and the astronauts feel safe in their shuttle and the space station.

I saw Dalton smiling in the corner of my eye as he climbed into the Space Shuttle simulator. I turned and watched him climb out of the escape pod. No longer was he smiling, but he had an intense expression. He practiced survival techniques; however, he was slim if the astronaut had a problem.

Again, he disappeared into the ship with the other astronauts. Shortly, I saw him maneuvering himself through the side shuttle portholes. He exited with grace no other astronaut displayed. He is a natural for this job.

He shouted, "What a rush!"

I was somewhat envious of him and his opportunity. I genuinely wish I could go with him. Unfortunately, there were so few Space Shuttle flights left.

When Dalton finished training, I ran up and hugged him as hard as I could.

Dalton, "I don't understand the Government's view on shutting down the Manned Space Program. It's amazing the entire technological areas benefitted medical improvements and even in our everyday living."

Dalton said, "Yeah, since 1976, over 1,500 documented NASA technologies have benefited the U.S. industry, improved the quality of life, and created jobs. But surprisingly, the Space Shuttle Program alone has generated more than 100 technology spinoffs."

I stated, "The artificial heart technology was a spin-off from the Space Shuttle fuel pumps. Dr. Michael DeBakey, the renowned heart surgeon, led to the development of a miniaturized ventricular assist pump by NASA."

Dr. Greg joined the conversation, "How about the Space Shuttle thermal protection system used on NASCAR racing cars? It protects drivers from the extreme heat generated by the engines; zoom, zoom, zoom."

Dalton, with his medical expertise, stated, "Do you know about the devices built to measure the equilibrium of Space Shuttle astronauts when they return from space? Major medical centers widely use them to diagnose and treat patients suffering from head injuries, strokes, chronic dizziness, and central nervous system disorders."

I kidded, "Sometimes, I think I could use a device of me being a dizzy blond. But, Dr. Greg, your many girlfriends probably need heart replacements from you breaking their hearts."

Dr. Greg bantered, "I will show you heartbreak. Just wait. I will get you for that one, Susan."

Dalton kidded, "Greg, I don't blame you. She is pretty cruel."

We all laughed as we left the building but knew the technology would soon end with the termination of the Space Shuttle flights and the government funding. It just wasn't fair.

# Chapter 39 - Deep-Space Brine

The following day, I fixed Dalton's brunch. He didn't have to meet the rest of the crew until 1400 at JSC. I didn't want Dalton submerged in 60 feet of deep Atlantic blue waters. It scared me thinking about all that water on top of him. But I knew the training would prepare him for his trip into Earth's orbit. The underwater training is as reliable as flight software. The liquid space home has been dependable since the government implemented the undersea habitats in the 1960s.

Dalton kissed the nape of my neck. Chills ran down my body as he said, "How's my Nancy Drew doing this morning?"

I rolled my eyes, "Sure, good job, Nancy Drew. Unfortunately, I did such a good job I got kicked off the case."

Dalton answered, "Let it go. You need to start concentrating on the MECS Experiment. Please attend a meeting about the MECS Experiment tomorrow. Then, we can drive to NASA together. I will attend an Underwater Habitat debriefing while you go to the MECS Experiment meeting.

The following day, we drove into the JSC gates. It felt good to be on campus again. I said, "Dalton, do you know why they call the JSC campus?"

"Is this a quiz? It seems I remember something about it. Go ahead and tell me," he said.

"Well, when they developed JSC, NASA constructed it as a college campus, so when NASA no longer uses it, it can transition into a University. Unfortunately, they numbered the buildings as built, so the numbers weren't in order across the entire community. The construction numbering system makes it confusing trying to find the correct building," I explained.

"Hmm, with the Space Shuttle being retired, it may just happen. JSC may just become Johnson Space Center University," Dalton said.

I glared into his eyes, "I don't want to think about it."

Dalton parked in front of Building 1. We walked briskly toward Building 1, the astronaut's office location. Security is tight: instead of one guard, they had two. They rechecked our badges before we could enter the building.

I was going up to Room 656 for the MECS Experiment meeting and said, "I'll see you later."

Dalton said, "Not if I see you first." It was so corny I had to smile.

I entered the room, which had a large table with mission posters all along the walls. I relished seeing the posters. It gave me satisfaction knowing I had participated in most of the Space Shuttle missions. Now, I was working in another capacity.

I sat down in a chair nearest the door. I felt unsteady; I wondered if the board would ask me the information I could not answer.

Remember, you have to say, "I'll get back to you, mañana." Then, just put a big smile on your face and nod at the strangers entering the room.

Simultaneously, Dalton sat down on the floor next to a very knowledgeable expert. It was the NASA Undersea Research Team project leader and simulation supervisor.

He deliberately began speaking, "No environment on Earth can capture the essence and isolation of space better than the ocean. It is not a simulation but just an exercise. It's what we call a mission analog and as close as you will get to living and working in space. You will be isolated for three days before the mission. Still, monitoring will happen at the mission control specialists in Houston and the National Undersea Research Center (NURC) in Key Largo. The National Oceanic and Atmospheric Administration owns the Aquarius, operated by the University of North Carolina-Wilmington. You will don scuba gear and float down to the Aquarius.

During your undersea stay, you will conduct your scientific experiment. The rigorous schedule includes building a temporary structure on the seafloor as NASA might one day build outside the space station, possibly the moon."

Dalton said, "Sir, I didn't know about The MECS Experiment transferred to the Aquarius. When was I going to be told?"

The expert said, "There is a meeting right now on the floor above, informing your MECS team about the event."

Dalton almost left the room but decided he needed to hear the rest of the presentation. He was not happy about the secrecy but told him, "Please continue."

He said, "Certainly, but most importantly, the astronauts will be able to test their mental stability. It's crucial when they are in isolation on the ocean floor's extreme environment. In addition, it develops communication and team-building skills.

Astronauts can survive in the undersea environment because of a physiological phenomenon known as "saturation" diving.

The technique is because, after about 24 hours at any depth, a diver's body becomes saturated with dissolved gas, mostly nitrogen," said the NURC director Steven Miller. "Once the body is saturated, decompression takes place in the time necessary to bring a diver gradually back to pressure at sea level. This procedure will ensure that the diver will not go into bends. It is the same regardless of how much time you spend underwater.

Remember, before you return to the safety of the surface, you will have to undergo 17 hours of decompression inside the Aquarius. If any team member were to surface accidentally, you could die, so be very careful not to emerge prematurely."

Astronaut Dalton Masters said, "We take this mission very seriously. In a simulator, you get to test your skills against a log of different emergencies. However, here in the extreme environment of the ocean, where you are out of air, you are really out of air."

The presenter continued, "This is why I am impressed with the importance of this simulator. This environment is not friendly. You can't open the door and go home. Home is not accessible, just like when you are on the space station. It is not accessible. U.S. Navy Captain George Bond pioneered saturation diving in late 1950. The answer to the human quest is to break the physiological barriers that limit the amount of time scuba divers can spend underwater.

After the first 24 hours in the habitat, divers can spend as much time as they need outside to conduct their research when nitrogen saturates the body. In the past, divers have been able to live in relative safety for up to two months. But problems, primarily with ear infections and skin abrasions, make 10-day missions more practical and comfortable for the aquanauts; any questions, aquanauts?" [10]

Everyone sitting in the room understood it was a mission that had no room for error. The wrong decision will cause death. They were all silent. Each was thinking about their vulnerability being deep under the water and in space.

"Additionally, the Aquarius mission will only be for five days so that you can conduct your MECS Experiment underwater," he said.

Dalton smiled, "This is an unparalleled undersea adventure. I can't wait."

During the same time in the MECS meeting, Ken sat next to me. His demeanor and body statue are mammoth above me, making me feel small. He acted as if this was his program and I was just his assistant. I didn't like it.

The MECS NASA Director began reviewing the last time the MECS Experiment flew. He had charts displaying Astronaut Dan Fletcher's bodily functions. It had the project successes and failures up to the time of Dan's murder. Chills ran down my spine. I wanted everyone to stop scrutinizing the information. Remember, this man is an Aerospace hero representing the Space Industry for eternity.

I had to put my feelings aside, realizing this was just facts and nothing but the facts.

Eventually, the Director asked, "Is the MECS Experiment ready to fly?"

Ken began to speak, and I interrupted, which sounded very awkward. I turned my back to Ken and started saying, "The experiment is in the final stages of development. The MECS team has met all phases of development successfully. Of course, success depends on the final stage. The technicians perform the final tasks on the night before the launch. This step is imperative to finalize the solution. The MECS team is

---

[10] By Tim Friend, USA TODAY

ready and prepared to complete the solution and fill the tubes with the crystallization solution. The MECS Experiment has no restriction for flight. This payload is ready to fly."

The Director asked, "Are you ready to sign the Ready to Fly Authorization?"

I smiled, "Yes, I am." The admin moved the NASA authorization form in front of me. She handed me a pen, and I signed the document authorizing Dalton's MECS Experiment readiness to fly. I felt confident we would finish the payload. It would load on the shuttle upon completion, just in time to fly to the International Space Station.

The Director said, "I will file the final paperwork and said, "We are ready to fly. Does anyone have any reason that we shouldn't fly?"

Ken stood up. My heart stopped. What did he know that I didn't? He said, "The MECS Experiment is ready to fly. What happened last time will not happen again."

My face turned red, so much for being transparent. But, of course, the same scenario wouldn't happen. Leona was not part of the program. She wouldn't be able to sabotage the MECS solution. This behavior was inappropriate. I would talk to him about this as soon as we left the meeting. I was the lead, and he was undermining my position using politics. I hated politics.

We both walked down to meet Dalton. There were too many people around us to address this matter. Dalton came out the door, and as he did, Ken walked away. I called out to Ken, but he continued getting on the elevator. He was soon out of sight.

When Dalton and I got into the car, I reviewed with Dalton what had happened.

Dalton said, "Don't worry. Ken feels responsible, and he probably didn't realize how everyone would perceive the situation."

I made a face and asked, "Would he do that to you?"

Dalton said, "No."

His answer confirmed I needed to speak with Ken about his inappropriate behavior. I didn't like it.

The next day, we flew to Miami on a private NASA jet. I

accompanied Dalton to the ocean scientist ship, the Aquarius, off the coast of Key Largo. It was a beautiful day with a soft, warm breeze playing in my hair. I turned to Dalton and put my arms around him. I wouldn't see him for a whole five days. But I knew this experience would be a chance in a lifetime to witness the ocean's beauty underneath tons of water with all the sea creatures.

The Captain announced, "Let's find the large life support buoy, which supplies air and power to the Aquarius."

Of course, he had already set the GPS, which took us directly to the Aquarius.

I could see the bright yellow school-bus-size habitat on the surface.

I said, "See the large life-support buoy, which supplies air and power to the Aquarius."

Dalton said, "Yeah, the five-day mission undersea is equivalent to thirty to thirty-five days of research with normal scuba diving. Five days should give me plenty of time to get my research evaluated."

I was very excited and said, "Dalton, I wish I could go with you on this incredible undersea adventure. Maybe I should be an astronaut, and then I could do this too."

"Susan, we only have room for one astronaut in this family," he said.

"I believe there has only been one married couple in the history of married astronauts, and they even went into space together. I heard they sealed their relationship in outer space. What a thrill!" I grinned.

Soon, the boat slowed down, and the Captain threw out the anchor. The boat bobbed like a cork on a fishing pole. The boat Captain motioned Dalton and the rest of the crew to the stern of the boat.

Dalton turned to me, gave me a quick kiss, and smiled. I said, "I'll miss you."

He responded, "You wouldn't say that unless it was so."

I thought it was so as I watched the aquatic astronaut divers jump off the boat. The divers swam directly to the 82-ton structure. I could barely see the 120-ton base placed anchored onto the seafloor. It had a gazebo with a transparent dome, which I deducted supplied their air beside the entrance. The large umbilical connected the habitat to the life-support buoy that floats overhead.

I could hardly see Dalton enter the Aquarius through the wet porch and moon pool at one end of the structure. Dalton disappeared into the building.

I gasped. I felt separation anxiety. It was just a short time, but leaving Dalton underwater tugged my heartstrings. I didn't like the danger under tons of water in the deep blue brine.

The captain raised the anchor, and we headed to shore. My face said it all, no smiles but just a reflection of my time with Dalton. I could see his face, feel his kisses, and his hands moving over my body.

Dalton had no time to think about me. Once Dalton was inside the porch, he removed and stored his gear. He showered off the salt water and dried off his body.

He said to Dr. Greg, "Try to get off as much moisture as possible to keep out any water from the already humid habitat."

Dalton dried off twice to remove the water from his body. His hair was not much of a problem since he had shaved all the remaining hair off. He was thankful for this.

Dalton scoped out the cozy quarters, which included his lab, kitchen, and sleeping bunks. He counted six sleeping bunks for himself, Dr. Greg, and two scientists who performed life science experiments. They made introductions, and Gregarious Greg smiled and said, "Have you seen any mermaids down here?" The scientists took offense to his comment and turned to begin working on their experiments.

Dalton responded, "Well, Dr. Greg, you know they don't want to share with you. However, I will keep a lookout for any mermaids down here and send them your way."

Dr. Greg said, "Yeah, thanks. Just make sure the video camera is on, and you get my best profile."

*Dalton thought Dr. Greg was a workpiece, but he had grown to admire his intelligence and egotistical personality, humongous Greg.*

Dalton took the bunk closest to him. Dalton took out his

laptop and signed on since he wanted to send Susan an email before returning to Kennedy Space Center. He wanted her to know how much he cared for her. It just wasn't the same without her being next to his side.

He and Dr. Greg settled into their new home. Dalton threw his gear under the bed. It was definitely cozy. They began planning the King's payload and the installation of the new hardware. Dalton felt pressure in his chest. He excused the feeling of being in an underwater environment. It certainly was a different experience.

Later that evening, he called Susan. Again, Dalton used the video camera and the Internet service.

Susan settled into the room when she heard the computer ring.

"Hi Susan, I'm certainly missing you," Dalton said.

Susan heard in the background.

"I'm missing you too," Greg said, laughing.

"Well, boys, I'm missing you both," I said.

"Susan, this is such a great experience. Tomorrow, we will set up the mock MECS Experiment and begin researching to see how the crystals develop undersea," he said.

"Well, while you are performing the MECS experiment, I will fill the tubes with your special formula. Then, I want to have it completed to load onto the Shuttle. It will be a successful mission," I said.

"I know. The most important success is to have the King completely cured of prostate cancer," Dalton said. Then, I said, "He will be living proof the formula works."

It was almost as if Dalton was right with me in the room, but he wasn't.

Dalton said, "Tomorrow is full of live teleconferences with mission control. We will also have a live Internet chat with schools across the country on the NASA Quest website: **www.quest.arc.nanas.gov/projects/space acquarius/2002/index.html**.

You can also do a virtual walkthrough at **www.uncwil.edu/acquarius**. It should be exciting. Please check it out."-

I asked, "How large are your quarters?"

"Believe it or not, this is about the same size as the Space Station,"

Dalton responded, "It's a great place to perform pre-mission exercises and ensure all our safety issues are corrected?"

I said, "What time is your internet chat scheduled?"

Dalton said, "1400, my Dear. I had better go; Dr. Greg has someone to call, and I'm tired. Need to get my beauty rest."

I laughed, "So do I; goodnight, my darling."

# Chapter 40– Body Dragging Exercise

Early the following day at KSC, I participated in the Body Dragging Exercise. Once again, a mockup simulation practiced astronaut escape on the launch pad in case of an emergency. Since the astronauts could be disabled, they would need help in leaving the cockpit. That assignment went to me as the extra person since an assigned mission technician could not make it.

The mission technician lead began, "A practice run removing the astronauts from the Space Shuttle, either the ground or the escape basket, is required to ensure the astronauts' safety. Fortunately, we have never had to do this. However, it's a known fact that astronaut's bones deteriorate in space. So be careful with them."

The fourteen-mission technician would have the honor of carrying the disabled astronaut from the white room in the orbiter to the escape basket or out of the shuttle when it had landed. This position was difficult. Not only would the astronaut's life be in danger, but the mission technicians. So, instead of astronauts, we took turns as the incapacitated person.

I was next, "Please be gentle; I can already feel my back hurting. I need help!"

I pretended to be in pain, and I moaned, "Help me, help me!"

It was fun being carried by new friends to the escape basket at the top of the launchpad. I felt safe with them carrying me.

I hoped the next imaginary astronaut wouldn't be the heaviest crewmember.

Well, they chose a nice-looking, muscular man. After that, it was my turn to carry the debilitated astronaut, whose weight was twice mine.

I wanted to impress the stranger who was breaking my back by not showing any signs of weakness. But unfortunately, his dead weight made it difficult to move him toward the escape baskets.

The lead technician gave orders, "Everyone picks him up simultaneously."

I did my best while my red face broke out in a sweat. I wanted to have a massage and take care of my damaged muscles. Unfortunately, being a technician is not all it's cut out to be.

He kidded, "Don't you guys drop me. I am a top gun astronaut-- expert iceman, cool as a cucumber."

"No, you mean, you're hot and heavy as a tree trunk on fire." I returned.

He gave me a cold look; *I couldn't help but wonder why. The hair on the back of my neck stood straight up. After all that had happened, I was suspicious of everyone and everything. The lifting of dead weight was not my cup of tea. My body didn't like manual labor. I was getting too old for this type of work. I thought this day would never end. I looked forward to a hot bath with bubbles to soothe my aching muscles. I wanted away from this iceman. I wondered why the stranger hadn't given me his name.*

*I thought, if I must do this one more time, my body will break. I was so glad this exercise was over. Never would I volunteer to perform body dragging. Now, auditing didn't seem so bad.*

Furthermore, I had to return to JSC and begin the MECS audit. Fortunately, the NASA jet was returning to Houston tomorrow, and I would see my sweetheart again.

## Chapter 41 –MECS Audit

Once aboard the small NASA Lear jet, it felt very cozy, only holding eight passengers. Then, the pilot came over the speaker.

He said, "Good afternoon, everyone. I am so pleased to have you onboard a NASA flight heading to Houston, Texas. We will be arriving on time or a little earlier with the wind flow of the jet stream.

"For your pleasure, we have snacks, sodas, and alcoholic beverages. Drink and be merry.

"Now, to the safety features. In case of an emergency, a mask will fall from overhead. Please put the mask over your face and pull until the tube extends. Breathe normally; the plastic bag will not inflate, but oxygen will flow. After you have the mask over your face first, then assist anyone who may need help. Then, sit back and enjoy the flight home."

The flight back to Houston was uneventful until the jet fell in an incline, and suddenly, the masks dropped.

The pilot announced over the intercom, "We have decompressed. Don't panic. We are not in danger, but I must lower the plane so you can breathe normally without the masks. So please relax, and don't worry. I have everything under control."

I could see the fear on everyone's faces. Grown men turned pasty white, and tears ran down their faces.

Without removing my mask or leaving my seat, everyone passed their trays for me to put them away. I knew if we crashed, we couldn't have food, plates, and dishes flying around the cabin.

It felt like an eternity before we landed at Ellington Airport. Everyone kept staring into each other eyes. I wondered what they were thinking. Yet, I was calm, knowing that it was my time. I had found the love of my life and experienced what many women had never enjoyed.

When we arrived, one of the men kissed the ground when he got off the plane. I laughed to myself; if they had gone through what I have, this was nothing, absolutely nothing.

I immediately went to the JSC astronaut laboratory. The wall displayed the standard safety sign, "No Food or Drink Allowed."

The white sterile laboratory provided a protective barrier from germs and debris. Inside were two refrigerators and stainless-steel tables with hard, uncomfortable stools provided for the laboratory technicians. The cold, sterile, barren room reminded me of an operating room.

Before I could enter the white room, I had to suit up. I found the white room uniform lockers. I picked out and put on a gown, gloves, and a surgeon's hat, which completely covered my blond curly hair. I walked into the white room full of test tubes sealed in germ-free wrappings.

I remembered Dalton's complete instructions and told my MECS team, "Fill each tube with the correct amount of solution. The MECS consistency requires the exact proportions in the experiment, or it will fail. Patty and Connie, I want Ken to mentor you. Please fill the tubes with the exact chemical proportion detailed in the MECS Test Preparation Sheet (TPS). Each quality control person will test the capsules. Ken, you will be the final eyes of quality assurance."

I saw Ken standing next to the refrigerated cabinets. He gave me a great big smile, "I certainly will be the last step. It's so great to see you here. I guess you are ready to perform the final audits on the micro-crystallization tubes."

I said as I took out the audit checklist, "Yes, I am." I immediately checked the temperature of the refrigerator. It was compliant. I wrote down the objective evidence on my checklist.

Ken led me back to their workbench. A tall, masculine, dark-haired man was sitting on the bench. It was David, who was on the MECS team.

I smiled, "Hi, it's good to see you again. I'm going to perform an audit of the MECS Test Preparation Sheet (TPS)."

He didn't look me in the eye but slowly said, "It's good to see you again,"

I asked to see his bench certifications for chemical equilibrium, which requires the complex mixture's submission.

He opened his wallet, which contained his certification. I checked for the date to ensure it was up-to-date. Then, I asked, "May I have your certification for soldering, etc.?

He removed them from the drawer and handed them to me without eye contact or emotion. The hair on my neck stood straight up. I couldn't help but think that he was a very strange bird. He had no emotion on his face. But, again, I documented the objective evidence.

I inquired, "What is your job description?"

David deliberately answered. I saw a glint of pride when he said, "I am the Life Science Experiments lead engineer for the MECS Experiment."

I inquired, "What does that mean in layman's terms?"

He methodically said, "I calculate the chemical equilibrium composition and properties of complex mixtures. Then, to put it in plain English, I ensure that the experiment states the theoretical rocket performance, so the tubes are shock-tube parameters for the incident and reflected shocks."

I tried not to look surprised by his explanation. David was quite knowledgeable. Funny, when Leona and I filled the tubes, I didn't have a clue about the rocket performance. I asked, "Do you have a Test Preparation Sheet (TPS)?" The document explains to the technician how to perform the MECS experiment.

He looked around and brought out a notebook full of paper. He handed it to me.

I said, "Could I have a copy so I can inspect the paperwork later?"

David said, "Of course." He handed it to the laboratory administrator, who immediately began making a copy outside the laboratory door. When she completed the task, I randomly picked a section and began auditing the functional requirements.

I said, "How did you retrieve the tubes?"

David immediately said, "I checked them out of the Inventory Laboratory."

I asked, "Could I see your procedures before you take me to the Inventory Laboratory?"

*He opened his desk and retrieved his procedures. I thought to myself that most employees keep outdated procedures on their desks. He should have retrieved them from the electronic library. I was right when I asked him to show me the library database. Yep, it was an outdated copy.*

He looked nervous and said, "I should have known better."

I documented the anomaly and said, "It is an easy mistake, and generally, the solution is education."

Next, he showed me his stamp form, which allowed him to check out the tubes.

I asked to see his stamp and compared it to the stamp on the TPS. Next, we went to the Inventory Laboratory and checked their stamps. I also requested to meet with the Laboratory Administrator, and she showed me the Technician's Stamp Log. I asked for their training log to ensure their required training was current. All were in order.

Next, I began checking the tubes individually to ensure each stamp coincided with the stamp log. I found one that was out of date. The name had Ken's stamp number on it, which was 001. What was he doing stamping off the MECS tubes? I needed to report this anomaly. I had to take personal out of the equation. Just report only the facts, nothing but the facts. Now, I have found two non-conformances.

Subsequently, I checked the refrigerators' temperatures in the correct range to keep the MECS formula compliant. I sat down in front of the refrigerators, thinking about how wrong the experiment went last time and how right everything looked on paper.

I remembered Leona marking the tubes. So, I methodically checked each tube and didn't see any anomalies.

No one in his or her right mind would try to pull the same stunt again. This time, Dalton's life could be in danger. I hadn't mixed the formula this time, but I was the auditor to ensure no anomalies, and I was the MECS project lead. The technicians assigned to implement the application are each required to have Top Secret security clearance. That gave me some comfort until I remembered Astronaut McKnight and Leona, who had the exact clearance. He was an astronaut, for God's sake. He was a powerful, well-respected man but an accomplice to murder and treason.

His Hippocratic Oath meant nothing to him. I couldn't figure it out as he died in space, as did Dan Fletcher. So, I told myself to concentrate on the audit and think about other things tomorrow.

I concentrated on auditing the tubes, their approval stamps, and their formulation dates. All seemed to be in line except one.

I asked David if I could meet with the NASA Quality representative. An intelligent young woman walked over and introduced herself. She was slightly built, with a beautiful smile, and I couldn't help liking her. Her name was Claudia.

I asked, "Is your stamp on the tubes?"

She immediately answered, "Yes, here is my stamp. It is 001. I performed 100% coverage for stamping each tube, along with Patty and Connie. I'm a stickler for compliance."

David had a half-grin, "Yes, she is."

Apparently, David was relaxing under the audit pressure.

I smiled, "I can believe it. I need to return to my office. Thank you for your time. I will be releasing my report tomorrow. It is the final signoff for the flight. Oh yeah, could you give me a list of everyone who has had access to the MECS tubes and the technicians who worked on the formulas and their stamp numbers?"

As I walked to the office, I contemplated what paperwork to analyze. Since I hadn't witnessed the formula formulation, the subsequent best adherence to compliance would be to review the paperwork. Unfortunately, it is inherent that humans make mistakes, not on purpose, but just by being human. Just because you make a mistake on the paperwork does not mean you made a mistake on the formula, but all would be suspect.

Before I left, I received the additional paperwork. Before the night was through, I knew that I would be back in the laboratory, checking each of the tubes for compliance. I could not leave any stone unturned. I would make sure my honey would be safe. I would do everything humanly possible.

I immediately dug through the 300-page individual sign-off for each step of the TPS documents and on the label to show the tube's completion. I heard a gasp in the back of the room. I tried to see who made the sound, but no one was there. I walked toward the sound and found no one in the area.

I saw a shadow out of the corner of my eye. It reminded me of the dark, menacing figure in my sailboat's stateroom. Panicked, I walked very fast into the restroom, holding back nausea. Yes, I wanted to throw up. I was scared, very scared. The fear was almost too much. I had to convince myself that it wasn't real so that I could complete the audit. It was my mission and responsibility. I could not go home until I finished the MECS Final Audit. I took three deep breaths and headed back to my office. The weight of the TPS felt heavy. I secretly wished I still attended high school when life was much easier with fewer responsibilities.

I put the TPS on the desk and began at the very beginning, looking at each step. Then, I got out the stamp control log and traced the steps with the stamp log. This check showed if unauthorized personnel had performed the tube formulation.

I felt like an investigator for the CIA or Colombo. I evaluated every step twice. I wanted to do it a third time, only I wouldn't have any sleep. It was already three-thirty AM when I finished studying the data.

I reminded myself one could look at information too much and miss the obvious. I wanted to report the information accurately, so I stopped the auditing process and formulated the Audit Report.

Who will be the recipients? What is the least common denominator for the data root cause analysis?

I was dead tired, but I didn't want to leave the report and the data unattended. I sent Dalton a text message at his underwater home telling him I wouldn't be home. I curled up on the floor, which was horribly uncomfortable. I used the 300-page TPS as a pillow.

I finally fell asleep out of exhaustion. As soon as I went to sleep, the nightmare crept into my dreams. Again, my heart felt like it stopped, but subconsciously, I felt my heart beat fast. A voice came from out of nowhere with the familiar threatening sound. I couldn't believe my ears. My mouth opened to shout for help, but I knew this time no one would hear. I was alone, except for the unknown person without a face shouting menacingly, "You will die."

I was so scared I could not move. Suddenly, without control, I began to whimper, to cry. A deep emotion took over. I wanted to stop crying, but I could not. Paralyzed, I became overcome by the fear of tomorrow, of the night, and of the person who was stalking me.

Why would they want to kill me? I hadn't harmed anyone. I realized they wanted to kill the auditor I had become. They didn't want me to discover their existence or report my findings. Who had murdered Dan? I don't even think they want the experiment performed again. Why would they want me dead? I began crying again, but this time harder. I could not focus on reality, and then I saw a shadow coming toward me. It got closer. I wanted to get up and run but could not. I picked up the TPS, trying to shield myself. The figure got closer and closer. I began swinging the TPS for protection. I closed my eyes and heard a familiar voice.

"Susan, are you okay? Don't be afraid; it's just me, David," the voice said. Thank God it was David, the MECS engineer.

He said, "You need to go home. It is too late to be in the Astronaut Laboratory alone. Take your work with you. I will walk you to your car."

I felt embarrassed since he had seen me as an emotional wreck. I drove back, sad, to the hotel and took a long-overdue, hot, steamy shower. I crawled safely into bed, thinking how I missed Dalton and hoped David wouldn't mention how I crashed and burned in the lab. *But I thought, why is David at the laboratory in the middle of the night?*

As the sun rose, I put the final changes on the MECS Audit Report. After completion, I asked myself, *Should I call Dalton to review the MECS Audit Report?*

I realized it wouldn't be independent if I did that. I would attend that day's debriefing report when everyone else got the results."

The following day, I felt the weight of the world on my shoulders. I had only found one major anomaly and one minor anomaly. You would think I should be happy, but I wasn't. I felt as if I had missed an essential piece of the puzzle. *What was it?*

I stopped at the JSC NASA front gate and showed my badges. A sign near the gate indicated a high-security level. I wanted to ask why but knew they wouldn't disclose why. Then, as we entered the NASA Astronaut Building, Ken came running up to us.

He asked, "Did you find anything out of the ordinary?"

I said, "I will be reporting what I found at the meeting. So, you will have to wait."

Ken knew I couldn't disclose any audit information until the meeting.

The NASA Director of Astronauts called the meeting to order.

He began, "I want to welcome our most distinguished project lead, Susan Masters. She supports Doctor Dalton Masters' most impressive MECS Experiment with his Royal Majesty Karl Ásgeirr XIII as the recipient of the MECS Experiment. We truly have a unique situation that provides international coverage. I want to impress on everyone in this room the importance of an error-free space environment. We truly have a unique situation that provides global coverage. I want to impress on everyone in this room the importance of providing an error-free space environment. It is up to the whole organization to check, double-check, and triple-check your processes and procedures.

First on the agenda are the results of Susan's MECS Experiment audit. The documentation proved verification that no one tampered with the MECS capsules. In addition, all the TPS steps were quality-checked and performed correctly. Susan, could you give us your report?"

I stood up, looking into everyone's eyes. Then, I handed out my report.

It merely stated, "Two anomalies found in the formulation of the MECS formula. One non-conformance was a stamp validation on a TPS step that didn't have current certification. I documented another non-conformance due to an outdated procedure on the desk of a technician. It shouldn't be a problem since the current process procedure is the online library. I found the outdated procedure on the desk, but not used."

The NASA Director of Astronauts' smile withered. Finally, he stood up and asked, "Who didn't have a current certification?"

I said, "Ken."

Ken immediately stood up and pulled out another certification, stating it was up-to-date. His face was a deep crimson as he handed me his certification. I noticed that Brenda Cortez, Quality Director of RUSH, had signed it. How could she sign for Ken? I needed to call Pam, the NBL manager, and ask what was going on.

I didn't feel comfortable with Brenda being responsible for the stamp assignments. The paperwork seemed to be in order, but I still felt uncomfortable. *Had I missed*

I kept remembering Dalton, saying, "The secret is in the timing. The serum's final ingredient must be placed in the bottle right before the flight at KSC and refrigerated immediately, or the solution will lose its potency. Please handle each drop as if it's the most precious life force in the world."

I wondered if Ken or Brenda Cortez had tampered with the MECS formula as I left the meeting. Now, there was a link between Brenda and Ken through RUSH. Ken had access to the formula both times. I often wondered if he had played a part in the space murders. In my mind, this question was still unanswered.

After the meeting, I called Pam at the NBL, "This is Susan. I have been auditing the MECS Experiment TPS and discovered Brenda Cortez had signed off on Ken's stamp authorization."

Pam was silent and said, "This is a mystery to me. I don't understand how she is getting so much responsibility. I received a memo stating her new responsibilities, including her stamp authorizations. But I tell you, she is power-hungry. She still hasn't even finished the Mishap Investigation. It's almost as if she doesn't want to do the Mishap Investigation. I ask her about it, but she ignores me."

I said, "Who is giving her the responsibility? Who sends the memos?"

Pam responded, "Human Resources signed the memos. They are always changing personnel, so the last few were from different people. None of this makes sense."

I sighed, "I guess everything is in order if Human Resources is sending the memos. Of course, things change all the time. One more thing, what can you tell me about David, the MECS engineer and technician?"

Pam paused, "He is a strange bird. He is an insomniac and comes to work at strange hours during the night. David doesn't socialize much, and he pretty much keeps to himself, but I've noticed lately he has a smile on his face at times. The smile is new for him."

I said, "Interesting; wonder where his smile comes from?"

Pam said, "Someone said that he possibly has a new girlfriend."

I said, "Well, there is no harm in that. Everyone needs someone to make you smile."

Pam giggled, "Yes, even David, the quiet engineer, but who is this someone?"

## Chapter 42– The Last Dinner

Dalton finally returned from the underwater laboratory training, as excited as I've ever seen him. I listened to his stories about the crew becoming fish underwater and how successful the MECS Experiment performed in this adverse condition. He had bonded with Dr. Greg Humongous. He laughed, "Greg kept looking for his mermaid. I told him that you are my mermaid and that he could never find a beautiful mermaid, my wife, but he kept looking for his mermaid."

I said, "Watch it. I may dye my hair bright shimmering seaweed green like a mermaid, and you may not like it if I were to grow a fishtail."

He laughed, "You are so right. I like your tail just as it is."

It was 15 days before the mission flight, and I was panic-stricken. I didn't want Dalton to go into space. I had bad feelings. He was going into space in an unfriendly environment with possibly hostile people. I knew he would have to go back to NASA Kennedy Space Center, and I would follow a little later. He would catch a ride on the Space Shuttle and be responsible for curing King Karl Ásgeirr. *Blast that King; why did he have to get sick? Why should Dalton put his life on the line for royalty?*

I knew it just wasn't royalty, but for everyone who had cancer.

It was my last night with Dalton in our home before he left. When he walked into the kitchen, I poured him a glass of cabernet sauvignon.

"Darling, let's toast your last night at home," I demurely said and kissed him passionately. I heard bells.

Dalton said, "I think we have company. I will answer the door."

A few minutes later, I walked King Karl Ásgeirr XIII. Secretly, I died inside. *How rude.* It was our last night together before the flight.

As if the King could read my mind, he said, "Dalton, thank you for inviting me over tonight. I know you didn't want me to be alone."

Dalton smiled and said, "Susan and I are pleased you are here."

I looked at him funny, and he said, "Oops, I forgot to tell Susan you were coming."

I smiled and said, "What a lucky girl I am to have two charming men joining me for dinner."

I poured the King a glass of wine. We clinked our glasses together, and the King made a toast.

I stood between the two men, and the King said, "To my new and special American friends. I want to tell you how much your support means to me. I have been alone for so long, even though people surround me all day long. I now feel I'm a part of the research that could save many people, including myself. It is only because of the great man standing in front of me and the woman behind the man, pretty Susan."

Dalton laughed and said, "You know it is true. Susan is the most beautiful woman in the world."

I blushed, "Guys, you really haven't had enough to drink to make such compliments, but I will take them."

Both men just stared at me.

I broke the moment and turned to begin dinner, "Dalton, please start the grill. I prepared a salad and baked potatoes, so all you have to do is your magic on the grill."

The King and Dalton went out onto the patio to begin grilling the steaks.

I set the table and put the salad and potatoes on the plate. I wanted to hide as I sat down and felt very confused. Instead, I was alone until the notorious King Karl Ásgeirr XIII entered the room. He looked dashing, a true King. I found myself staring into his eyes. I could not take my eyes off him when he said, "Are you happy to see me?"

My heart stopped. "Well, King, you are the last person I thought I would see tonight."

The King said, "Do you want me to leave?"

I said, "No, but I would like to spend some time with my husband. It's stressful for me for him to leave. I don't want him to go."

The King said, "I know. I'm so sorry that I came, but I'm

so scared. It is my last chance for survival. Your Dalton is my only hope."

I felt horrible. I shouldn't have told the King how I truly felt. He is just a man, royalty or not, and he doesn't know what the future will bring.

I said, "I'm sorry if I made you feel not welcome. But, of course, you are welcome. So, let's have a wonderful meal and enjoy our last night together."

He perked up like a little boy, smiling from ear to ear. Then, he said, "Thank you, Susan. You are such a classy woman."

At that time, Dalton came in with the steaks. He placed them on the table, and we ate.

The King asked, "Dalton, I heard you can grow the crystals in gravity."

I said, "So you mean you can grow the crystals on earth."

Dalton said, "Yes, we did it underwater; they are not perfect, but close. I believe that's why Leona and Dr. Greg wanted the formula. They could create all the biochemical weapons to destroy humanity in the major countries in the world. They or some major entity could control the world with this technology.

"It's hard for me to imagine that they were so close. It's not something I don't want to repeat." I said. "Tell me it won't happen again. I don't want it to."

"That's not all, my Susan. Listen carefully. The seed crystals don't contain sediment in a microgravity environment and grow into a perfect crystal structure. When the solution dehydrates, water removal across an osmotic membrane often allows large, perfect crystals for molecular structure analysis. However, the crystals are fragile and have possible damage from spacecraft re-entry g-forces or post-flight harvesting procedures. Therefore, we will keep the crystals on the Space Station."

"How do you use the capsules? Will you be harvesting the crystals at the space station?" I asked.

"Yes, that is the plan. I am going to teach resident American astronauts to make the crystals," Dalton explained.

The King asked, "Can you teach me how to make the crystals?"

Dalton said, "I'm afraid not since it is a top-secret experiment, but you are the MECS host. So, it will be your cure, but no information on the formula."

After the conversation, we didn't mention the days to come but the days after the mission. What we would do and where we would travel.

I said, "I hope you don't mind, but I don't want to go to Sweden again, but someplace warm. So, Dalton, let's go back to the Bahamas. I want to swim with the pigs at Staniel Cay and go to Exumas Park. This time, I want to stay on the south side of our private beach. The beauty of the shimmering blue water is mesmerizing."

Dalton grinned, "Wherever you want to go, I will go. All I want is my baby to be happy."

I continued, "The Atlantic Ocean is so transparent, aquamarine, and multiple colors of blue that contrast with the cobalt blue skies. The skies remind me of the heavens in Texas, where the skies are larger than life."

Dalton smiled, "Heaven is anywhere you are, Susan."

The King looked very sad, "I guess it is time for me to leave. Thank you so much for dinner. It has been an incredible time, and I'm glad I didn't have to spend my last night in Houston alone. I do appreciate your Texas hospitality."

We walked him to the door, and The King leaned over and kissed me on the cheek goodnight. My cheek burned from his lips.

Dalton didn't notice the redness as I blushed. He took my hand and led me to our bedroom. "Susan, I want this night to be special. I blew it by inviting the King to dinner as a guy, but I know how I would feel. He is dying, and this is his last chance for survival. He is another guinea pig, Fletcher. I have so many questions, and this time, I will be executing the experiment. Instantly, I will know if it is successful or not. No one will be manipulating the numbers. I am responsible this time."

"Dalton, whether it is successful or not, just come home to me. If I were Queen for the day, I wouldn't let you go into space. It is so dangerous. I can't lose you," I said.

Dalton said, "My beautiful Susan, you are not going to lose

me. It is only 220 miles above the Earth. You could drive 3.3 hours to get there or sail on our sailboat 55 hours to the Space Shuttle in a day and 1/2."

I laughed, "Yes, it is not that far, but it is a very unfriendly environment."

Dalton said, "Let me show you friendly." He gave me a long, sensuous kiss, with his lips traveling down my body, making me tingle all over. My mind traveled to the king's kiss on my cheek. I immediately felt uncomfortable, and Dalton could feel my body tense.

He asked, "What is wrong?"

I quickly recovered and said, "I'm missing you already."

Every touch, every kiss, made me warm inside. We had a relationship that most people never experienced. My heart throbbed with the tenderness of our past and the excitement of our future.

Afterward, that night, I tossed and turned; I didn't sleep. I lay next to the man I adored and wanted to climb inside of him to keep him safe from harm's way. I knew I had done everything possible to ensure the quality was perfect. But *what is the price of quality? Is it worth my husband's life?*

## Chapter 43– Astronaut's Cottage

It was good to be back in the Astronaut's Cottage at KSC. The simplicity and beauty of the cottage made me feel at home. The memories came back from our romantic escapade to the beach.

Quickly, when I saw the astronaut's family, I was brought back to earth. The designated astronaut accompanied each family member throughout the flight. All were in this room. I thought they hadn't assigned anyone to me. I wondered why. The same muscular man who participated in the body-dragging exercise program entered the room.

I gasped as he walked up to Dalton and introduced himself as my designated escort. "I'm Dean Milton. I am an astronaut in training. I have not completed my formal training, but I'm appointed to be Susan's escort."

Dalton said, "I'm sure you will take very good of my beautiful wife."

Dean responded, "You can be certain I will."

I stared at him for a very long time. His assignment to me didn't feel right.

He smiled and said. "I will see you tomorrow."

I said softly, "Of course."

Dalton whispered, "Let's go to our room. It will be a long time."

Suddenly, I said, "Let's take a swim."

He laughed, "Now, why didn't I say that."

"You know we have to be careful since there are children around." I giggled.

As we ran down the beach, we left a trail of clothes. It reminded me of Hansel and Gretel, leaving a trail of breadcrumbs.

Dalton jumped into the shimmering waves cresting in the moonlight. I followed and remembered our last beach trip.

The water felt very warm and very delightful. The silky, salty sensation of the clear blue water felt incredible on my skin. Dalton put his arms around me, and I felt so desired. I wanted this night never to end.

He kissed me tenderly, holding me tightly. I wanted him to hold me forever.

Dalton said, "You know this mission is hazardous. When I took astronaut training, I knew the risk of my life, but the risk was always less than our space accomplishments. When I took the training, I didn't know you existed, but now I do. I want to live a full life with you."

Before I could say a word, he kissed me again. I wanted to find a way to keep him inside me by imprinting his memory onto my brain. Then, I would be alone, and he would be in a mysterious space as dark as the ocean before me. Since time began, both space and sea have secrets waiting to unravel. Dalton would certainly unravel the mysteries of cancer.

Dalton ran his hands over my salty, slippery body, which brought chills to my skin. I felt the shivers run across my skin. My arms surrounded him as he raised my hips to match his. The water swelled behind us as we rode the wave up to the crest and down the backside. I sighed with anticipation. I knew he was meeting my rhythm. Breathlessly, I hung onto him as his hardness entered my body, matching the thrusts of the waves. I felt time stood still while we were in the luxurious water.

Suddenly, a bright light was blinding me. Simultaneously, our eyes searched for the lights on the beach. Instead, the brightness scanned the water.

I asked, "Are they looking for us? Who has the high beam searchlight?"

Dalton said, "Move Susan slowly toward shore. Just be calm, don't panic. I believe they are searching for sharks."

As soon as he spoke, I saw fins skimming the surface. My heart raced. I wanted to panic, but I knew any fast action would be the end of us. The carnivorous beast can travel faster than we can move. It happened so quickly; I saw Dalton hit the attacking shark on the nose with his fist.

I felt like I was going into shock when he screamed, "Susan, get out of the water fast."

I looked back as another shark was coming. Dalton swiftly turned and began coming toward me as fast as he could. My heart was going to explode out of my chest. Suddenly, I felt something brush against me. I screamed.

I realized Dalton was right behind me, and he had touched my leg. We turned in time to see both sharks were heading at us.

I yelled, "Hurry, Dalton, hurry."

We both darted very fast across the water. I knew if we didn't get out of the water, we would be the sharks' dinner or mangled or dead.

It seemed like an eternity until my feet hit the sand. We were going in slow motion. We both kept running away from the beach when our feet hit the sand. I didn't want to take any chances that the shark would come onto the beach and get me. Dalton was right behind me. I turned to see the superficial bite on his arm. Dalton, my hero, had thwarted the attack.

I found my shirt and swiped the spot of blood with my tee shirt.

"Dalton, we could have been seriously injured," I said.

"Yes, but we got out just in time. The searchers must have been trying to warn us. NASA always keeps watching over us. For a minute, I thought terrorists were attacking us," he stated.

"You have protection from NASA, but even NASA has no control over sharks," I said.

Dalton laughed, "You can say that again, but I believe there are a lot of sharks working at NASA."

I chuckled, "I know. Should we tell the others about the shark attack?"

Dalton said, "No, let's keep that information to ourselves; no need to alert the others. We are the only ones that are crazy enough to go swimming at night. Next time, let's go during the day when the sharks are not feeding."

"Sounds like a plan," I said, thinking how close we could have been to dinner.

We went back to the cottage, where everyone was sitting and talking about the upcoming flight experiments.

Dr. Greg said, "Dalton, I'm glad you came in. I want a re-familiarization of the MECS Experiment. Tell me how I can help you as the payload specialist/physician?"

233

Dalton said, "It is a cancer experiment. We grow the micro-crystallization cells in test tubes and then insert them into the arteries that lead to cancer. The formula of micro-crystallization cells encapsulates the cancerous tumor. The good part is the medicine is not spread to the rest of the body, just the targeted areas."

Greg said, "I understand. I'm sure when we are up in space, I will assist you with the experiment."

Dalton responded, "Of course, you are my assistant. Susan will place the test tubes into the containers for shipment on the Space Shuttle."

The King overheard the conversation, and he inquired, "Since Greg is assisting you, I would like to learn the technique so I can promote the technology to others who need the experiment."

Dalton said, "Well, gentlemen, we can begin in the morning on learning the MECS experiment."

The King said, "I would like to understand the basic components of medicine. It is going into my body, so I want to understand how it works and what it will do to me."

Dalton said adamantly, "The components of the MECS formula are confidential, and there will be no disclosure of the information. It is complicated; soon, it will be the countdown, and I'm tired."

I said, "As a matter of fact. I need to work on the MECS tomorrow. I don't know where the time has gone."

Dr. Greg said, "Neither do I."

I said, "Well, tomorrow, I will audit the capsules."

Dalton said, "Yes, we need those results. Yes, soon, it will be the countdown."

"Let's all go to bed. It is getting late, and we need to be fresh in the morning," I said.

Everyone began laughing when The King said, "Sounds like the best offer I had all day."

"No, that's not what I meant," I said.

I headed over to audit the MECS laboratory to ensure the capsules loaded onto the Space Shuttle in the morning. When I walked into the laboratory, I stood, Ken, hovering over the capsules like a mother hen.

I said, "Hi, Ken. You are here early this morning. What do I have to honor us with your presence?"

Ken responded, "I want to make sure the MECS hardware equipment loads with the capsules onto the Space Shuttle. I don't want any room for error. It is my baby too. My company built the equipment for this purpose. It is my hardware payload. I am responsible."

I said adamantly, "It is Dalton's payload, or should we say The King's Payload. Everyone here has a stake in the payload, but I need to do another audit to ensure we are *Ready for Flight,* or should I say *Go for Take-Off.*"

Ken blew up like a blowfish but didn't say a thing. He knew he was wrong. Ken had such an ego, wanting to take all the credit. Ken did build the hardware, but he didn't create the formula. His hardware design is successful because of Dalton's input and hard work. Dalton went to his manufacturing plant all the time, giving advice. It was a team effort, but the bottom line wouldn't be successful without Dalton.

As the technicians completed the last ingredient, I moved over to the trays and began methodically auditing each tube, the label line by line. I still saw the anomalies that Dalton had said were just fine last time. The red dots on the capsules identified anthrax the last time. My hair stood up in the back. I could not have the capsules be wrong since the paperwork allowed the capsules to fly. Still, I would recheck the tubes to ensure the MECS solution for the experiment was perfect, and The King would be safe.

I sat down at the desk and wrote a Red Flag alerting the NASA executives about the red dots. The red dots are anomalies and shouldn't be on the MECS tubes. It is the NASA executive's decision whether these tubes should enter space again. I felt like it was déjà vu. Unfortunately, I had done all that I could. It was out of my hands.

# Chapter 44– Pre-Flight Quarantine

Crew training came early the following day. The technicians fitted Dalton into his very own Aerospace Team Escape Suit outfit, a bright orange jumpsuit. Should I say many brave men who entered space had worn his reuse outfit?

His Extravehicular Transportable Unit suit is also well-worn. The redoing of the suits repeatedly displayed the tattered and torn memories of scientific space research.

I touched the remnants of yesterday's glorified days, and my heart exploded with pride with today's adventures. The dedicated technician handled the hardware with excruciating care. I asked, "How do you repair and clean these tattered gloves?"

He smiled, "We do it with our procedures developed by the engineers and, of course, with tender loving care."

I had so many questions about the process, "Can you tell me about the crew quarters."

He said, "The small building is called astronaut crew quarters. You have to obtain a personal contract badge and a physical to prove you don't have any bacteria, which can cause a health problem to the astronauts."

A beautiful dark-haired woman came to escort us into quarantine. She looked exotic, greeting us with an enticing smile. It was Nani, the food engineer.

Nani said, "Soon Dalton and the other astronauts would go into quarantine. They will stay in quarantine for ten days before the flight. It ensures the astronaut team shouldn't get sick."

I unexpectedly had an idea and asked Nani quietly, "I was wondering the possibility if I could help cook during the quarantine of the astronauts. I'm a pretty good cook, or I can be a number one bottle washer."

She hesitated and said, "Well, you have to have a physical first, but we do need help. Unfortunately, we don't have enough hands and feet to help with the money shortage from the political situation. Susan, you are famous in your own right and have aerospace experience, which gives you the expertise to do this mission. I'll tell you what I'll do. I'm going to make a formal request later today to obtain permission for you to join the quarantine team."

I said as I hung up the phone, "Thank you so much for making the request. Please don't tell Dalton. I want it to be a surprise. Talk to you later. Goodbye."

"I will call you later and let you know," Nani responded and walked away.

The following day, Nani called, "We are bending the rules, but you can go into quarantine with Dalton and the other astronauts. Bring enough clothes for a month because you will be there for the duration. The dormitory has beds, but you cannot cohabitate with Dalton, even though you are married. The food engineers will cook for the astronauts, but you can help. I hope you like having hot sandwiches made of Italian pesto chicken on brochette. I need to know if you are lactose intolerant or have any allergies. We can change the recipes if you have any requests."

I said, "Oh, you don't have to go through any trouble for me, but I am allergic to lettuce."

"It's no trouble at all, no lettuce for you. We perfect the recipe, even if it means going back and forth multiple times to the grocery store. It is our philosophy. We have quirky thermal stabilized items such as radiated items, beef, fish, or depending on what you want to cook."

"That sounds appealing," I said.

"Yes, it does as long as you put enough acid into it. It really won't matter. We vacuum-packed tuna in a thermos with tomato sauce in the space industry for two years. Still, the government regulations in grocery stores will last forever. The rules are more stringent in space than for the food industry."

"What food is everyone's favorite?" I asked.

Nani said, "Everyone likes the shrimp cocktail. It's spicy and keeps the taste buds alive in space."

"Sounds great; I want to eat everything. It all looks good." I said.

Nani laughed, "Look at me. I did taste everything, and I put on the pounds. It's a downside to the best job in the world, wonderful delectable foods. Let's hear what you can cook."

"Just plain ole' country cooking; my Mom taught me how to cook the country way," I said.

"I want you to know this is not normal practice. It should be fascinating for everyone involved; I mean everyone." Nani said.

"I can't tell you how excited I am. Thanks for letting me participate." I said.

When I got to the quarantine area, everyone was ready for entertainment, eating, and cooking. The rooms had computers and television, for an astronaut's desire. It was a vacation away from a vacationland. The room had offices that contained computers, printers, and telephones. Oh, I thought the purpose of quarantine was to prevent the spread of contamination and for entertainment. No one would want to flee this scene. It reminded me of a college dorm with the best technical equipment ever.

All the astronauts entered the room, and I was in awe of their presence.

A beautiful blonde-haired woman came up behind me and beelined toward my husband. I recognized her. She was Astronaut Kati-Linda, a Mission Specialist with a notorious reputation for trapping men. It certainly was a dichotomy with her high rank as an Airforce Colonel. I guess it was okay for men, but it felt funny knowing this about a woman colonel. The astronauts began speaking in a language I didn't understand. Their aerospace terminology was beyond my comprehension. I didn't have the education and background of either military or astronaut training.

Kati-Linda said, "Dalton, I've heard so much about you. I want you to know I'm a fan of yours."

Dalton responded, "Well, thank you, but I've heard about you and the testing you have done on the F-16 fighter jets."

She answered, "Yes, it is the first of the US Air Force multi-role fighter aircraft. It is the world's most prolific fighter and able to withstand higher g-forces than the pilots. What a rush. I just love the adrenalin of flying."

Dalton looked at her with his cute smile, "Yes, that's why they called it the Fighting Falcon made by Lockheed Martin."

"Yes, it is," Kati-Linda said.

I could have sworn she was flirting with my husband. It made me feel very uneasy. This incident confirmed I was supposed to be here during his quarantine.

Unfortunately, my old trust record began playing about questions I didn't want to repeat. It's like a broken record. Can I trust my husband? Just because you are married doesn't mean they are going to be true. My stomach felt sick, but I couldn't let on that this was bothering me. I needed to divert my energy into cooking.

I walked into the kitchen, and there stood a beautiful, exotic Nani. I said, "Can I help you?"

"Of course, you can. I want to find out your specialty. What would you like to cook? I will go shopping for organic foods and prepare them whenever possible. Also, I have a list of astronauts' allergies.

"Dr. Greg, or should I say as we call him Humongous Greg, has a garlic allergy, so we can't cook anything with garlic," Nani explained.

"I started laughing. I've seen Greg, and he is not large. He has an incredible physique and a beautiful smile, which would charm your Mother. How absurd that sounds, Humongous Greg." I said.

At that moment, Dr. Greg walked through the door. I couldn't help myself. I laughed so hard that I doubled up. When the door swung back, I saw Dalton and Kati-Linda deep in conversation. My laughter stopped, and my heart sank.

Dr. Greg was watching my face and said, "Where did the big smile go? I want to reintroduce myself. My name is Greg, Humongous Greg, but you can call me Greg."

He started laughing and said. "I know what everyone says behind my back. Let's have a drink. I need something to quench my thirst."

I didn't realize it, but behind me was a full bar. "Let's do have a drink. I want a gin and tonic. I wonder if we have limes." I inquired.

Dr. Greg looked in the refrigerator and pulled out a lime. "Well, my lady, I can make you your drink of choice."

He made me a gin and tonic. Then, he pulled a Shiner Bock

from the refrigerator.

"I can see you are a real cowboy. Of course, only a cowboy would drink a beer made in Shiner, Texas." I teased.

"Of course, I'm a cowboy. I went to Hook'em Horns: The University of Texas." He said as he raised his index fingers, and little fingers were bending over. He reminded me of a bull, a giant bull, that is.

"Now, I know why they call you humongous Greg." I laughed, "You are just larger than life, and everything is bigger in Texas, or should I say humongous."

He was just adorable, and his laughter was contagious. I found myself forgetting my insecurities and just having fun. Quarantine isn't so bad. I had heard quarantine at KSC is even better.

I sipped my gin and tonic, feeling very comfortable with Payload Specialist Dr. Greg. He was going to fly the bird. The lines of the Shuttle are magnificent. I had the image sketched onto my brain. So, I said, "Greg, please tell me about yourself. How did you become an astronaut and a physician?"

"It is my first spaceflight in real life. In my dreams, I've been to the moon many times, flying high above the earth. I've logged 3,200 hours in 41 different aircraft. Flying is my game. When I was young, my Mom always knew where to find me. She could find me in an imaginary plane my Dad and I had put together. My outfit consisted of broken sunglasses used as goggles, my Dad's big muffed hat, and overalls. With my outfit, I was ready to fly. It led me to study geography in detail. I wanted to know about all the obsessive little flyboys." Greg explained.

"You have an impressive flying time, little flyboy. Well, what made you want to become an astronaut? I inquired.

"My first word as a baby wasn't Mama nor Dah, but *a plane*. I was obsessed with planes. I would point to the skies. You know I still am. It's what I do. Flying on the Shuttle will be the ultimate rush. I wanted to be the best professional space traveler in the world, who is an astronaut, pilot, and physician." He showed me how he pointed like a child to the skies.

"Funny, that's what I called Dalton earlier. He is a

professional space traveler. I even wanted to be a pilot. Greg, everyone dreams of flying, whether it is a plane or makes-believe wings. I've always enjoyed being near planes. My Dad took me as a child to the airports. I was in a bi-plane as a two-year-old. I thought I could walk with the angels surrounded by the fluffy clouds. I felt closest to God up in the clouds." I explained.

"I know how you feel; I experience that each time I get behind the yoke. It is incredible. I am blessed. I figured I needed to become a physician, so if I ever crashed, I could fix myself." He smiled with a satisfied look and slowly walked out of the kitchen. "Catch you later."

Nani and I watched Humongous Greg leave the kitchen. Nani said, "That's the most I have heard him talk since we met."

I turned to Nani and said, "He's incredible. Now, how can I help you?"

"Yes, you can. I'm going to make a casserole, strawberry shortcake, and salad with fresh bread. Please begin making the salad. I will start on the casserole. After that, I will make a homemade chicken pot pie." She said.

I smiled and began combining spinach, tomatoes, boiled eggs, avocado, green onions, and mushrooms. Thoughts came into my mind about the surreal environment. A warm feeling came over me. Here I am with my man, sending him into space — the most dangerous zero-gravity environment.

The astronaut quarantine was full of life and anticipation for the upcoming flight. Everyone was preparing for the astronauts' last meals before takeoff. There was a special bonding between some strangers and friends getting ready to have their last meal.

Dalton was joining the crew this time, and he would be risking his life to perform the MECS Experiment on the King of Sweden. The King hadn't arrived yet. Everyone was excited to meet royalty. I've always thought the astronauts portrayed themselves as Kings and Queens; however, he's a real King this time. The King of Sweden made a pass to a married woman, me. Suddenly, I wanted to get some fresh air but could not leave the area.

I decided to go into a vacant room, looking for a place to be alone. There was a comfortable chair waiting for me. I was ready to perch when, out of nowhere, the King appeared.

The King joyfully said, "Here is the newlywed, Mrs. Masters."

Blushing, I said, "Well, this is a surprise."

He countered, "I wouldn't want to miss our last dinner before takeoff. I hear they prepare everyone's favorite food. What is your favorite food?"

"Well, you know they didn't ask me, but if they had, I would have requested grits and eggs," I said.

He made a face and said, "What are grits?"

The ridiculous look on his face made me laugh. I said, "You know I'm a southern girl, and, in the south, we serve white hominy grits made from corn. It's perfect for you, and it has iron and B vitamins." I laughed, "It may stick to the roof of your mouth."

"Well, I'll have to try it someday. It sounds delicious and gooey. I know you are just the person who will introduce me to southern cuisine." He said merrily.

We sat down on the swing, and I asked, "How was your stay at the Russia Uri Gagarin Russian State Science Research Cosmonaut Training Center?"

"It was interesting. The Russians have very stringent Russian rules, but one rule is different from NASA's. They indulge in lots of vodkas. On top of that, Russian women are beautiful. What a deadly combination. Nevertheless, of course, you are far superior in looks compared to Russian women. I hear they have their stash of vodka on the Space Station. Over and over again, they told me that their collaboration with the international partners would help humankind to solve the problems of mastering space." He said.

I retorted, "The space partners' participation in space is the future of Earth's civilization."

"I know it is the future of my existence. If Dalton's experiment is successful, I will live a long and fulfilled life. If not, they say I will die in 2 months. The cancer is spreading very rapidly. In a way, this is my last payload. Dalton is the key to my mortality." The King said solemnly.

Dalton walked up to the swing and gave his contagious laugh. "How are you doing, King? I didn't know you had arrived. It is a pleasure meeting you again."

The King stood up and shook Dalton's hand.

"The pleasure is all mine. What an exciting environment." The King said, looking directly at me.

Dalton noticed. He cleared his throat and said, "Susan, I would like your assistance."

I immediately got up and made my way inside. I said to Dalton when we entered, "The King makes me feel uncomfortable."

Dalton retorted, "Susan, you are a beautiful woman, and men will always admire you for your beauty and your intelligence. So don't let him bother you. He is the key for me to go into space."

I kissed Dalton, "I will try to ignore his stares and innuendos."

In the background, I heard the kitchen bell. I said, "It's time to eat, and I'm hungry."

We walked into the dining room hand in hand. This time, we had servers. I was in the presence of all the astronauts. It was such an honor.

Everyone was busy talking with Commander Mike West. He was a tall man with dark hair who was very serious. We sat down next to him.

The Commander cleared his throat and made an announcement, "I want to thank everyone for being a part of the national human-crewed space flight. We are going to perform one of the most important MECS payloads ever at the Space Station. We have a most honored guest, King Karl Àsgeirr XIII, who is here to join us. Along with the King, we have a Nobel Prize winner in Medicine, Dr. Dalton Masters. It is an opportunity in a lifetime. I'm very proud to be entering space with some of the best astronauts in the world. We've trained together at the NBL, Space Crew Equipment (SCE), Ultra Vehicular Activity (UVA), and the Johnson Space Center and Kennedy Space Center simulations. We are ready to fulfill our mission. Let us take the time to pray."

I looked around and saw tears forming in some of the astronaut's eyes.

Commander Mike West cleared his voice and began to speak slowly and deliberately, "Thank you for blessing us on Earth and in Space. Please, dear Lord, protect us while we are away. Give them the comfort of knowing we are in your hands on both Heaven and Earth. The food laid before us is a banquet, and we are truly blessed to eat this food in your name. Dear Lord, give us guidance and direction during the STS-995 Mission. Please provide us with a safe return in your name. Amen."

Everyone said in unison, "Amen."

We began eating as joy illuminated the room. Families were so happy to be together. I wanted to be along with Dalton but knew this, indeed, was an aeronautical family. All their support was with them.

I knew what he was saying. I said, "Goodnight, this was a wonderful dinner." Dalton walked me to my room. It was very lonely in the empty room. I missed his arms holding me through the night. It was going to be a very long 11 days of isolation until launch. I sat in my room all alone, thinking about Dalton. I didn't want Dalton to go into space. I didn't feel comfortable about him going into Space. Maybe I had a suspicion or just a woman's gut feeling. The audit left me feeling uneasy. Ironically, I had formulated the MECS formula. After the failure last time, NASA put more controls and procedures on the entire MECS process. It's a privately owned experiment, but they had the power to manage the formulation of the formula. You could say, their way or the highway. I hope that their extra controls will make a difference.

*I thought about why NASA had developed the Quarantine phase. It was a safety step to ensure the astronauts didn't get any diseases before going into space. Nothing would be more miserable than to be sick in space. Not to say it hadn't happened, but the astronauts would have to live through their misery.*

Quarantine in the past received terrible press. When the Apollo program took place, NASA biologists, geologists, and engineers had different views. You should say that the engineers didn't want to take the time and money to perform all the expensive quarantine processes.

I remembered moon dirt certainly got into the Apollo spacecraft. Astronaut Buzz Aldrin emptied a bunch of moon dirt from his shoes at Kennedy Space Center. Photographers had moon dust all over themselves from the cameras. If there had been any microorganisms, they could have infested the Earth and destroyed humankind. If extraterrestrial life existed, no one would ever know it. NASA drastically reduced the geologists' limited funds because of the limited infectious organisms identified.

NASA was sloppy and didn't put any controls or plans in place. As a result, they could spend an enormous amount of taxpayers' money on international welfare.

The only positive discovery from moon dust is that plants grew more significantly in the lunar soil.

Instead of NASA capitalizing on breaking down the moon dust into a fertilizer formula, NASA didn'thing. Farmers were willing to pay good money to produce a superior plant using lunar fertilizer.

NASA's reaction didn't make sense. Now, we are not developing a Moon Base, which could possibly end international famine and hunger. China is currently building a Moon Base. Thus, America is losing the Space Race. All of this didn't make sense. My head began hurting. Soon, I had a horrific headache and needed sleep.

## Chapter 45 –Launch


Today was the day the astronauts would be going out to the launch pad. It would live on this magnificent Earth be a night launch, which I thought was the most beautiful launch in the world. The following contrail lit up the whole sky. I thought to view the Launchpad, "Everyone is an Astronaut, which is positioned laterally with the Universe. We travel through days to find splendid beauty throughout the world. I wanted to join them."

The astronauts were already in the Space Shuttle. Astronauts Payload Specialist Dr. Dalton, Payload Specialist/Physician Dr. Greg, the King/the payload, Mission Specialist Kati-Linda, and Commander Mike West. They were strapped into the rocket with tons of explosives to send them into space. However, they felt weighed down by their suits. With gravity, they could barely move.

Dalton said, "I can't wait to get weightless."

"Me too," said Greg.

The mission closeout team would complete their closeout preparations in the launch pad's White Room.

Dalton began checking out the cockpit switch configurations. Then, he began performing the air-to-ground voice checks with Launch Control and Mission Control.

Dalton commanded the mission technician, "Rene' check the orbiter's crew hatch and check for any leaks."

Rene' answered, "No leaks, Dr. Dalton. I will complete the White Room close-out and retreat to the fallback area."

Over the radio, they heard "T-20 minutes and holding." The NASA Test Director conducted the final launch team briefings and completed the inertial measurement unit preflight alignments.

You could feel the excitement and adrenalin as the proficient teams worked like a well-greased machine. I watched the transition of the orbiter's onboard computers to launch configuration. I heard the following commands, "T-15 minutes and counting. Start the fuel cell thermal conditions, close orbiter cabin vent valves, and transition backup flight system to launch configuration."

Chills ran up and down my body. I never thought I would be in the Launch Control room. Again, life had taken me to places I never thought possible. I silently said a prayer, "God, please keep my Dalton and the crew safe, Godspeed."

I didn't know I was holding my breath when Ken came over and said, "Breath." Then, I heard "T-9 minutes and holding."

At that point, I knew it was only a matter of seconds before takeoff. I knew it was the final built-in hold, and the great minds were figuring out the final launch window determination.

She heard, "Activate flight recorders."

I heard the response, "Flight recorders activated."

The final go/no-go launch poll decisions were made by the NASA Test Director, Mission Management Team, and Launch Director.

The commands blasted into my ear, "Start automatic ground launch sequencer." A few seconds elapsed, and she heard, "T-7 minutes, 30 seconds, retract orbiter access arm; the T-5 minutes, 0 seconds, start auxiliary power units."

I wanted to close her eyes. The tension is too much.

I heard, "T-5 minutes – 0 seconds, arm solid rocket booster range safety safe and arm devices."

My hair on her arms tingled, "Please keep Dalton safe."

Another command sounded, "T-3 minutes, 55 seconds, start orbiter aero surface profile test, and do the main engine gimbal profile test."

Then, "It's T-2 minutes, 55 seconds, retracts gaseous oxygen vent arm or beanie cap."

Closer the countdown, "T-2 minutes, zero seconds, crew members close and lock your visors."

I wish Dalton didn't go on the flight. I didn't want him to go. The sinking feeling was weighing me down, which had me in a quandary. I knew Dalton's life's dream was coming true, but he was my Dalton. I had always heard that if you let someone go, they will return. He had to return.

Then, "T-50 seconds, orbiter transfers from the ground to internal power." Dalton had control. It was up to them.

Another command, "T-31 seconds, ground launch sequencer, is going for auto sequence start."

Nothing or no one could stop the Space Shuttle now; they had passed the time of no return.

Then, "T-16 seconds, activate launch pad sound suppression system."

Another command, "T-10 seconds, activate the main engine hydrogen burn-off system."

Now, "T-6.6 seconds, the main engine starts."

The NASA Test Director said, "We have a takeoff."

Everyone shouted with happiness and the thrill of a successful takeoff. The astronauts were on their way to the International Space Station.

I was the only one that had tears running down my face. I was so afraid that the approval of the red dots was a problem for the flight. I didn't understand why. Now, it was too late.

## Chapter 44–Docking


The Space Shuttle finally docked with the International Space Station at 1051 CST to deliver the King's payload. Also, it had 14 tons of cargo, which is essential for the orbiting laboratory's continued operations.

Commander Mike West guided the orbiter to a docking with a pressurized mating adaptor on the station's Harmony node. The two spacecraft were flying 220 miles above Earth between Australia and Tasmania. Before docking, when the orbiter reached a range of 600 feet from the station, Atlantis performed the nine-minute Rendezvous Pitch Maneuver, or "backflip."

West said, "Okay, guys, we are going into a backflip to have our pictures made." West rotated the orbiter backward, enabling Onboard Space Station Astronauts Chris and Nancy to take high-resolution pictures of the shuttle heat shield.

Chris asked Nancy, "Please send the images to the ground experts and managers to assess images of the health of the thermal protection system tiles."

Nancy sweetly smiled, "Sure will, Chris, only if you will play your guitar tonight and sing for us."

Afterward, they opened the shuttle and station hatches and received the new crew aboard the space station. As the hatch opened began, a big welcome aboard party. They celebrated Nancy's tenure as an Expedition 21 flight engineer.

Dalton asked, "Nancy, how does it feel to be the last station crew member to return to Earth on the Space Shuttle?"

Nancy stated, "It feels sad. I'm just so upset that the Soyuz spacecraft will soon fly for future station crew launches and landings. It's a sad day for America."

Kati-Linda, the shuttle Mission Specialist, removed the MECS payload bay and handed it off from the shuttle robotic arm to the robotic station arm. Then, Dalton and Greg relocated their spacesuits for their planned spacewalk to perform an update of the MECS capsule.

They reviewed the plan for tomorrow's spacewalk. Payload

Specialist Dr. Greg heard a noise at the POD Bay Door.

He asked, "Dalton, did you hear something? Someone's outside trying to get inside the Space Station."

Then again, a faint knocking sound was at the door. Dalton's hair came up on the back of his head.

Dalton responded, "No one is out there."

Dalton thought Greg was having space hallucinations. It's not good.

"I heard a noise; someone must be out there. We need to open the door and let them in now. They may die being on the dark side, away from the sun."

Greg issued a command in a stern voice, "Open the door now, Dalton."

Dalton said, "Don't be ridiculous; you must be getting space hallucinations. It's probably a piece of debris, possibly a tiny rock or piece of metal. Unfortunately, debris could pierce the outside of the space station or cause a hole big enough to destroy the space station. We can't open the door, or the space debris will come into our holding area, and we will die without oxygen."

Suddenly, Greg realized how ridiculous he sounded and said, "Dalton, let's install the reflective shield for the MECS capsule. We can add it when we perform the spacewalk to check out the MECS capsule."

Dalton said, "I will discuss it with the mission manager, Kati-Linda, to get permission. I think it is a great idea."

The noise mysteriously stopped. Subsequently, the atmosphere began to lighten up.

Greg got some MMs and water and gave some to Dalton, "Let's try to spin water."

Dalton laughed, "Of course, I don't know the first thing about doing that trick."

"We'll let me show you," Greg said as he took a gulp of water and let the water swirl before him, using his finger as a pivot.

Dalton mimicked Greg as I watched.

I couldn't help but tease the guys, "I think you have a water fountain. Pretend you are at Trevi Fountain in Rome and make a wish that your life will always be wonderful."

Dalton rebuffed, "How can I work on perfection? We have a perfect life together. Greg should be so lucky."

Greg said, "Ugh, you are making me sick."

His Majesty said, "I heard what you said, and I agree you do have a beautiful wife; she is perfect. I have a wish, but I'm not going to tell anyone."

I was so glad they didn't televise this segment. The King's voice made me feel uncomfortable. I turned in embarrassment. I know everyone in the room saw me blush. I couldn't wait until Dalton and our life was back to normal.

Both men floated as they gulped the water at the same time, which concluded their show.

Over to the side, I noticed Kati-Linda watching the display of male competition. She was laughing at their playfulness. Finally, she brought out a bunch of M&Ms." "You guys want to play. Just watch me."

She threw up two M&Ms and seductively caught them with her tongue. She playfully used her lips to bring them into her mouth. Her beautiful dark auburn hair floated in the air, surrounding her face like a picture in a frame. I almost died. She is so sexy. I thought the guys' mouths would catch her M&Ms themselves. Instead, their tongues were wagging, and their mouths dropped, which I thought was impossible in zero-gravity.

I saw for the first time Greg looking long and hard at Kati.

She looked at her audience and smirked sassily, "Can you top that?"

Greg immediately answered like a high school kid, "Oh, I can watch you all day. You are talented. Dalton, now I know my wish."

Kati-Linda said playfully, "And what would that be?"

Greg floated over to her and kissed her on the cheek.

Unexpectedly, they held hands, floating in space, looking deep into each other eyes.

I thought, but he didn't say a thing, "Could this be the first romance started in space? I doubt it."

King Ásgeirr said unexpectedly, "I'm exhausted. I'm going to lie down."

I felt sorry for him; I knew his face looked weary and drawn out.  Cancer must be taking a toll on his body.

The King placed a Velcro pillow, attaching it under his head.  Funny, Velcro's use for space is that the Space Shuttle seats wouldn't fly away in zero-gravity.  Some astronauts need the comfort of home, using a pillow with Velcro.  The pillow provides that need even though it does not support their heads.

The King suddenly turned and said, "Good Night, Susan.  I hope you sleep well tonight."  Then, he entered his floating bunk bed quarters located in the crew quarters.

Dalton said, making a face.  I guess the King gets the royal treatment since there are only four bunk beds.  I think I'll just get a sleeping bag and attach myself to the wall."

I watched as he pulled himself into the sleeping bag.  I began to laugh.  I knew he was listening.

He looked and said, "Goodnight, sweet Susan.  Please get some rest so we can begin the experiment upon your arrival first thing in the morning.  Sweet dreams.  Nighty Night Sailboat.

"Remember, you are the center of my universe, even in space:  I'm patiently waiting to come home to our world.  Goodnight, my sweetheart, Nighty Night Sailboat."  I said back, remembering buying a wonderful children's book in the Bahamas with that name.

I turned and told everyone, "Be here early and ready to work tomorrow.  I suggest everyone get a good night's rest; I will see you at 0600 sharp."

Everyone said, "Nighty Night Sailboat."

As I walked out of the building, I wished I could be in space with Dalton and feel zero-gravity again, not for 30 seconds.  I knew in space, there is no up and down since there is no gravity.  I wanted to explore the sensation of weightlessness.

The navy-blue car was waiting for me.  The driver asked, "Where can I take you?"

I answered, "I am going back to the Astronaut's cottage.  Alone, this time, my stay is with the Astronaut's family.  I feel so special to meet the spouses and learn about their family members in space."

Internally, I thought, "Just like me, my spouse is high above.  Space is a mystery, and my Dalton is solving the mystery of cancer."

I went to the cottage, and it seemed everyone was retired for the evening. It was my bedtime, but I couldn't sleep. The porch looked inviting as I walked outside, remembering the times Dalton and I shared at the cottage: our lovemaking, my struggles with self-doubt, and internal conflicts.

Now, ironically, the person who caused most of my current insecurities has been released from prison. Leona is somewhere out there. This revelation gave me chills. Previously, I had some comfort knowing she could not get into Kennedy Space Center even though she knew all the security rules and regulations. I wondered if she could sneak through the gates or even come by sea.

I had to stop thinking of Leona. The authorities would apprehend her and lock her back up, hopefully forever. It is where she belongs in the criminally insane facility for life. I still don't believe in mind control. Especially if her grandfather invented mind control and inserted the long development device into the twenty-first century, it is just unbelievable.

I walked outside, looking at the beautiful stars. They twinkled in the sky, brightening my heart. I knew Dalton was sleeping with the constellations, which traveled faster than any plane on Earth.

I walked back in and heard a noise in the kitchen. I froze. I was the only person awake in the Astronaut's cottage. I thought everyone else was asleep or had gone into town. Maybe someone had returned.

Did I dare go into the kitchen? How I wished Dalton was with me. His protection is what I need right now. I peeked around the corner and saw a blond-headed woman standing in the kitchen. She looked like Leona. Was it Leona? I froze in my tracks. Sweat beaded from my forehead into my mouth.

I backed up, and the lady turned around, seeing me. It was Mike West, the Commander's wife, Loretta, getting a cup of tea.

She said, "Would you like to join me?

I took a deep breath and said, "Sure."

I sat at the kitchen table, and she handed me a cup of tea.

Politely, she inquired, "What would you like in your tea? You know chamomile tea will help us sleep."

"Please, just stevia," I said.

She looked frail and thin. Her hands were shaking, and she started crying. Her outburst of emotion caught me by surprise.

She said between sobs. "It is challenging to have my husband so far away with danger at every corner."

I said, "You have to remember everyone is trained to know his or her job comprehensively. NASA has taken every safety precaution possible. I want to be in space, myself." I smiled, trying to elevate her fears.

"I understand, but this time, I have an ominous feeling about the mission. I don't know if you believe it, but I have extrasensory perception and dreams." She said sadly.

I seemed puzzled by Loretta, whom I had never met, "We all have fears, but we can't let the fear get the best of us," I said.

"Mark my word." She said, "Someone will die in space again. I feel it, but I don't know whom. If we can figure out whom, we could prevent another unnecessary death. But, believe me, whoever it is, they don't have to die."

I wanted to run away and hide in the bedroom under the covers. I didn't need this conversation. The Commander's wife must be crazy. I drank tea as fast as I could.

I said, "Well, it must work because I can't keep my eyes open."

She gave a crooked smile and said, "Goodnight and sweet dreams, Nighty, Night."

I quickly turned and went straight to bed, but I didn't have sweet dreams. Instead, I dreamed of death on the Space Station. Leona ran in and out of my dreams with her maniac, crazy laughter, and threats of killing Dalton and me.

## Chapter 45–Mission

Tossing and turning all night long, I welcomed daylight. The alarm went off, and I turned it off as soon as possible. I jumped out of bed and dressed. I had a quick breakfast and walked onto the porch, where the navy-blue car was waiting for me.

I opened the door and asked, "Take me to the Mission Control Center."

As I walked into the room, I heard the astronauts' wake-up song, "Good Morning Starshine," on the loudspeakers" Oliver. The music brought a smile to everyone. How true are the words? The earth says hello. There was my Dalton eating his breakfast with a straw, sipping his eggs, grits, and sausage from the same container. It sounded disgusting, but he enjoyed his breakfast. He looked up, saw me, and said, "Good Morning, Sunshine."

I smiled and said, "Hope you enjoyed your zero-gravity sleep. I know your bones certainly won't hurt you. No weight on your body. It must be nice."

Dalton said, "It has its benefits, but I'd rather be sleeping with gravity. I think it takes time to acclimate to close quarters. You certainly can't be anti-social or claustrophobic."

I kiddingly said, "Don't talk while you are eating. I wouldn't like you to get sick and choke to death. The pepsin in your stomach would make you miserable. Anyway, it would be difficult to do the Heimlich maneuver without gravity."

Dalton finished his meal when the King entered, "Good morning, Susan. You should have had my view in the crew cabin. I could see all the stars. If engineers built NASA spaceships at a reasonable cost, civilians could fly into space. I might see the same."

Dalton interjected, seeing the King reaching for a cup of coffee. Dalton said, "Please don't eat or drink anything until after the MECS procedures. It will be a couple of hours to begin since Dr. Greg and I will perform a spacewalk to inspect the MECS capsule and install a reflector. So, we shouldn't be too long."

The King didn't look too happy but said, "Well, you boys get suited up and get to work."

Dalton and Greg began the tedious process of putting on the Extravehicular white suits. Greg had stripes around the legs of his suit, and Dalton's suit had no stripes. It is a visual identification method.

Inside the Station, the crewmembers powered up the Robotic workstation inside of Destiny, checking connections made by the spacewalkers.

The Space Station cabin pressure matched the spacewalk's atmosphere. The hatch opening allowed Dalton and Greg to float out of the space station. They checked the MECS capsule connections for debris repair and installation of the capsule debris reflector.

I watched while they diligently worked on the repairs and installation of the MECS module 238 miles over the Atlantic Ocean.

Without an indication, suddenly, Dalton's vital signs started going off the charts. Something was wrong. His breathing was labored and intermittent. He was gasping for air and the need for new oxygen. My heart stopped. What was going on? He was in distress. His hands quickly moved to his chest, realizing he had to conserve his breath. Desperately, he looked around for options.

Commander Mike West said in a firm voice, "Dalton, can you tell me what is happening?"

Dalton said in a raspy voice, "My oxygen."

Commander West commanded, "Don't speak, and make your way back to the Space Station immediately."

Astronaut Greg said, "I will escort him."

My heart stopped. What's happening? It had never occurred during a spacewalk. Dalton seems disoriented.

Greg led Dalton's by his hand back to the Space Station. Greg opened the hatch and guided Dalton into the chamber. They had to wait for the pressure to equalize before entering the ship. Dalton's body functions were distressed. He was still getting some oxygen, but not enough for regular breathing.

It was almost like someone had tampered with the oxygen intake. But at least Dalton was in the pressurized cabin waiting for equalization.

Finally, they got the go to take off the space helmets. Greg took Dalton's helmet first. Dalton's face was gray-blue as he gasped for breath. Finally, Dalton took a deep breath of oxygen, and his coloring started changing to normal.

My eyes filled with joy, seeing that he could breathe again. I wondered what caused this condition, but I knew he wouldn't have to do another spacewalk.

Houston Mission Control came over the intercom and said, "Astronaut Masters, vital signs are back to normal. He is not in distress. His oxygen levels are at the standard composition. The next shuttle status report is in two hours."

Dalton went inside ISS. Commander West said, "Dalton, rest until you feel better. The MECS Experiment will not be performed today but will be tomorrow."

Dalton argued, "I'm okay. I have to start the experiment today, or else we will not have time to complete all the steps."

Commander West said, "Take two hours to eat and rest, get composed, and start the MECS Experiment. If I see any signs of oxygen cyanosis, I will go directly to your sleep quarters with an oxygen mask. Then, Kati-Linda, perform the risk assessment of Dalton's air pack to see why it malfunctioned."

Kati-Linda said, "I will begin immediately."

Greg said, "Yeah, let's eat Dalton since our suits already smell like steaks, and it's beginning to make me hungry."

The King said, "I'll have my steak medium-rare." Everyone laughed.

# Chapter 46 – King's MECS Experiment

The King floated back and forth anxiously in the Space Station biomedical pod.

He thought, "Dalton will perform the MECS experiment, and I don't know anything about the formula. How will it affect my body? I have to ask him some questions."

When Dalton was rested and ate, he returned to the biomedical pod with Greg.

The King almost pounced on Dalton when he entered the pod. "I have some questions before I get into the capsule."

Dalton responded, "Go ahead and ask away."

The King asked, "How are capsules formed?"

Dalton said, "Okay, do you want the short answer or the long?"

The King answered, "I want the long answer."

Dalton took a deep breath and said, "The formation of multi-layered microcapsules, about the size of a red blood cell, will combine the two liquids. One uses water as the solvent and another secret liquid. When I bring both liquids together, they become low unmixable conditions. The contact with the opposing unmixable solvent causes some dissolved polymer to come out of the solution. Then, they form a composite polymer film. The unmixable liquids will form stratified layers in Earth's gravity, with the densest solution on the bottom and the least dense solution on top. Thus, the polymer skin forms a planar sheet at the interface between the two liquids. Hence, the polymer membrane traps neither liquid. However, in microgravity, there are no sedimentation or buoyancy forces. Thus, surface tension causes each immiscible liquid to pull back from the other liquid, forming liquid spheres. Simultaneously, in the presence of certain surfactants, the polymer membrane forms especially coat the aqueous liquid sphere, thus forming a liquid-filled micro balloon (microcapsule). When the aqueous polymer solution contains dissolved drugs or proteins, the resulting microcapsules entrap those dissolved molecules as part of the liquid sphere within the polymer membrane. Does that answer your question?"

The King said, "Enough already. You are confusing my mind. I guess we should start the experiment that will save my life."

Dalton said, opening the capsule while Greg helped the frail King into a lying position, "Well, that is the plan."

I was surprised to see the King's skin color had become yellow and grey. He looked jaundiced and not well at all. He was declining at a swift pace.

# Chapter 47 –Payload Begins

Susan contacted MECS's team, David, Patty, and Connie, on a direct line to a Houston JSC conference phone, "Have you set up the application for the payload MECS data?"

Patty said, "Connie is testing the application with dummy data."

Connie piped in and said, "It is working just like it did last time you did it perfectly. We are ready as soon as King Karl Ásgeirr is ready."

Dr. Greg Humongous appeared to look as confident as always. He floated around the white sterile laboratory, looking at the equipment.

"Dr. Masters," Greg stated, "When you begin the MECS procedure, I would like to monitor your performance on the implementation plan."

Dalton said, "Sure, Greg, please monitor step-by-step the implementation plan. Let's get this show on the road. First, I'll insert the catheter into the subclavian artery below his sternum while the King is in the capsule."

The King winced as Dalton inserted the catheter. After connecting the capsule and equipment, Dalton used the MECS syringe to introduce one cc of the crystallized solution into the catheter.

Dalton said, "After the next ten days, I'll sample your blood to monitor the progress. The capsule will substitute as a CT Scanner to visualize the size of your prostate tumor. Also, I'll measure your vital signs. Then, I'll calculate the results three times a day, 0700, 1400, and 2000, and downlink the results to Susan's team for analysis."

Greg said, "I must admit this capability is unbelievable. Do you have an estimate of when the MECS formula will reduce his tumor?"

Dalton explained, "If it is like last time, there should be an improvement each day like Astronaut Dan Fletcher. The numbers will be downlinked, showing the micro-crystals are ready for use to encapsulate the tumor. The weightlessness in the zero-gravity environment will promote the perfect shape of red blood cells. It will become a more efficient carrier to the target cancer site. The series of events triggered by the increase of pure oxygen attached to the capsule. The downlinking of data will be analyzed not only for the King's safety but to document a baseline of the results for future experiments."

Listening, I said, "This event will change humankind's healthcare services but also cancer research and the cost. It will possibly eliminate expensive cancer medicine and medical equipment. In ten days, the MECS will complete the cure. It's totally mind-boggling."

Dalton said, "Well, yes, it's possible. Unfortunately, the cancer business would be out of business."

Greg and Kati-Linda began engaging the connectors to the King's body to perform the baseline physical.

Dalton began recording the events with his PA voice recorder, "All of Astronaut King Karl Ásgeirr's XIII vital signs are normal."

He continued, "His medical diagnosis since take-off is the destruction of his white blood count from cancer. Therefore, we will begin his treatment in a systematic process using the MECS Payload Medical Operating Procedure at 1300."

I asked, "I am using the same program as last time. Is there any additional information you need for MECS data collection?"

"No, just that the information is accurate." Dalton requested.

"It will be accurate. I will have Connie and Patty graph the results, identifying any differences sorted by the categorization of his vital signs." I explained.

"That would work just fine," he said as he began sorting out the preliminary data.

I said, "Each time the data downlinks, I want a report by date and time. Please deliver the report to me promptly. Please print the report in poster size. I want to be able to glance at the King's information at any given moment. Dr. Greg, I'm sure you'll confirm these numbers as we go along."

Greg repeated, "I will confirm the numbers and downlink

the number after Kati-Linda has entered them."

Dalton said, "I will administer the drug delivery to the King."

# Chapter 48 – Payload Implementation

On day two, we watched the monitor as Dalton reconnected the wires to the transmitters.

Soon, Kati-Linda began downlinking the payload data from the Station. Next, she imported the data into the database, creating the nominal functions' base point from Day 1 of the MECS Experiment.

I observed Dalton carefully removing the crystallized medicine from the tubes. During the long journey in orbit, the precious drug had grown. He used a syringe to transfer the crystals with his steady hands.

He inserted the valuable medicine into the catheter. The King's forehead dripped with sweat as he grimaced.

Dalton, seeing his adverse reaction, asked, "Any problems, King?"

The King responded, "It feels so cold, like someone has put dry ice inside me. I can feel it freezing as it travels through my veins, heading toward my prostate. It amazes me how quickly the circulatory system operates. The sensation is intense, and it stings."

I sympathized with the King. Astronaut Fletcher had said the same response.

Patty printed off the updated MECS Program Report and gave it to me. I reviewed the vital signs. Dalton questioned The King again. "King, how do you feel?"

The King said, "Well, I feel uncomfortable, but it's a warm sensation throughout my body, tingly, just tingly. Actually, after the shock of coldness, I feel quite warm inside."

Dalton said, "Please prepare the data, categorizing the information by his primary functions."

Two hours later, Connie produced the graph, as I requested. Unfortunately, it demonstrated few vital signs. I looked at the MECS Program Report and emailed it to him.

Subsequently, Dalton analyzed all the graphs from the MECS Program Report. Again, he noticed a slight improvement but nothing notable to report.

Dalton was pleased with his first glance. He wondered if the numbers were showing improvement or were just a fluke, "I'm observing an improvement in the numbers, but this is just the beginning of the MECS project. I will keep you in the capsule for another two hours, allowing your body to rest in a controlled environment. Greg, please administer the antibiotics to prevent any rejection or infection from the catheter and drug. Greg, please go ahead. I'll observe the procedure."

Dalton grinned from ear to ear. "Your teams' MECS Program Report (MECSPR) helps me analyze the results at a glance. I'm so pleased with the second day of the experiment; only eight more days to go."

The following two hours passed very quickly. Finally, Dalton told The King, "It's time for you to get out of the capsule. It has been a total of four long hours, and I know you want to stretch your stiff legs and body."

Dr. Greg unhooked The King's electrical leads, except he didn't dare remove the catheter. It would remain in his body for the duration of the experiment. Finally, the King pulled himself out of the capsule. "I feel so much better. I can't put my finger on it, but I do. Maybe the zero-gravity environment is making me giddy, or maybe I got too much pure oxygen."

Dalton said, "Let me recheck your vital signs." He called out the numbers while Kati-Linda inputted the downlinked data.

I converted the numbers into the MECS Program Report. The report would be published nationally and internationally on news stations and newspapers everywhere in the world. Dalton had requested the report printed on poster-size paper.

When the report returned, the label said Day 2 – MECS Experiment.

Dalton analyzed the results from the baseline and updated the team, "There is a subtle difference in the King's white blood count. After the next treatment, we will do a CT scan and measure the tumor. The capsule's design performs a CT scan. For the record, gentlemen, the CT scan capsule's technology is patented and classified, so don't ask how it works. I'm just getting a little aggravated about the many inquisitions about the top-secret experiment."

Dalton sat back and observed me for a second, "You know, I don't know anymore. All I care about is the King's safety and the success of the MECS delivery system. If it fails, the Space Medical Exploration Program (SMEP) will be in jeopardy." Finally, he gave a big sigh and turned away from me, "All I care about is the King and the experiment."

He turned his back away from the screen. My questions reverberated in the tone of his voice, causing tenseness throughout the room. I could feel his agitation.

"Dalton." The King began talking, "I feel so wonderful. Finally, I'm beginning to feel normal. I feel like I'm King of the Hill."

The Payload staff laughed at full volume. I doubled up with laughter, causing tears to run down my cheeks. Everyone's laughter was uncontrollable from exhaustion and tension. It started from the first two days of the program's constant concentration.

"Now, it's time for a rest for everyone except Susan, David, Connie, and Patty."

I turned toward Dalton and, for a brief moment, stopped analyzing the MECS information. Then, he called, "Ladies and gentlemen, please listen."

"Here are the results of the past two days," he said professionally. "The King's vital signs demonstrate an improvement."

Everyone clapped with excitement.

"Could this be a good day, or do the vital signs change in space? How does the MECS work?" I inquired.

Dalton began explaining, "The answer to your questions is complicated. The King is in zero-gravity, and that does affect his body. The blood system is complicated in space. To pump blood through vessels, one must compensate for gravity by using numerous one-way check valves located in the veins in your body. These trap the blood with each beat of the heart. The entrapment allows the blood to travel back up to the heart. In zero-gravity, the one-way check valves don't work as efficiently as on Earth. The Venus side returns blood to the heart. It will be the location where I will insert the catheter below the subclavian vein. The vein will pump the crystals to the tumor surrounding the cancer.

In space, your body will respond the same as when your feet swell on Earth, but without gravity, fluid collects around the heart. It's almost an overload, but you can urinate to get rid of the water, resulting in changes to your blood volume to 88% compared to the amount it was at launch. Amazingly enough, your body adapts to space just like it adapts to cold weather; it gets a new reset point.

The oxygen attached to the capsule will trigger the micro-crystals to release the treatment from the catheter. Now that is how it works."

"Dalton, now I understand the importance of documenting any differences. I'll have Connie develop another application to generate controlled statistical analysis and build 88% capacity. It will provide configuration control, ensuring the accuracy of the numbers. It will show the minute differences in the King's vital signs." *I thought to myself, I will make Dalton proud.*

## Chapter 49 - Status

The tests showed significant changes rapidly. I had my team diligently transfer the numbers into the metrics database. The CT Scan prints of the prostate tumor recorded substantial progress.

The King displayed excellent spirits. His skin became less yellow, and the grey had gone away.

The King taunted her as he threw a Frisbee at Kati-Linda.

It floated directly above her head, and Kati-Linda jumped off the walls sideways, catching the Frisbee afterward and doing summersaults.

Her eyes crinkled, laughing, "I got it. I'm the first woman Frisbee Space Champion out of this world."

I silently wished I were playing Frisbee in space with my heroes. The public enjoyed watching the playfulness of the King. He won their hearts.

Daydreaming, I felt Dalton was genuinely the most interesting, sexy, and intelligent man I had ever met.

## Chapter 50- Payload Test

I saw the King staring directly at me. His eyes had a twinkle, and he looked like a new man. I turned away. His presence made me feel uncomfortable. How could he try to communicate with me through his eyes right in front of my husband? He had no shame.

On Day 5, another MECS Program Report was ready. Again, I couldn't believe my eyes. The results are incredible. Excitedly, I reported to Dalton, "I will uplink the report results. The numbers demonstrate substantial improvement!"

Dalton's eyes got huge, "I need to confirm the numbers and verify the accuracy of the report. So, I'll hold any comments until I complete the validation of the statistics."

The King drifted into the Payload Station room. I looked at his face, and he looked significantly healthier. His face looked relaxed, and it beamed with happiness that glowed throughout the Station. Not far behind him was Dalton. The two began throwing the Frisbee.

The King turned somersaults, smiling and making faces in front of the televised screen, "No pain, Dalton, no pain. I haven't felt this way in years. What do you have in that formula of yours?" I evaluated the King; his eyes didn't reflect any pain.

There was no sign of pain in his eyes; my thoughts were interrupted, "King, let's run another CT tomorrow morning and measure the tumor. I want to evaluate any changes."

Homogenous Greg commented, "I'm excited for the King, and he is acting like a new man." He said in his best Swedish accent and requested, "It is good to be the King." Everyone began laughing as Greg pretended to duel using a flight glove as a scepter.

The King said, "Yes, it is good to be the King, and I am the King." Then, he bowed down in front of the camera and gave everyone a wink.

Everyone laughed, and all the women swooned over the King except me. Dalton became serious, "Dr. Greg, please prepare more crystals for tomorrow morning and the King for the capsule tomorrow morning. I want to run another CT scan and the standard test of his vital signs. Please analyze the reports, which show a gradual improvement. It is the midway point of the experiment, and I want to re-examine the tumor's progress. I'm curious about improvements in his vital signs. Please perform an additional test of his hearing and vision. A full examination is in order at this time. So far, I'm thrilled with the MECS Experiment results."

"Dr. Greg, you are instrumental in the success. Thank you for all your assistance and competent work.

The King exclaimed, "The crystals have magic in them. I can feel them working.

# Chapter 51 –Payload Results

The following day, the King entered the capsule to commence the additional testing of his hearing and eyes using the CT Scan. His heart pounded with anticipation. He knew they would test his eyes first.

Dalton said, "The ophthalmology equipment is in the capsule. The eye chart is displayed on the glass portion of the capsule above your eyes. Stay perfectly still inside of the capsule. I'm going to use electronic control to turn on the eye chart. An eye cover moves over your left eye first, and then the chart illuminates on the glass cover of the capsule. I want to baseline your vision."

The King exclaimed, "Do you want me to begin at the bottom line?" He began reading, "e G A u R S T."

The cover concealed his right eye. Once again, he read the chart effortlessly and, like an auctioneer, "Little e, big G, big A, little u, big R, S, and T. Yes, I can see. Yes, I can."

Kati-Linda laughed in the background, "King, you are nothing but a showoff."

Dalton said, "No sign of cataracts, left eye is 20/20 vision. The right eye is 20/20. Vision is normal."

Quickly, Dalton commanded, "Let's execute the hearing test."

The King eagerly responded, "Not a problem."

Dalton said, "Let's get started. King, please position the headset on your ears. They attach to the side of the capsule. As I said before, the hearing test will be conducted in the capsule using the computer's signals. The King, raise your fingers on your right hand each time you hear a frequency. As a former military pilot, this should be an old hat for you. The advantage is the capsule acts as the perfect sound-free chamber. We can't even begin to duplicate this quality of hearing test on the Earth."

The King raised his fingers to Dalton when he first heard the tone. The King could hear the lowest frequencies. Dalton monitored the computer as the software proceeded through the audiology exam.

The King beamed, "I can tell you right now that my audible range is excellent. I hear all the tones. As soon as the King got out of the chamber, he began playing with Dalton's stethoscope, turned to Greg, and pretended he was playing a horn.

Both scolded him, taking the stethoscope from his ears; "You break the equipment; you'll have to pay for them."

The King said, "I can afford to replace it; I have lots of money."

I thought about how egotistical he was, but he was well. His PSA numbers were now normal. MECS healed the King.

He began being obnoxious and very arrogant, and I like this new behavior. He was no longer humble.

## Chapter 52 - Attack

That night, I tossed and turned, feeling restless and discontent. I felt clammy and feverous as sweat drenched my body. I couldn't sleep.

The frightening nightmares were now embedded in the back of my mind, replaying death and destruction. Unknown black shadows were following me, waiting at each corner; I turned in my dream. The black shadows were taunting me everywhere I went. Whether in my car, at my home, or even in the streets, the black forms loomed over me.

Were these forms friendly or sinister? I didn't know, but I felt off-balance all the time. I looked forward to Dalton coming back home, lying beside me with our arms intertwined. Maybe the black forms would disappear after the mission. I don't think I will ever let Dalton out of my sight.

Even though NASA is my protector, I still didn't feel safe. Something is wrong, deadly wrong. I felt it in my bones.

Voices kept telling me. *You need to go to the MECS Laboratory.*

I kept staring at the clock. The hands moved ever so slowly. The clock hands made a sound of a click, click, and click as if it was a pendulum swinging back and forth over my head. The noise was driving me crazy.

I got out of bed; I couldn't take it anymore as I paced around the astronaut's cottage. I tried to comfort myself with the familiarity and the fresh smell of the ocean breeze. It reminded me of the happy times we enjoyed the beautiful and quaint cottage. I enjoyed the porch surrounding the cottage with the swing. I sat down on the swing, rocking myself back and forth. Then, in the corner of my eye, I saw the black shadow staring at me. I quickly turned away but eventually looked back, where the ominous black shadow still watched me.

The words vibrated through my body, "You will die, and so will your loved ones."

I turned away a second time, but when I gazed back, the shadow was gone. It was gone just as fast as it appeared. I had to get away from the cottage with the sinister black shadows that lurked in the darkness. I immediately called NASA transportation. I had to see Dalton check his monitors. Could the black shadow be trying to warn me of what may come?

I called NASA transportation for a car to bring to the MECS Laboratory. I waited impatiently. Going to the lab would allow me the opportunity to ensure Dalton's safety, and I would feel safe at the NASA MECS laboratory. The MECS Laboratory is the place where I felt closest to Dalton.

When I arrived at the laboratory, the lights weren't on, and it was dark. No one was around when I turned on the fluorescent lights and inspected every corner. Everything seemed in order.

It would be some time before the rest of the crew would enter the building. The astronaut's wake-up call wouldn't be until 0600. I immediately performed a mini-audit using an existing checklist. I checked off each of the questions one at a time. First, I checked the monitors displayed the standard calibration, specifically the astronaut monitors. They all displayed in the normal range. Next, I stopped to observe the quietness on the Shuttle. It was very peaceful. Dalton was sound asleep. His vital signs were slow, and he showed no signs of distress. I was relieved. What would I ever do without my Dalton? Everyone was asleep; at least, everyone thought so at ISS and Mission Control.

I stared at Dalton, sleeping like a baby. He looked very tranquil, but it looked strange for him to be tethered to the wall floating in the zero-gravity atmosphere. I chuckled to myself. I do believe he could sleep anywhere. The lights on the shuttle were very dim. Silence penetrated the modules except for the oxygen compartment, which had a low, monotonous buzz. I continued to monitor all their vital signs when I noticed a change in the King's monitor. His heartbeat began accelerating, and I could see the perspiration on his head. He began to disconnect his wire, which monitored his vital signs. He carefully took one wire off at a time. Finally, his monitors shut down completely, stopping the recording of his vital signs. Surprised, I wondered what he was doing.

He continued to lay in his sleep compartment, not moving. The look of anguish transformed his handsome face into a demonic expression. When the King emerged from his sleep compartment, he still had a determined, disturbing, twisted appearance. I studied this man's face, who had the weight of the world on his shoulders.

The King moved silently in space toward Dalton, who was asleep with no care in the world. The King's forehead dripped in sweat. He stopped and surveyed the area as if watching for any other movement as he proceeded toward Dalton. Finally, he reached his destination, stopping and watching Dalton's peaceful face.

I knew Dalton's contentment came from the success of curing the King. He had succeeded in making the King a whole man, cancer-free. The reward for all his hard work and disappointments is the cancer cure for the King. Now, the King, cancer-free, could fulfill his royal destiny and continue to lead his country.

It was difficult for me to focus on the TV monitors with the muted lights, which caused poor visibility. Finally, I tried to concentrate on the fuzzy screen, but the Space Station shut down for the night.

I listened for the morning song to wake up the others, but to no avail.

The King floated soundlessly over Dalton and glared viciously. I couldn't tell what he had in mind. Maybe he wanted to question Dalton about the experiment, or perhaps he didn't feel well. I sat looking at the monitor when the King put his hands around Dalton's neck and began squeezing tightly. I gasped for air, unable to defend myself. Hands grasped around my neck, squeezing savagely. Pain emanated throughout my body. I tried to speak, to shout, "Help me. Don't kill me."

Fighting for my life, I clenched both hands into fists and began beating against the unknown dark force. I thrashed back and forth. I felt my eyes bulge from the threatened attack. I tried to scream, but I could not. The executioner's hot breath breathed against my naked body. Not being able to move, his rough hands tightened even more ferociously. My life was ending.

My inborn fight for survival renewed my strength. I fought desperately to protect myself. I grabbed the perpetrator's hands, pushing them away as hard as I could. It was useless; I didn't have the strength to fight anymore. Immobilized, I thought I was having a nightmare. I slapped myself into reality. I was not dreaming, and this was not a nightmare; it was real. It could not be happening to Dalton, trapped in his makeshift bed.

I screamed frantically, trying to wake up the other astronauts. Dr. Greg heard my heart-wrenching scream. He saw my anguished face on the camera.

I yelled, "Help Dalton!! The King is trying to kill him!!"

Greg quickly saw the attack and sprang toward the vicious assault.

Dalton fought off the wicked king as his eyes bulged from the intense grip around his neck. The King looked like a madman but was no match for Dalton's and Greg's strength. Prostate cancer had drained the King's strength.

Dr. Greg maneuvered himself to the back of the King and put his strong arms around the King's back, gripping hard like a vice. The King could not move.

Greg and the King were holding on to each other performed backflips. It looked like a war dance.

Greg turned the King around, and Dalton tied his hands with the sleeping compartment's tether.

Dalton shouted as he rubbed his neck, "King, what in the hell's going on?"

King Karl Ásgeirr XIII roared, "Dalton, I demand the MECS formula for my country. I mandate you to give Sweden the MECS formula to protect my country using chemical warfare and curing cancer. The MECS formula will boost our economy. Give it to me or, I will destroy you and Susan both financially and professionally."

Dalton and Greg looked at each other with disbelief and threw up their hands in the air.

Greg said, "King, do you realize how ridiculous you sound. Dalton just saved your life from prostate cancer, and this is how you repay him? I think you may want to rethink this whole situation. Dalton can take assault charges on you or even attempted murder. I am a witness, so is Susan and NASA records our every move. King, do you think you could bully or even kill Dalton into giving you the MECS formula. It is an impossible situation I have ever seen."

The King began profusely crying as he apologized to Dalton and Greg. The King, the stately man, looked like a weak, broken man. I couldn't believe I had once thought him charming and a strong King.

Dalton finally spoke diplomatically, "King, I can't give you the MECS formula for either. The MECS formula saved your life, which is the most precious gift of all. There is no price on life. Susan, this is what I want you to do. Are you listening to me, Susan?"

I said, "I'm here, listening."

Dalton spoke very deliberately, "Send *the Message* we created before I left."

He repeated, "Susan send the message containing the MECS formula to all the pharmaceutical companies in the world. I want it to be available globally to everyone and anyone who wants it. Susan, erase the MECS formula with the special chemical warfare ingredients along with its application. The MECS will never be for the destruction of humankind. It should have never existed. I am not going to have something I invented for humanity's welfare used to destroy the very essence of life."

I said, "I will do it immediately."

Before I could move, Ken entered the room and put his hands on my shoulders, holding them tightly, saying, "Dalton, I heard what you said. But, please don't do it! RUSH will pay you more money than you could ever spend in a lifetime. Cancer is a big money-making business, and RUSH does NOT want its business to stop! Chemical warfare will allow them to take over the world."

I felt I was in a bad science fiction movie. Then Ken's hands moved from my shoulders up my neck and squeezed savagely.

I froze in fear. I gasped for air, unable to defend myself. Pain emanated throughout my fragile body. I tried to speak, to shout, "Help me, don't kill me!"

Struggling for my life, I clenched both hands into fists and began beating against the known dark force. I thrashed back and forth as my eyes protruded from the aggressive attack. His rough hands surrounded my neck. My inborn fight for survival renewed my strength. I grabbed the perpetrator's hands, pushing them away as hard as I could. It was useless; I didn't have the power to fight anymore. My life was ending.

Ken screamed to Dalton, "In the name of Allah, I will not kill Susan if you give me the MECs formula."

Dalton shouted, "Stop it, Ken. What are you doing? Keep your hands-off, Susan! Allah?"

Ken shouted, "I want the MECS formula."

I thought desperately, "How could it be, Ken? I never thought he might be a follower of Islam. He's Dalton's best friend and partner. What has happened to him? How could we not have known?"

I continued to fight desperately against Ken. He applied even more pressure on my throat. The nightmare had returned, but this time, it was real. I felt like it was déjà vu when Leona was choking me. Again, someone from my first sail with Dalton was trying to kill me.

Dalton said, "I will give you anything you want. Stop your attack. Please, I beg you, my friend."

In the distance, I heard someone enter the room. I couldn't tell who it was. Who was the person fighting Ken off me? Ken began to release his rough, strong hands from my throat.

I began coughing, trying to catch my breath when I saw David, Leona's boyfriend. How ironic? Leona tried to kill me, and her boyfriend, David was saving me. Unfortunately, Ken's size and weight overpowered David's small frame.

I called out for help! I heard the security guards yelling for me to open the door. I realized the door locked from the inside, and no one could get in.

David fought violently against the mad man with the pure strength of adrenalin. He punched Ken over and over in the kidneys. Ken groaned with pain.

I heard more knocking at the door. Again, I tried to make my way over to the door. Ken tripped me as I passed, and I fell to the floor, hitting my head on the edge of the desk.

I was dizzy, and my head hurt, but I had to save David.

I could make out blood running down over David's eyes. Ken had scratched David's face above his eyeballs. I slowly pulled myself up on the desk and shakily made my way to the door.

David managed to pick up a Silver Snoopy, NASA's award given to an employee for exemplary work ethics supporting the astronauts and significant contributions for mission success. Unfortunately, it was glass with very sharp edges.

David began hitting Ken in his face repeatedly with the sharp object. Ken put his hands in front of his face to protect himself without success. Again and again, David swung the sharp object hitting him on the back of his head. Blood spewed from Ken's head, covering his body. Soon I could not recognize Ken for the bright crimson red blood. Ken staggered toward David. He hit him one more time, as Ken fell to the floor with blood gushing from his head.

Then, the room filled with stillness; there was no motion, and silence filled the air.

I sat there, motionless and in shock; I couldn't move from my throbbing head. So, the unknown assailant, the perpetrator in my nightmares, was Ken, our friend, we thought.

David put his arms around me for comfort. He covered my trembling body with Ken's bright red blood.

I whimpered, "Is Ken gone?"

Solemnly, David got up and checked Ken's pulse, "Yes, he is dead. He will never hurt you again."

Dalton asked urgently, "Susan, are you okay?"

I began to cry in disbelief about what just happened and my aching head. Sniffling as I spoke, "Yes, Dalton, I will be okay. Now, I'm just confused. Ken almost killed David and me. You worked with Ken for many years to destroy cancer. It was his life's work, too. So why did Ken sell himself to the devil? Why would he do this?"

Dalton said, "I guess he got greedy. His wife wanted more and more from him. He had told me he would have gotten a ten percent bonus if I sold the MECS formula to RUSH. I would receive approximately 600 million and Ken 60 million dollars.

"Ironically, RUSH wanted the formula not to be marketed. It would destroy the money-making cancer industry. Cancer makes more money than any other disease on the planet Earth. I told him I wouldn't sell the formula to anyone, absolutely no one. He got so upset, but not in a million years would I think he would be capable of murder. Susan, please send the MECS formula out immediately to everyone: pharmaceutical companies, hospitals, research centers, and anyone who may need it. Make it public knowledge and put an end to this dreaded disease and RUSH. Also, destroy the MECS formula for terrorist warfare. It is in a special file named Susan. Yes, we will destroy cancer in our lifetime."

Sadly, looking at Ken's stone-cold body, I thought of the black shadow who warned me about Ken's destruction.

I said to Dalton, "Aye, aye, Captain."

Dalton said, "This is the right thing to do. It will end the chaos in our lives. The MECS formula will eradicate cancer if it is available to everyone.

He took a deep sigh and continued, "Now, we can have a normal life and not be used for target practice anymore. Unfortunately, in life, we cannot direct the wind, but we can adjust our sails. Unfortunately, my one close friend Ken didn't realize the ramifications of his thirst for riches."

I pleaded with a heavy heart. "I am so ready to adjust our sails and go back to the Bahamas, but I'm not sure this will end the chaos. Remember, the MECS formula is also a terrorist warfare weapon. If everyone has the formula, it will be no time before a terrorist figures out the MECS warfare weapon formula. The whole world would have chaos, not just us. So, I don't think we should send out the formula."

Dalton said desperately, "Susan, do this now, or we will never be safe nor have our freedom. We will always be looking over our shoulder, waiting for another attack."

I sighed as tears burned my face, and the taste of salt coated my lips, "I know."

I walked away as I heard Dalton calling for me. I didn't look back as NASA's personnel and security rushed through the door.

I knew in my heart I had to do what was needed to keep the formula safe from those who would harm humanity, even if it meant going against my love, Dalton's wishes.

## Chapter 53 – Susan's Poetry

The pen captured my thoughts in the magic of my adventures.  These adventures are words of the heart fashioned with the rhythms of life and soul.

At every reunion, there is a time when the lover has already returned to the heart.

## The Fear- Chapter 1

A woman sits alone.
No one seeing
No one hearing
Gray hair falling down
Hands crooked around
No one cares
No one dares
Eating without grace
Features without a face
Lifeless of heart
Happiness apart
Calling to one
Wanting to run
But the Fear
Keeps the tears
Streaming through day-to-day
Gleaming to silent prey
To no one but
The Fear

## Clear Blue Water – Chapter 1

Deep in the clear blue water
Gliding just knowing the way
The sails and lines hard over
To venture in seas, we play

From West Palm Beach to West End
Buying conch and lobster so sweet
Anchoring just in the sand
Boat slipping away while asleep

Deep in the clear blue water
Gliding just knowing the way
Salvaging a basket part
To take from yesterday

From West End to Great Sale
Dinghy to coral shore
Using the engine, not the sail
Nothing there to explore

Deep in the clear blue water
Gliding just knowing the way
The sails and lines maneuver
To venture in seas, we say

From Great Sale to Carter Cay
Exploring the shore of conch shells
Bahamians singingly
Not waiting but taking a quick sail

Deep in the clear blue water
Gliding just knowing the way
Turtles and fishing as Dover
To peril in seas, they play

From Carter Cay to the Fox Town
Having dinner at Shell Café
Playing and drinking Kalik down
High seas in dinghy to May Day

Deep in the clear blue water
Gliding just knowing the way
Dolphins playing together
In the bow parting to play

From Fox Town in Spanish Cay
The rich and famous hide
Seeking all the privacy
Hide away from their demise

Snorkeling and fighting the current
Beautiful sunset at dinner
The touch, the kiss, the living spent
The peace in the days forever

Deep in the clear blue water
Gliding just knowing the way
The sails and lines hard over
To venture in seas, we play

Making the way back to Great Sale
Stopping at Mangrove Cay
A quick dip from the rail
Speedy return to West Palm Beach

Deep in the clear blue water
Gliding just knowing the way
Seeking home with sails hard over
The venture ending the play

In the Clear Blue Water
Abaco's, Bahamas

## Paradise – Chapter 2

The Island sun
Calls to us all
Hearing the fun
Waiting the fall
Wakening the soul
Touching your body
Rising just to see
Wanting not to be told
By the Island sun
Calling to us all
Breathing life to one
Not catching the fall
The wind in my hair
Blowing in your face
My body so bare
Not leaving a trace
In the Island sun
Calling to us all
Shaping of a run
Breaking the fall
Kissing your sweet, moist lips
Tasting the mixture of us
Chills in your fingertips
Breathlessly the lover's rush
From the Island sun
Called to us all
Leaving not to be done
Ending of the fall

In Paradise
Nassau Bahamas
01-19-02

## Yesterday, Today, and Tomorrow – Chapter 3

### Yesterday

A chance, a meeting
Somewhere retreating
Into life without a plan
But time sifting through sand
A smile, a boyish look
Grasping pleasure took
Repeating a childhood sameness
Different places no less
Similarities are there
As clear as the morning air
To breathe a new delight
Friendship, newness, polite
A hand reached out to say
Come with me and let's play
From coast to coast
To life, we toast

### Today

My heart, my soul, takes a peak
Through laughter, I seek
A peace from within
At last, without sin
I am what you see
Not trouble-free
But a smile to speak
Sensuous weak

## Tomorrow

I cannot speak for tomorrow
Nor do I have a crystal ball
Only stolen time to borrow
From this tenuous self-built wall
For tomorrow's are in yesterdays
And yesterdays are kept in today
Remembering your glance
And charming romance
On cliffs by the enchanting ocean
A kiss, a touch feeling the motion
From crashing waves far below
Happiness to you bestow

## Yesterday, Today, and Tomorrow

# Forever In Time – Chapter 6

Crushing waves to shore
As the moon hides behind the cloud
With the wind sounding roar
Hearing a voice faintly so loud

Can you catch the wind?
Can you catch the moonbeams?
Can you see waves blend?
Can you see what I have seen?

Sending shivers to my soul
Taking each inch of my body
A touch that is much like a hold
Speaking softly somewhere in me

Can you catch the wind?
Can you catch the moonbeams?
Can you see the waves blend?
Can you see what I have seen?

Looking through the dead tree
As the moon surrounding rays
This was done before with thee
Saying long ago from today

Can you catch the wind?
Can you catch the moonbeams?
Can you see the waves blend?
Can you see what I redeem?

Reflecting on the time before
Fluttering of my delicate heart
Leaving me desiring much more
Recalling not wanting for us to part

Can you catch the wind?
Can you catch the moonbeams?
Can you see the waves blend?
Can you capture this scene?

***Forever In Time***

# The Rain

Wetness surrounding her body
One drop falling at a time
Endless thoughts roll to the sea
Seeking softly words that rhyme
One drop falling at a time

Feel the warmth touching.
Feel the warmth brushing

Across the fingers to her lips
Rolling toward sensuous hips

Shimmering droplets from within
Glimmering droplets from within

Of wetness surrounding her body
One drop falling at a time
Endless thoughts roll to the sea
Hearing lightly words that rhyme
One drop falling at a time

Feel the cool singing
Feel the cool bringing

Engulfed throughout your life
Seeking solitude while in strife

Shimmering droplets from within
Glimmering droplets from within

### The Rain (continued)

Of wetness surrounding her body
One drop falling at a time
Endless thoughts rolled to sea
Breaking through the words that rhyme
One drop falling at a time

Feel the heat chasing
Feel the heat raising

Wetness in a kiss hovering
From head to toe covering

Shimmering droplets from within
Glimmering droplets from within

Of wetness surrounding her body
One drop falling at a time
Endless thoughts crush to the sea
Screaming out words that rhyme
One drop falling at a time

Feel the love lying
Feel the love hiding

The last drop fell upon her head
Seeking solace within his bed

Shimmering droplets from within
Glimmering droplets from within
Raining in my Soul

## Seeking – Chapter 20

The Icy Palace
Covered in snow
Delicate Lace
Comfort and glow

Flashing fast downhill
Laughing to the thrill
Lovers holding hands
Crossing frosty land

The Icy palace
In the Rockies, high
Away from the race
Reaching to the sky

Driving through hidden pathways
Giggling with happiness and play
The danger not aware
No sign of any scare

The Icy Palace
The white wonderland
A secret place
With closeness at hand

Always Seeking
Vail, Colorado

Blanket of Stars – Chapter 27

Covered with a blanket of stars
Surrounded by moonbeams from afar

Hold me close forever by your side
In the blanket of Stars
With your true heart, I will always hide
Not ever to be apart

Come be there as I cover thee
With the blanket of Stars
Celestial beds for us see
Wrap the sensuous heart

Covered with a blanket of stars
Playing in outer space as we are

Under the Blanket of Stars

## Kiss my Soul – Chapter 27

I'm so afraid
Of tomorrow
My life is frayed
Sad with sorrow

Kiss my lips
Reach my soul
Seek my heart
Watching I told

I'm so afraid
My life protect
Just you have made
Love resurrects

Kiss my hand
Touch my soul
Take my heart
Keep me whole

I'm so afraid
Of distant past
As I will lay
In your love, surpass

Kiss my breast
Speak not to me
Now I rest
Always with thee

Not afraid

## Safe Inside - Chapter 37

The touch that links us together

Answers not questions

Making what was now forever

Wholeness in sanction

Reach for my hand, always knowing

Sanction in Believing

In the look, the smile, the loving

Believing the searching

Every inch covered in kisses

Searching the ending

Beginning with the ecstasy

Safe inside resounding

Safe Inside

# Rejoice – Chapter 38

As the darkness falls
Turn thy head to see the light
Think of times to recall
The continuous journey, the flight

Help me; God takes the pain
Into life, I do remain
Seeking no one to take blame
Before you, I am lame

It has been my home
Solitude all along
I am not to belong
Take me your throne

Hold me close in your arms
Comfort me with your charms
Keep me away from life's harm
In eternity, keep me warm

Rejoicing as the darkness falls
Turning thy head to see the light
Thinking of times to recall
The ending, the journey, the flight

Rejoice

# Chapter 54 – NASA Spinoffs

These are just some of NASA spinoffs from the Aerospace
A program that has made our lives better in today's world.

**Bioreactor** - Developed for Space Shuttle medical research,
this rotating cell culture apparatus simulates some
aspects of the space environment, or microgravity, on the
ground. Tissue samples grown in the bioreactor are being
used to design therapeutic drugs and antibodies. Some
scientists believe the bioreactor will routinely
produce human tissue for research and transplantation.

**Diagnostic Instrument** - NASA technology was used to
create a compact laboratory instrument for hospitals and
doctor offices that more quickly analyze blood,
accomplishing in 30 seconds what once took 20 minutes.

**Gas Detector** – This is a gas leak detection system,
developed initially to monitor the shuttle's
the hydrogen propulsion system, and used
by the Ford Motor Company in the production of a
natural gas-powered car.

**Infrared Camera** - A sensitive, infrared, hand-held
a camera that observes the blazing plumes from the Shuttle
also is capable of scanning for fires. During the brush
fires that ravaged Malibu, CA, in 1996, the camera was
used to point out hot spots for firefighters.

**Infrared Thermometer** - Infrared sensors developed to
remotely measure the temperature of distant stars and
planets led to the development of the hand-held optical
sensor thermometer. Placed inside the ear canal, the
thermometer provides an accurate reading in two seconds
or less.

**Jewelry Design** - Jewelers no longer have to worry about inhaling dangerous asbestos fibers from the blocks they use as soldering bases. Space Shuttle, head shield tiles offer jewelers a safer soldering base with temperature resistance far beyond the 1,400 degrees Fahrenheit generated by the jeweler's torch.

Land Mine Removal Device - The same rocket fuel that helped launch the Space Shuttle is now being used to save lives— by destroying land mines. A flare device, using leftover fuel donated by NASA, is placed next to the uncovered land mine and is ignited from a safe distance using a battery-triggered electric match. The explosive burns away, disabling the mine and rendering it harmless.

**Lifesaving Light** - Special lighting technology developed for plant growth experiments on Space Shuttle missions is being studied to treat brain tumors in children. Doctors at the Medical College of Wisconsin in Milwaukee is working with light-emitting diodes in a treatment called photodynamic therapy, a form of chemotherapy to kill cancerous tumors.

**Prosthesis Material** - Responding to a request from the orthopedic appliance industry, NASA recommended that the foam insulation used to protect the shuttle's external tank replace the heavy, fragile plaster used to produce master molds for prosthetics. The new material is light, virtually indestructible, and easy to ship and store.

**Rescue Tool** - Rescue squads have a new extrication tool to help remove accident victims from wrecked vehicles. The hand-held device requires no auxiliary power systems or cumbersome hoses and is 70 percent cheaper than previous rescue equipment.

The cutter uses a miniature version of the explosive charges that separate devices on the shuttle.

Vehicle Tracking System - Tracking information originally used onboard Space Shuttle missions now helps track vehicles on Earth. This commercial spinoff allows vehicles to transmit a signal back to a home base. Municipalities today use the software to track and reassign emergency and public works vehicles. It also is used by vehicle fleet operations, such as taxis, armored cars, and vehicles carrying hazardous cargo.

Video Stabilization Software - Image-processing the technology used to analyze the Space Shuttle launch video and to study meteorological images also helps law enforcement agencies improve crime solving video. The technology removes defects due to image jitter, image rotation, and image zoom in video sequences. The technology also maybe useful for medical imaging, scientific applications and home video.

# Chapter 55 – Email from Dr. Dennis Morrison, PhD

Renne',

Was I correct that you didn't know about the project we had reviewed by the Fort Detrick Defense Research Labs? They thought our concept of encapsulating Ciprofloxacin (antibiotic) in tiny microcapsules that were inhaled after an anthrax spore exposure would be a novel and effective way to treat the terrorist type of anthrax powder exposure. The microcapsules would be the same size as the anthrax spore & I can alter their surface charge to have the same characteristics; therefore, the Cipro microcapsules are taken up by white blood cells policing the lungs and taken to the regional lymph nodes just as the anthrax spores. Hence, you would have a type of direct local treatment right where the anthrax spores end up before they have a chance to begin multiplying.

On two space missions (including Columbia's last flight (STS-103), I made those microcapsules of Ciprofloxacin and Doxycycline so we could get started (& those experiments).

Of course, we never funded the project, so it sits on the shelf, waiting to be proven effective. It could be the first Inhalation/ sustained release treatment against inhaled bio-weapons.

If this gives you ideas for your new book, let me know & we can talk more about it.

Dennis Morrison, Biomedical Ph.D., retired
NASA Scientist

# Chapter 56 - Pictures from
## Renne' Siewers' Aerospace Career

Renne' Siewers attends the Extravehicular Activity Astronauts Ceremonies with astronauts who performed the spacewalks on a mission.

Granddaughter Payton tours the NBL.

Neutral Buoyancy Lab is the largest astronaut training swimming pool with a mockup of the International Space Station for astronaut training. Water simulates what it is like in space.

Neutral Buoyancy Laboratory Astronauts' training being lifted into the water since the EVA suits are very heavy.

Granddaughter Payton, at the NBL Viewing. Center.

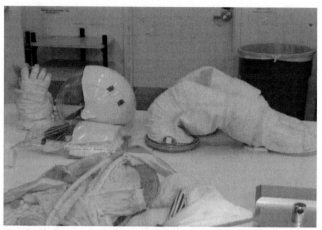

Technicians working on Astronaut's EVA Flight Suit,
but now the astronauts work on their suits.
They have a problem with the helmet filling with water
with water, so they use a hose for breathing if this happens.

Renne' attends a Voluntary Protection Program (VPP)
function during Halloween with astronauts Flight Crew
Equipment (FCE) and Extra-Vehicular Activity (EVA) suits.

Mission Close-Out Crew

With parents Bill and Wilma Overstreet, Jon
and Renne viewed the Space Shuttle launch at
the Vehicle Assembly Building (VAB).

.

Successful Launch.

Bringing Space Shuttle Mockup home
to Houston for an exhibit.
Unfortunately, Houston didn't receive
one of the original Space Shuttles.

<u>*Science Fiction, Espionage, Romance,*</u>
<u>*Murder Mystery in Space:*</u>
AEROSPACE: The Last Payload
AEROSPACE: The King's Payload, *Sequel*
AEROSPACE:  The Rebirth Payload, Trilogy

Relationship:  Real Stories
Moving On…"NEXT"

Poetry:
Sensuous Poems Through Times
<u>*Nighty Night Sailboat Children's books (Educational):*</u>
Nighty Night Sailboat (sailing terms)
Noche Velero (bilingual Spanish/English – (sailing terms)
Nighty Night Sailboat Goes to Spain
(Spanish culture - provision a boat)
Santa finds Nighty Night Sailboat
(Children who move or may not be home for Christmas)
Nighty Night Sailboat in the Bahamas
(Bahamian culture – going through customs)
Nighty Night Sailboat Celebrates Key West Birthday
(What to do in Key West - Making new friends)
Nighty Night Sailboat Searches for Pirates
(History of Blackbeard – Bullies)
Sailing Angels Crew for Nighty Night Sailboat
(Doing a Good Deed
Nighty Night Sailboat takes Juni to the Hospital
(What to expect at a hospital or doctor's office.)
Nighty Night Sailboat Meets an Astronaut
(spin-off Aerospace Technologies)
Dash Gordon
(About doing good for Special Needs)
Dash Gordon His Story
(Why he created The Dash Gordon Foundation)
Dash Gordon Foundation "A Night To Remember" Pageant
Ladies who compete in a Special Needs Pageant to be Queen.
Rainbow of Hope Texas
(Young Adults Special Needs Equine Therapy)
The Piggish Birthday
(Making a bad situation a good situation)
Check out Amazon KINDLE or
https//www.sailadybooks.blogspot.com
Do A REVIEW:https://www.amazon.com/review/create-
review?ie=UTF8&asin

ISBN-: 9798863015682

Printed in the United States of America
Illustrated by Sailor Renne' Siewers
Book Design by Sailor Renne' Siewers

# RENNE SIEWERS FIRST PLACE WINNER

Swish, Swish, the Mistake

I Promise

Love of the Sea

African American genre fiction

Military genre fiction.

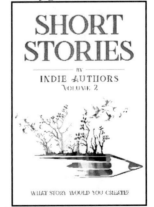

Action/Adventure genre fiction.

Order short stories on  http://IndieLector.Store

Made in United States
North Haven, CT
07 November 2024

59987845R00190